Finding Miranda…

She was tied in some elaborate way, with more than enough rope to keep her from getting away. But nothing seemed that messed up. And it was so natural those blankets under her: it looked like she had wanted to stretch out on the floor to get cool.

I felt the inside of her palms; they were as soft as I had felt them earlier that evening. A little springy. I moved her fingers, and they flipped back like thin dead fish. The walls were starting to swim. I walked out, locked the door, and I went back downstairs, three steps at a time, and threw up in the sink.

"Call 911," I said with a furry echo in my sinus that rang through my whole skull.

"Tell them to come because Miranda's dead," I said.

THE ROPE JUGGLER

Judson Blake

STARK HOUSE

Stark House Press • Eureka California

THE ROPE JUGGLER

Published by Stark House Press
1315 H Street
Eureka, CA 95501, USA
griffinskye3@sbcglobal.net
www.starkhousepress.com

ISBN: 978-1-951473-88-4

Book design by Mark Shepard, shepgraphics.com
Proofreading by Bill Kelly

PUBLISHER'S NOTE:
This is a work of fiction. Names, characters, places and incidents are either
the products of the author's imagination or used fictionally, and any
resemblance to actual persons, living or dead, events or locales, is entirely
coincidental.

First Stark House Press Edition: June 2022

To MK
....for valuing the small.

1. The Angel's Wing

It was the afternoon before the night when Miranda got killed. And later I wondered if something in the day, maybe some little detail, had anything to do with it. Because for sure there was plenty about the woman that I never knew till the fracas was over. It was a lovely day in summer, so brilliant it makes you think it will go on forever, just made to take it easy. Only thing was, at that moment Sam was digging at me about the woman and he wouldn't let go.

"You're living on whimsy, man. You call it freedom. Freedom's for patriots. That's not you."

"All I mean," I said a little perturbed, "is I can do what I want and think what I want, just like everybody else."

He smirked, and the clear light of afternoon sun cut a skeptical shadow under his eye.

"You're talking crap," he said without looking at me.

I hated it when Sam talked to me like that. It meant more coming from him. Well, maybe I wasn't being really clear, that particular moment. I wanted him to give me some space right then. I stuck around him because I liked him. And underneath I still believed that if I had some of his practicality and a little more luck, then finally I'd get the good time I wanted with the woman. He was catching me on my blind side, really, which was my partly fantasized affair with Miranda.

Why fantasized at all? Well, because lately she had no time for me. And I was having trouble letting go. I had this confusion, you see, between love and lust and what you might call too much memory of a good thing. I was going to keep asking her even when I knew the answer. I'd ask her again tonight, if I could find her.

"See, that's the thing about you," said Sam in a speculative tone. "You got a naïve streak, Milo. Big time. That's why you got involved with the woman in the first place. Anybody else would've told you, what for? What's that going to get you? So she's a fox. She the only fox in town? She lives in your building, so how can you ever get away from her? Ever think of that?"

"I don't want to get away from her."

"Now you say."

"Have you ever loved anybody? You don't know how I feel 'cause you never cared for her in the first place. You told me that."

"Oh, I saw who she was, I left it at that," Sam said. "She wouldn't look at me. And it's not like she'll go out with anybody. I think it's damn strange she'll go out with you. You're not in her league. She must have rocks in her head. I mean, nothing against you, Milo. You're a good-looking guy and all, I don't mean that ..."

"Wouldn't be my first mistake," I said. But I had the feeling I was missing something even when I said that.

"Yeah, well, you could pick a better mistake to make. That chick's mixed up in some heavy shit. Don't ask me how I know 'cause I don't know her directly and I'd rather not say. But I wouldn't have nothing to do with her. You don't even know the kind of people she runs around with. She ever introduce you to any of her friends?"

"No."

"What I mean." He nodded. "And there she is in the same building."

He pursed his lips like he was going to spit, but he didn't spit. Just the thought of it made him antsy and discontent. I should have listened to Sam. He was a good friend and he always told me what he thought. But the way I was feeling then, well, there was nothing going to persuade me against my natural desire for the woman. She was more than a fox. She was the sexiest woman I'd ever encountered. Who wouldn't be affected? I looked out the window of the Creation Cafe at the cars spinning past on the avenue. Today it was hot. But I had air conditioning in my place. I didn't have to sit here.

"She used to like me," I said thinking back. "Maybe she still does, in her way."

"Means nothing. Nothing," he said. "You're not paying attention to your best interests, Milo. This thing with that woman is out of hand. You got involved. Your problem is how to get uninvolved. Stick with the woman you got. People have seen you with her. Everybody talks. That's the world we live in. You think rules are for everybody else, not you. That you're something special."

"Where'd you get that? I've tried all my life to be ordinary. Being special just gives people a better target to shoot at."

Sam chuckled.

"You're like that guy over there."

He poked his finger and I turned to see a man who slumped against a lamp post. While we watched, he nervously left it to walk in a circle and return to the other side of the post and lean again. It was Beremy, a harmless nut you'd see in the neighborhood. He wore a heavy jacket that made no sense in this weather. He had a blotched tan and a smile that made him look enormously happy about whatever was going on. He had a pattern you'd see sometimes: he took a few prideful steps one way, checking his cell all the time, then he turned and retraced himself and did it over again, all with the look of intense concentration. He'd greet you with an air of knowing who you are when you'd never met. I felt hurt by what Sam said but I tried not to show it.

"Um, how so?"

"He gets one thought in his head," Sam grinned as he scratched his temple. "And he can't let it go. Then he gets another, and what then? He can't let that one go, either. That's bad, my friend. You don't know it, but that's bad."

Sam told me a story once, about a woman he loved when he was quite young. He wanted money and a friend offered to get him in on a real estate deal in Oregon. The woman was beginning to like Sam, and maybe if he had persisted, who knows? But that wasn't like him. He got impatient and Oregon began to look good. It was a sacrifice, it was a hard choice at the time, but he would always shrug it off and get that icy sharpness in his eye of someone who would even kill if he had to, to get what he needed to live in his own way. It was clear he would never let a yearning like I had get in his way.

Sam was one of several bachelors in my building. He worked out at a gym and it showed in his arms: sinewy and hard. He had been a jockey once, and he hadn't lost his shape. But all that was some time ago. I never heard him talk about work. I guess he made enough to last him the rest of his life. He sat now with a relaxed air and one hand clasped behind his coffee. On his arm was a tattoo of Gibraltar with a fish flying over the crest.

"I gotta go," I said. We paid and went out on the sidewalk where the heat was like a bath in hot sand. He had to go somewhere and I was going home, so we parted there.

I crossed the street and made a point of giving Beremy a familiar nod. I tried to meet his eye.

"Bitchin' day," he said. He shrugged in the incongruous heavy coat. "But it'll rain tonight."

How was I like him? I decided it was Sam's idea of a joke. I walked two extra blocks just for the feel of the heat and the summer day. There were eager mothers pushing strollers that bristled with levers and bottles and neat rags to pamper the next little mishap. There came students with fantastic hair, off for the summer. Lovers not caring who saw them, they could only see each other. With no particular plan I doubled back along a shady street.

The evening was hot but clear the way it can get in summer. The sun was low and there was a young moon. If you didn't think to look, you could miss her; but no, in the vault of blue there she was, a pale sliver cocked like a joke, and as she seemed, alert to all the odd goings on among us strangers down below.

Up the street Holly called me from her car. She'd seen me walking. Over time we had gotten used to chance encounters where each thought the other might be. It had become a little game we played where you always win.

"Hey, big fella," she said cheerily with that sensual grain in her voice. She was wearing a flowery dress that fit her like summer dresses do. I crawled in next to her feeling good, feeling the heat flow from her body. But there was something odd in the air when I reached over to kiss her.

"Not here," she said. "I'd feel ashamed." She was a little irritated. Like an electric charge it came out at me and I backed away.

We took a breath and looked at each other. She was trying to be serious, I could tell that. I could get her to explain, maybe, if she was in the mood, but I didn't know if I was ready for that.

"Why don't we drive around to my place?" I said.

"Where'll we park?"

"There'll be a place."

She got the car going. I really liked Holly. We had been seeing a lot of each other over the last few months. She really liked me, too. We usually got along fine, and she had no idea about my leaning over Miranda. Today it was probably the heat that got her. On the ledge between us there was a shopping bag full of things. I pawed through it wondering what her tastes of the day might be.

"That's just some stuff I got," she said with that casual-not-really-casual sound in her voice. There was a big stalk of broccoli, romaine lettuce, a sack of kiwifruits, couscous, a cheese that I liked, and a bottle of wine. Two onions, and a small can of peas. There was even a bottle of soap. The triangular torso of Mr. Clean, friendly household eunuch, always ready to serve, came smiling up at me.

"You remember we planned to fix dinner tonight," she said testily. For some reason I felt lonely when she said that. It was one of those times when you can feel lonelier with someone than when you're out on your own. It was strange like that.

"Oh. Well, I don't know, Holly ... I don't think that we really said it all that definitely...."

Her lip stiffened. She was silent a moment while the car tooled along. A clutch of teenagers with painted jeans split up to let us pass. I watched as Tarragon Street came into view. There were children playing on the stoop of my place. And down the street another group was jumping double-dutch amid music and screams and laughter. A couple of housewives sat on the sidewalk in chairs they had brought out. How I liked that. This was what home was about, wasn't it? People you knew, doing things for reasons you could understand. None of the craziness the city is famous for: domestic fights, stupid crimes, nonsense like that. That wasn't Tarragon Street. To one side I saw a pair of sunshades and purple-red lips watching as we approached. Suddenly my ankle developed a terrible itch and I bent down to get a good scratch, my head sunk low. But my feet were slipping on something even as I did that. I looked around. The floor of the car was awash with unopened junk mail and magazines. There must have been twenty magazines. They had torn covers; some were mashed and badly folded. And titles? This you had to see: *Modern Bride*, *House and Garden*, *Bride To Be*, *New York Weddings*, *American Bride*, and more. What got into Holly? Couldn't she clean her car?

After a moment I brought up my head. We sailed by and the sunshades stayed still, unseeing but not unseen. Stern and weightless, they belonged to a distant Apollonian goddess with lips like you never see on anyone real. It was Miranda.

The music from the radio drifted out; some oldies station:

"... I'll be trewwww ... and I'll neverrrrr leave yew ..."

"Don't you get tired of listening to that stuff?"

Her finger flicked a button and the air was silent. Even that struck me as odd: Holly's car seemed to make no sound at all.

"Holly, honey, I don't feel so good. I don't think tonight's the right night, okay? We could do it on Saturday, that would be better. There'll be plenty of time then. Yeah, I really think so. On Saturday. Whatta you think?"

The silence was like a ship cruising in airless space. We glided past Neptune before the next street. Kids shouted as we passed, their voices came thin and far away. It was the silence that prevailed.

"I'm seeing my sister Saturday," Holly said, like it was hard to get out the words. "When're you going to grow up and start thinking about other people?"

"How can I think about other people? I don't know half the stuff that's in my own head. What about that?"

"You should learn to take responsibility for things you say. At least you could do that."

"I know you think I should, Holly. But hey, give it some thought. I'm 31. I have some things I haven't really fleshed out yet, you know?"

"You don't mean half the things you say."

"Well, exactly. Cut me some slack."

"You're emotionally unreliable. Has anyone ever told you that? You're the Great American Flake. Flake! You hear? And Saturday is out."

"Well, the next day, then. Yeah, Holly, then I'll be in a good mood. I just got off work. I need to be alone right now, you know? You're sometimes that way too. Aren't you? Sure you are. It's just, you know, one of those... things I gotta work out by myself. Why, just imagine: did you know there are people in New York working for less than a dollar an hour?"

"Don't make fun of the poor."

"... and once a month a space rock the size of a truck hits the atmosphere of Earth, but nobody hears it. Doesn't that worry you?"

"Stop talking nonsense," she said and then she hissed: "This is not a rehearsal."

"Exactly my point. It's a reenactment. A restaging of all the things I've ever dreaded.... Think about that, for a change. Reenact ..."

"I wonder how you keep a job."

"Not only that, but when I do the Tarot, Holly, it's obvious, like a letter in the mail, that the Widow means me no harm. I do a good job for her. You got to trust something, Holly: not everything can go bad all at once."

"You're skating on thin ice with the Widow, I'll tell you that. One day she's going to drop you like a hot piano. And I'll laugh. I'll just laugh."

"Aw, come on, Holly. Know what? I started reading that book you gave me: *Reassuring Ideas of the Modern Age*. It's meant to help you organize your thoughts. Like, think about it: when does real life begin, anyway? Hm? I dunno. Let me finish that before I answer more questions. Okay?"

I waited while she said nothing, then I said "Okay?" again.

"You'll be a punch line in my life, if you live that long."

"Well," I said looking wistfully out the window, "nothing can stop a sour idea whose time has come."

Holly and I sometimes had little conversations that sounded like non sequiturs. It was one of those odd things that people do when they're getting used to each other and growing close. It usually worked to clear the air and get over rough spots that showed up now and then. Well, it didn't work this time.

"So fine," she said, but it was only an instant before she gunned the car. The stream of trees and people rushed by in a gray whirl. When Holly got angry, I warned myself, she had a bit of a mean streak. Well, I have to admit very often I found that attractive, one of her charming sides. But maybe not right then.

She skidded to a stop at the corner, just for an instant. I had an idea that was my chance. I unlatched the door, my arms reached out like eucalyptus branches floating in air. My feet scrambled for purchase on the swamp of magazines. My knee crunched on the dashboard. The car lurched and the heel of my hand scraped the street. Did I imagine her foot propelling my ass as I sailed out? Her tires squealed beside my ear, the door still open. It hit the bumper of a parked car and whacked shut. She squealed between two trucks and didn't stop.

I rolled out of the way as another car missed me. I stared after Holly but she never looked back. I just sat there, stunned. My body was yelling in pain, my mouth wide open, but wouldn't you know it? I burst out with a wave of laughter. What a relief, to be free of her just like that! The sting in my hands and my knee were trifles next to the glee, the sudden release. I took a breath to calm down.

"You are not safe here," said a voice from the clear blue.

A gentle hand took my arm.

"You must get out of the street," he said with a delicate accent that harked from another time. It was Klondyke, one of the first people I had come to know in the neighborhood. He ran the funeral parlor across the street. A hearse was drawn up there and people in suits were milling about. The women in black veils. They looked and then looked away, disdain for the crazy guy who had unfairly cheated death. Traffic went by a few feet away. Smashed paper and amorphous food slopped the curb. I thought to myself: yeah, for real you're in the gutter now, Milo, with the paper cups and summer tar. And a mortician standing over you with a helping hand.

"You must be more careful."

I stood up. I dusted my hands and thanked him. He smiled his broad, kindly smile. His eyes looked back with indelible sadness. There was no misfortune he had not seen.

"I'm okay. Nothing a cool beer won't fix."

He mused, waving for patience to the group across the street.

"That was very rude of your friend. Why would she do such a thing?"

Often when I came home from work I passed Klondyke's Funeral Home, and sometimes I'd see him and we'd talk. I never thought much about it, but that afternoon even before he came over and I heard his voice, it was as if an angel's wing had reached out and lightly brushed my ear. It was one of those spooky feelings you get sometimes and you never know from where.

Looking back on it, that afternoon was strange. And the night to come was stranger still. And you know when things take an ornery turn there's the feeling that somewhere something could have gone differently, even if you can't think what. I had the crazy intuition even then that the past (that afternoon) and the future (that night) were tangled vines that could not separate themselves without some help. Afterwards I tried to remember everything, thinking that would make a difference in the worst blunder of my life. It became a puzzle lost in a murky forest so deep I'd never get through it. And somewhere—perhaps the angel knew—the pieces were being silently drawn together even while we were standing there in traffic by that grimy curb. Like Klondyke here. His kindly gesture of taking my arm. I felt such love for the man at that instant! He had plenty of other things to do. A funeral was in full swing and people were staring at us now. Why had he crossed the street to help me? Like the angel's wing, an invisible thread seemed strung out between us.

It was a curious fact that Klondyke knew the Widow Kytler, the old witch who owned my building. She rarely came around, though she kept tabs on everything. Years before, I had conned her into letting me be super for only a few weeks. I caught her in a time of need—thinking I could parlay it into a long-term deal if I worked it right, flinty as she was. Because I was all charm. And she had no chance in Hell of finding anyone as good at fixing stuff as I was. I ran her building and kept the tenants at peace, happy enough to stay quiet and pay the rent. And I had my own place in the bargain.

"Little difference of opinion," I muttered scraping off a bit of skin.

"Get her some flowers," he hailed as he turned. "And Haagen Dazs. It works miracles."

He went back to the black-clad crowd that could not mourn without him.

2. Slamming the Door

I wound my way back down the street, as far as the double-dutch competition. There must have been a dozen kids gathered around. The girl in the yellow dress held center stage. She was still going strong when I got there and there was a lot of screaming of "Go, go, go!" as the jump ropes whirled around her.

Then all of a sudden she tripped and stopped. The ropes stopped. Exhausted, she stepped out, shaking her hands like rags. She got a round of whistles and whoops, and it was hard to tell if she had lost anything or been defeated. The flaccid ropes strung out along the pavement and the child on one end looked around to see who would be next.

Somebody said something that made one girl slump and laugh. Then she straightened and they started the ropes whirling again. In and out, in and out.... Someone turned up music on the radio. Another girl, this one quite pudgy, stepped forward. There were whistles from the crowd that indicated she might be a favorite. She had fans. When she jumped in the middle, she was instantly on the dance floor, no one would doubt that. I stood watching her, fascinated while she danced alternately in two different steps to the music. After a minute of that she went with the faster rhythm. It seemed just the toes of her feet moved. Up. Down. Up. Down. Fast. But then she switched and kicked her feet out straight, and all of a sudden everyone cheered. The capper came after that: she let her arms fly out around her, occupying space for a split second that you'd swear the rope would cut off. Over her head. Back down. She spun in a circle. There was no stopping this girl. Her hands flew out like wings. No stopping...

Then, without preamble, she leaped out of the shell. She was breathing hard but she smiled a big broad smile, and they hooted for her being so good. I felt the glow, the great wonderful upwelling thrill of being a kid. All my muscles chilled. It was so great I felt like cheering for them all. I pulled away from the central space as if breaking magnets. I looked around at the trees. What a lovely evening it was going to be.

In front of my place (the Widow of course never came here, preferring the sanctum of her East Side aerie-penthouse) was a sycamore and a little open stretch of sidewalk where Tommy and Louis were drawing figures with chalk. It seemed partly a game of marbles, but they were very intent on it and the designs with the chalk were what was important now, though you couldn't tell why. Louis was a morose, kind of poetic kid a year or so older than Tommy, but they often played together that summer. Tommy was a ruffian; nothing scared him, he was just like his mother, Paula, who let you know right away when there was something she didn't like. Louis' taste in chalk went to radiating blues. Tommy liked boxes, but he might have been influenced by the hopscotch designs down the street. I had never seen these kids play hopscotch. Perhaps only girls played it. Letitia and Anne-Louise stood up above on the stoop looking down at the others, twisting their bodies as if they had a secret they wanted someone to guess. They greeted me as I approached and I smiled broadly back. They all liked me. None of them had seen my nasty incident with Holly, or even noticed my hands.

I knew these kids. They all lived in my building, an old hotel that had never really been converted, just rented out once the entryway had been rearranged. I had watched these children grow, and they all smiled when they saw me. I had, at one time or another, been into the apartments of most of them, repairing something or moving something. They were used to having me around. I would hear them talk about me, sometimes they would even mention things I had said. Admire me really. "Milo says," had some cachet I had heard, which could be a bit of saving grace in the rude and uncertain world of children. And it wasn't so unnatural, if you thought about it, because all of them, except for one of the girls, were children raised without fathers. And so (my fantasy here) maybe in some little way I took the place of a father in their kid's imagination. I was tall and had an easy smile. I let myself think in those days that I might become a symbol as they grew up. It was a nice idea anyway. An uncle maybe. Uncle Milo.

Louis squinted up and greeted me. I said hello and he said hello and then he went back to his drawing. No time to lose. Nothing was as serious as the exact scroll of color on concrete. It seemed to be a game, for they traded their chalk back and forth, all different colors.

"Milo," the woman called from behind me. I turned, knowing it was Miranda, and wanting to savor the moment of being just a little unsure it was really her. She spoke my name and it felt like a precious, unbelievable sound. Wasn't that something? She didn't take off her sunglasses to speak to me. She wore a maroon bandanna around her hair, as if it was late autumn and she wanted to protect herself from a little nip. And her gray raincoat. I had never seen her go out without it, even now in the brilliance of summer.

"Miss Dauphine," I said with a smile. "You're home early today. Or is it you're up very late?"

"Can we go inside?" she said curtly and went tripping up the stoop. She waited for me to open the door. We both crowded into the open entryway. I stopped to check my mailbox. As usual there was a fistful of junk and I paused to glance through in case there was anything special.

"Can't you do that later?" Her perfect lips, like you only see in cosmetic ads, took on a gorgeous pout. "I've lost my key. I'll have to borrow one from you."

"Well, I'll get you one," I said in a calm avuncular tone. I was an uncle, I wanted her to know. I looked her over, perhaps a second too long. Strange as it seems, there are some people who thrive on crisis; it's like that first morning shot for an alcoholic. They wouldn't know what to make of their lives if they didn't have something urgent to run to, some errand that just can't wait. She was like that some of the times I'd spent with her.

"Could you? I can get it back to you in the morning."

"Nonsense," I said, "I'll have Leonard make you up a couple."

I stuck the mail under my arm and opened the second door. Besides having a thick glass panel, it was reinforced with iron, the frame of sheet steel, a door you couldn't get through with a crowbar. I had installed it myself the week I moved in, with money I had wheedled out of the Widow. I had suggested that she had a liability, this being Brooklyn, and robberies down the street her tenants talked about.

We went in. My own place was at the back on the main floor. It wasn't the biggest apartment, but I had two bedrooms, the whole side on that floor, so how could I complain? As we entered she looked around, though God knows what she could see through her shades.

"Make yourself at home," I said and tossed my mail down. "It'll take me a minute to find the key."

Akbar, half-tabby, half-Maine coon, all imperious, mrrrrkkkigggggaoued to us and stretched his paws on the rug. He sniffed delicately at Miranda, then came back to me. Akbar the Faithful, The Ever Vigilant, wondered if she would stay.

"Have you seen Gerald?" called a voice from the hallway. It was Bernice, who didn't have much time with her kid, since she worked.

"Um, no," I said. "I just got in."

Bernice impatiently watched us, as though we might be hiding her son and not telling anyone. Her face was worn with no sleep and an unkind wrinkle to one side of her mouth, way before she should've had to worry about wrinkles. She smiled at Miranda but Miranda glanced away. Bernice scampered back up the stairs.

Miranda shifted her stance by the open door, but her air seemed to reach out and go everywhere: insistent, incongruous, distorted with steely silence. She and I had started an affair some time before I knew Holly, and in my mind we had never really broken it off. We saw each other now and then. We talked. I could remember now that she seemed very different back then, when, despite her veneer she had seemed at a loss, like a rain-soaked creature looking for any sanctuary. So much so that despite that long soft neck and her Egyptian eyes you could never forget, I at first hadn't quite believed she was a model. Why would a model live here? It had to be some tall tale, I thought. But then I had seen her portfolio with clippings from magazines and honest to God I had to admit: in front of a camera she was radiant.

Perhaps at one time I had not seemed so bad a date. For one thing, believe it or not, she didn't know for a while that I was only the super; I let on that I was watching over the place for a friend of mine, just till she (the Widow) got things under control. At least I was friendly, and not such an unknown quantity since Miranda knew where I lived and that I was always around in the evenings. I was a picture of stability then. I was amicable, and I had a job, what a lot of women want.

Now, however, as she stood there waiting for me, all that was gone. Sam's words rang in my ears like some church choir at a funeral. I had been stupid. I was a frog and Miranda, waiting there, was a swan. Simple enough for Sam, but it's hard to admit if you're the frog. Sam's view on things echoed like a vengeance come down on me, but despite all that I liked living in the same building with her. If she wouldn't go out with me, that wouldn't stop me asking.

And I was only the super! Well, I was six-two, good build and I kept in shape. I had an alert look in my eye since I didn't do drugs or drink much. Most supers I've ever met are gnomes. You wouldn't go near them. They're either fat from watching TV all day, or they're shrunken wraiths that spit in the flowers and do smack every night they can. Well, you might say the job was invented to corrupt you. It was just sitting around all day and waiting for something to go wrong, if you lived it that way. Being super sounded cool at first, what with the free rent and some cash besides. But it was a trap for a lot of people. I had struck it right with the Widow; she wouldn't give me money, but I got free rent and I could have my other job on the side.

Miranda had loved me for a short time. And I was certainly taken. Cartwheeling. Spinning, I was. Maybe that's what went wrong: we didn't keep our balance. I didn't. We had been passionate lovers almost from when we met. I spent my mental energies trying each hour to figure when next I could call her. I savored those precious surprises when she would call me. We spent hours just lying in bed not saying much of anything, just vague whispers that seemed hardly anything at all. We seemed to share everything.

Then, one day, in the space of a couple of days, everything changed. She certainly did. I seemed to slide out of focus for her. She got more busy. When we met, she stopped telling me things. I felt puzzled, but I kept on thinking I could recoup, reclaim the old situation. I pressed her about it, and finally she told me. Not like I was wrong for her, she said in an exhausted tone, but she'd become involved with someone else. She had so little time. She should have told me sooner, she said. She had known him longer than me and she really felt indebted to him for all he had done to further her career. She and I didn't really know each other that well, she let on. But she still would talk with me sometimes. We would even have tea together now and then. She would invite me in so she could know all the gossip about the place. It really seemed to interest her, what everybody did, how they were getting along. I didn't reflect on it then, but how would she know anybody? You didn't see her around much, she came and went too quickly for that.

I found the key. I almost hated to show it to her, knowing it was the only thing she wanted from me now. I moved to accompany her up the stairs.

"Can't you just give me that one?" she asked poking with her fingers. I smiled broadly, letting her see my face even if I couldn't see hers.

"Oh, it's no trouble. I'll get you a copy made. Anyway, I don't like to let out the last one. You can understand."

She was silent as I went up with her. On the third-floor landing Ms. Peretti greeted us, her round apron-draped form seeming to bubble out of the doorway. The hands of a child wrapped around her knee.

"Oh, Mr. Fyrish," she said with that infectious joy of Italians who like to cook. "I wanted to talk to you a moment, but if you're busy right now, no, no, it can wait ..."

I said sure, that I'd be back. Miranda walked past as if she were on some windblown escarpment with no time for a glance either way. Ms. Peretti smiled at us both. You could tell she assumed we were lovers. I wasn't surprised she said nothing to Miranda. No one seemed to know Miranda very well. She never had parties or even guests that I heard about. Which should have struck me as odd, since she would have lots of connections from her work. I decided that she kept her parties elsewhere, and her home here was probably just her place to sleep.

Miranda went before me on the next flight of stairs, just a couple of steps. I got a whiff of her perfume, not very strong, just the lightest air, unquiet, high-tuned, reminding me that a lot of guys would desire her. Bernice stood in her doorway and disappeared when she saw us. Then on the last flight up Miranda stood on the landing, and asked if I could hurry. Then she glanced away and waited. I opened her door; the same key fit both locks. I promised to return with a new set. Wordlessly she walked in. She turned and looked at me, as though what was I waiting for now? Then she slammed the door.

3. Miranda

I got the keys made at Leonard's down the street and came back
and checked my answering machine. Ms. Clamper's spigot still
needed fixing, and I had put her off last week. The roof was more
important, and at least I had gone up and slapped some roofing
compound on the flashing over Tartakauer's apartment, so maybe
that wouldn't leak if it rained. And it probably would rain, the
radio said. I resolved that later that night I would call Ms.
Clamper. For sure. Right now I opened a beer and slumped back
on the extra bed by the back window. Trying to think of something
healthy, something besides Miranda. I was in no hurry to take her
the keys; all it meant was that she would reach through the door
in her arrogant way and snap them out of my hand—and that
would be the last I'd see of her for another two weeks. I tried to
think of something else.

This building for instance. It had become my home without my
realizing it. Akbar had come along, for one thing, and a cat
always knows where home is. In the harsh world of New York
realty, in actual fact, I could be shoved out tomorrow by the
Widow on one of her crazy whims. Oh, you hear about real estate
prices going through the roof in New York, and you think maybe
it's not possible to lose money here, but it is. A lot of people had
lost. Two of my friends had gone bankrupt from bad real estate
deals. But not the Widow. She made money, I was sure of that,
because everybody in the house paid. You get to know these
things, even though the money never passed through my hands.
She didn't want to come near the place, which was fine with me.
Just that she came to the glass factory now and then, and I saw
her there. That was a strange thing about her. She bought glass
ornaments of all shapes and colors that we made at my job, and
her house I knew was full of them. Thousands of characteristic
glass vials, all different shapes and textures and stains. And very
pricey, she'd have you know. Did she ever put anything in them?
What could they possibly hold?

Through the screen I could hear voices off and away, and a radio
that tinkled like glass on the other side of a lake. It was really
quiet here. If I leaned over I could see part of the sky and the

waving tops of trees against a stream of clouds they seemed to own.

How my father loved trees. He knew the names of hundreds of them and he could spot a hawthorn or a pear tree at a stone's throw. He could tell the age by a glance at the thickness of the trunk, which wasn't so unusual, but he had some crazy ideas. When I was small he told me that what you thought and feared and hoped for when you walked by a tree were mysteriously known to the tree. That the tree remembered the things done around it and the people and if they knew about the tree and the part it played, he said, "in what's real in their lives." A tree, according to him, felt things and knew things about people long dead, and about children, and the lives they would lead just from having played under its branches. He was a man of another century, my father, to have believed all that, even though he told it to me as a child, and I didn't know enough then to take in the value of all he said. What son does? Then he got silent when he got older. It was no good to think too much about him now: when he died, I went a little crazy. I ran away to travel all over Canada and Mexico and finally hit on America, in particular this charmed and battered city. I washed up on its shores, exhausted really, not believing I could live any place again without being anonymous and alone.

But here, now, I could look out on the scrubby grass, a few stalwart honey locusts and a row of older plane trees that divided the backyards of what had once been gardens for a single family each. Sometimes at night, I imagined, you could feel the ghosts of those people talking to each other, whispering, telling stories. Under the trees were ragged lines of broken furniture and rotted refrigerators drawn off like barricades. Families gathered for the evening now, some talking, some watching television. It's funny: even as insular as people tend to be in apartment houses, still I knew one old couple in my building who had gotten to know each other over the years and regularly dined together: Mr. Mannheim on two and Ms. Renfrow on the fourth floor. Never heard a word out of them.

The phone rang.

Let it ring, I thought, but no, I thought, don't stick with a bad habit. I picked it up. It was Miranda on the other end.

"I'm sorry I was so testy with you, Milo," she cooed. "I've had a lot of things on my mind recently and ... well, you know ... I just get a little impatient sometimes. I don't mean to emanate bad feelings." Her voice sounded warm and rich and promising. She used the word emanate. She was so languid I had to remind myself it was the same woman I'd seen only an hour before. I took a deep breath.

"Oh, that's okay," I said.

"You did get the keys like you said."

"Sure. Sure, I got them, Mir." The name I had used once.

"And so you'll bring them up right away."

"Sure. I got a couple of stops to make and then I'll bring them right up."

Mr. Clean.

"Thanks. I even thought that ... well, I'll tell you when you get here." We hung up.

Well, now wasn't that just like her? I even tried to warn myself: if her tone changed so drastically, could that mean that ...? I had to quash the fantasies that started buzzing up in the air to the tune of the melodious trickle of her voice. She sounded so inviting. She knew how to do that. What sand castles wouldn't I build out of such alluring smoke-in-the-air? I didn't want to put it off now. I put a cap on my beer and said farewell to Akbar, who watched me leave with astonished longing.

Up at Miranda's I quietly knocked on the door. After a second and louder knock the radio went down. She opened up.

"Hi. Here are your keys."

She took them and thanked me. Then she stopped. She was wearing a white terrycloth bathrobe and her hair was done up in a turban.

"Can I make you some iced tea?"

I went in, passing within an inch of the misty, haunting perfection of her mouth. She closed the door with her hip and the smell of the shower came off her. She looked at me steadily, as if she expected me to tell her something important, or even make an advance. But then when I was about to, she broke away, resetting her hair in the towel. She looked at me with the steady gaze of a child.

"I'm glad you came up right away. I guess you give me a feeling of security, Milo. And I don't do you justice sometimes. I don't give you the credit you deserve. You're very special to me."

"Well, thanks. The feeling's mutual," I said.

She moved around, like a dancer experimenting with the space. It was Thursday, she said, she had the weekend free, so she might go out of town. I looked around at the place where I hadn't been in weeks. It was laid out just the same. Like she had just moved in and never changed a thing.

For instance, the way she had the bed arranged was the oddest thing. It was an heirloom from her mother's mother, she told me once. It was right opposite the front door in a sort of wide spot that might have been a vestibule or a breakfast nook at one time. The bed filled up most of that space, and you had to walk beside it to get to the rest of the apartment. Anyone else would have put the bed in the center of the next room, which was larger. The bed was heavy lathed hardwood after all, and you would want to show it off. It was part of her kookiness, I thought, maybe part of the way she thumbed her nose at the rest of us. She told me once that she wanted it to be the first thing she hit when she opened the door. A lover's dream, perhaps, but I had slept there only a few spare nights.

I walked past the bed into the second room. It was just like the last time I had been there, entirely empty, but with a closet on one side. It was big; you could stroll around in it. This was where she did her dancing exercises, and of course, why she couldn't put the bed there. I had installed a bar for her along one wall, and she had gotten two $300 mirrors, about the time I first moved in, because she couldn't get the previous super to do it. The floor was sanded down to show the yellow of the wood, and it was lacquered smooth. She had insisted on having that done when she moved in, she told me. I looked around.

"You never told me about this," I said, leaning beside a picture on the wall. It was the only thing on that wall. Except for the mirrors and the bar, the other walls were totally bare.

"I put that up a few weeks ago," she said. "Just an old picture. I had it tucked away."

It was a photo of Miranda and a small child, a toddler, on a sunny beach. The horizon of the sea was behind them, and the toddler was showered in surf. Miranda held a sun hat from blowing away and she looked into the camera while she held out the other hand for the child. Another woman, her face in austere profile, was staring away at the horizon. Her air was serene and blithe. I presumed the brawny shadow across the foreground was some man's. Underneath, it was signed in a flourishing lax hand, as if it were a picture only of herself: "Simone. With love and remission."

"Your kid? You never told me you had a kid."

"A friend's. I won't have a child till I'm at least 35. I'm much too vain," she said with the matter-of-fact way of someone who has grown into consenting to all her lacks. Vanity was part of her profession, part of her life just like a stump leg or a deaf ear. You couldn't get away from looking the way you did, even if you looked great.

"Well, you could change your mind," I said.

"No," she said solemnly. "I won't."

"Where is the child now?"

"Oh, out west, I guess. We didn't keep in touch."

The frame was done in a kind of lacy design someone had made by hand from cut-out paper. It was something a woman with lots of time would have done. But it was exactly the kind of thing you would never expect of Miranda if you didn't know her, as worldly and unsentimental as she appeared.

"You look better without sunglasses," I said.

"I know," she said, dead serious, as if it was the product of profound deliberation. She didn't smile, though she had the most winning smile, which she could make appear with the suddenness of a beacon off shore. She filled out her bathrobe as prettily as any woman I had ever seen. The high arch above her eye was graceful as a swallow's wing. A lot of men could forget everything looking at that face. I certainly had.

I passed into the next room and flopped in the lounge chair next to the rosewood hope chest while she got the tea. Here was her furniture: a couch, a hope chest, a writing desk and chair. Also, two lounge chairs and two large potted tropical plants. This room looked out on the back through filmy curtains and latticed windows. The feeling you got here was of warmth and freedom spread out for you. Off in the distance over the roofs the scape was radiant in the slanting rays of the sun. I could imagine the woman sitting here by the hour at perfect peace with herself.

At my elbow was the rosewood hope chest I remembered. Did people have hope chests anymore? Wasn't that kind of old fashioned? I had never looked in it. It was open now and a tumble of lingerie and pins and rings and pendants in small boxes were spilled out as if trying to abscond. An old Bible was set to one side.

"Mind if I look at your Bible?" I called down the hall.

"No, it's all right," she said.

I picked up the Bible but what was underneath it caught my eye: It was an open box of children's toys. There were alphabet blocks, a toy hammer, a little football, The Hulk in miniature, a painted rock, little green dragons and dinosaurs, a string of plastic cubes and spheres. I studied the Bible: it was worn and leather bound, the kind made for swearing oaths on. On a blank page at the front someone had penciled in a date: "1896 Cheri Williams."

Miranda came in with the tea while I was looking through the Book of Ruth.

I sipped the tea and asked: "How do you know it'll be a boy?"

She put the box of toys away, as if they should be safe from fire.

"Well, it will be one or the other," she said, "so whenever I'm near a toy store, I add a little ... that's why they call it a hope chest."

She closed the lid down. She hesitated just enough for me to slip the Bible back in. The chest seemed to belie her sophisticated image, being full of history and sentimental. Like her bed.

"Something bad happened to me today," she said. She looked especially sad. "I just got my purse snatched. Right out here. Two blocks from here. Before you came."

I looked up.

"Were you hurt?"

"No, just shook up. Insulted, really."

"How much cash?" I asked.

"Not a lot. Two hundred dollars. And a few cosmetic things. Junk mostly. But: phone numbers. Credit cards. My cell phone. My appointment book which has all my phone numbers in it. And my keys."

"Thought I saw a purse on your bed."

"Oh, not that one," she said.

I felt awful for her and told her so in the gentlest words I could find. I asked for more details, as many as she felt like telling me. Not that I thought it would do any good; you could never catch people like that, especially since they liked to operate on the spur of the moment in neighborhoods far from where they lived. She hadn't been watching when they approached her, she said. Didn't know where they came from. She had screamed after them, and a couple of other people had seen it. But the muggers were too fast. So, thinking that I might be home soon, she had just waited outside. That was all.

"Miranda, that's terrible. Did you call the police?"

She seemed to be into her own thoughts and didn't say anything for a minute.

"I'll call them tomorrow," she said. "I have to get to the bank first. I don't have a cent."

"Well, I can lend you some ..."

"Oh, if you could just let me have a hundred dollars till I can get to the bank ..."

"Well, I can get it." I fished around in my pocket. All I had was forty bucks. Her fingers delicately pursed them out of my hand.

"Anyway you should call the police."

She took a long breath and her eyes seemed to glaze over.

After a pause her voice came out weighty and brittle: "I know some people that fix things like that. I'll talk to them. Someone was following me. I hate that. Only creeps do that. Sick people."

"Yeah, well, nobody's going to get it back for you now."

"Yes," she hissed at me. Her eyes flared.

She wanted revenge, which was natural enough. And there was a tight knot of spleen you could see writhing within her.

"I could, if I wanted to, get them killed. You don't know, but I know. People disappear ... if you want them to bad enough."

She sounded like she had actually found some crazy consolation for her loss.

"Really?" I said. "Have to tell you, I doubt it, Miranda. You'll never catch those guys. One in a million."

"You know shit! Some people know more than the cops. People that'll give me anything I want."

"Call them," I said with a positive tone, knowing that any action at all would get her mind off the humiliation and hurt she felt. "You really should. And tell the police anyway. And if you can remember their faces ..."

"I can remember enough," she said. Her fingers tore at the towel and pulled it away. "Two black teenagers, both thin. A peaked leather hat one of them wore, and I got a good look at his face. I'll remember that." Her lower lip took on a pout.

She jerked her head around as though from a dance position, the long stream of her hair lapsed gracefully over her shoulders. She wanted to forget about the purse, and what that took was some physical release like what she did now. She propped one knee on the wicker chair by the window and ran her fingers through the thick mesh of wet hair.

"I have missed you," she said looking out at the evening coloring the sky. "Over all this time I should have talked to you more. You're different from other men. It's just that I've had a lot of other things to think about in my life. A lot of things that don't matter got in the way before. We should talk. Like we used to."

"Well, uh.... Of course. I'm always ready," I said. But Miranda wasn't fazed. I should have perceived that she had no idea of changing anything with me.

She looked out at the horizon of building tops and said: "I think I would be better off if I could start over, in a way."

"Of course. Sure."

She turned and the lithe long set of her back tilted out in the open space of the room. She was holding her robe in the front so it slid down from her shoulders. She arched back and the line of her spine rose up like the stretch of a predatory cat.

"Suppose," she said in her wandering way, "you knew a child that needed help, but you couldn't get close for fear of making matters worse, what would you do?"

"You mean, like the kid in the photo?"

"No I don't mean that. That's something else."

I paused, thinking she would tell me more, but she didn't, as if that were all there was to it.

"Forget it, probably," I said. She looked around at me.

"Hold me."

She slipped into my arms and cringed there as if awaiting some thunder or blinding flash. She was like a high flood when she moved onto me, touching every pore. My hands slipped into the familiar small of her back like marmots licking up honey. Everything about her felt so tender, I gently wrapped her in. My arms seemed to absorb soft radiance right through her robe. We must have gone on a long time there immersed in kissing and holding and warmth I could hardly believe I was coming back to. Maybe tonight, I thought. Yes, without a doubt ...

The phone rang and she broke away with an angry tearing

insistence mixed with indifference all at once. I turned back and slumped in the chair. What was so important about the phone? What was I, *foie gras*? What was our closeness that filled that precious moment? I was dazed. I was kissing you, you witch, I thought. Wasn't this a time, a special time we yearned for? Or was I kissing somebody else and you just happened to walk by?

I felt angry, but I stopped myself. I was just letting myself get dragged around by the nose. Miranda, in her special way, could do a mental pirouette and the world she lived in by herself would change and out of the blue it could become something new and unexpected. And it was your tough luck if you thought you were invited into that world too.

While she was on the phone I pointlessly gazed around at the windows. The orange of evening made the place seem smoky and luminous, and I could imagine her sitting here writing a letter at the little desk which didn't seem to have the space for any but those small intimate sheets of tinted paper with delicious scent that women cherish. On days like today, the evening here would seem to go on forever.

Bits of Miranda's voice filtered in from the other room.

"... of course, I know it doesn't ... but if you want ... We can ... no, not later. Well, if you're nearby, what's the problem? If you can't make it ... No. Now is fine," I heard her voice in the other room. She had plans. I wouldn't see her later. The soft touch in the small of her back was a fish that got away.

She lingered by the phone, but soon she came back and asked if she could freshen up my tea.

"Miranda, what's going on? You treat me like a hat rack. With a hat rack you could have more fun, I suppose. You want to talk more with me, and then you make a date with some other guy? And he's going to be here in what, five minutes?"

She frowned and looked at me like a scolded child. Part of her wanted to get angry at me for talking to her like that, but for some reason she couldn't muster true anger. At least I had touched a nerve.

"It's my physical therapist," she said seriously. "For my back. It's all out of whack. And when he's gone I have to take a nap. Just three hours of sleep is all I need. So if you could come back at midnight, that would be great."

That meant going to work tomorrow with little or no sleep, but that wasn't much of a price to pay.

"Um, sure."

The buzzer sounded by the door. Her eyes widened and it looked like she was going to do nothing. Then she ran to the buzzer and pressed it for ten seconds.

"You'll have to go now," she said. I felt a cool wind of giddy imbalance from her mood. Could it be she was upset about seeing her physical therapist?

"I'm sorry we didn't have time … "

She looked away and ran her fingers along the wood of my chair.

"We can make up for it," she said. "But not now. Later. Yes. Can we talk later?"

"Well … sure."

"Midnight. I have to meet somebody now. I'll be free at midnight. I want to talk to you. I've been thinking about you."

"Then why make me leave?" I was sitting down, with my back to the window and some mean streak in me made me want to see who had rung the buzzer. I waited like a block of stone. It seemed a restful and a calming thing to do. I just sat there.

"You shouldn't wait here," she said.

"What have I got to be afraid of, Miranda?"

"It's not that, it's just that it's … awkward."

By now she knew I was going to meet this guy, in the hall or wherever. We both waited. Soon there was a knock at the door. She went and let in a man I had never seen before.

He was tall and had the rounded face of the languishing overfed. His lips were delicately curled, like satin pillows that seemed to be made darker by poor circulation. He had a soft face that, I suspected, belied his actual age. Even so, he seemed to me in his early twenties. His eyes were large, heavy-lidded, and left the impression of imminent sleep. All in all he was not a trivial figure. He was rather handsome in a well-dressed sort of way, but when he saw me he looked away with some strange embarrassment that made me feel an undertone of arrogance. For a moment as I sat there I had a flare in my eyes of scorn for them both.

And I won't forget the way she looked at him that particular moment, her daunted stillness and silent gesture of waiting.

I wondered immediately how they had met. They had known each other for some time, I got the feeling. She would meet all kinds of people in her work, of course, but even so he seemed a strange figure. He could be a set designer or some exotic kind of stylist, I could believe that. He carried a briefcase, which he set down by the door. She talked to him at the door in a purring whisper. But even after some talk, and him straightening his suit coat from the stride up five flights, he still didn't want to meet me, and he actually looked away when we were introduced. His name was Vincent, and he was sweating.

This is my rival? I didn't believe that physical therapist stuff, but let her have her story, I thought. I'm not the one to upset a nicely stacked apple cart, even of ridiculous fruit.

Or could it be he was a diplomat-trained, bona fide, absolute, honest to God, on his mother's grave, a real hands on physical therapist?

"How do you know Miranda?" he asked. His voice had a no excuses tinny sound.

"Well, we live in the same building," I said. "How about you?"

"We ... ah ... met in the course of business," he said.

We were all stock still for an embarrassing moment.

And then, something came to me like a sudden intuition that lights up a whole room between people. It was one of those rare moments of clarity you sometimes get. I felt like a glimpse came to me of her, for the first time, as she really was. I had the crazy notion that I saw why she was with this character, though I could never have put it in words. I saw that Miranda perhaps really was a wounded creature, one who needed no more wounds, not another glancing blow. The world, whatever her world was, had done enough and she could take no more or she would crumble. I wanted to cherish her: seeing her and wanting to cherish her meant much more than the absolute fact that she was moving swiftly out of my orbit. Her distance, though it would determine what actually happened, was, at that instant, just a meaningless misfortune. Although I couldn't spell it out in x, y and z, in this formally polite encounter I saw an unnamable pattern behind what was happening.

The room felt very cramped now. It wasn't that there were too many guys. It was that there was too much ambivalence and questionable intentions. It was even getting hard to breathe. I just wanted out.

"I'd better leave you to your business," I said, getting up.

I edged around Vincent, noticing the tiny points of his fingers radiating from a pudgy hand, as he waved me away. Jeweler's hands, I had heard them called. I walked to the door, fully expecting them to let me leave without a word. But no, she ran into the hall after me and closed the door behind her. She touched my arm.

"Come back at midnight," she whispered. She obviously didn't want Vincent to know she had plans. What was she going to tell him? What did I care?

"When? Eleven?"

"No. No, midnight. Don't knock at all. Use your key. You might have to wake me up and knocking would just upset people. Everyone talks. Understand? Don't forget me. It's going to rain and I'm afraid of storms."

You know, I couldn't have imagined her saying that if she hadn't said it. Where was all her aloofness now? Her cold smug air at being pursued and dogged by the attention of others, where was that? Don't forget me, she said. She made sure we had eye contact then, after all this evasion, but by then I was so disgusted with her unpredictability that I looked away before she did and I headed down the stairs.

Forget? I wouldn't forget. I doubted she'd be there at midnight.

4. The Reef Hermit

I was hardly two steps down the stairway when a voice called me from above.

"Milo."

Tartakauer looked wide-eyed at me. The old doctor. I liked him, though I couldn't say I understood a lot of the things he said. He had the place in the odd corner across from Miranda's and he hailed me now as if from his perch on some deserted reef.

"Milo, it's going to rain."

Tartakauer had been there from decades before and he told me things I would never get from anybody else. His presence seemed ancient and arcane, embedded like the calcified mortar stuck in chinks of granite beneath the pilings. He motioned me back up and through his door.

"Yeah, that's what's supposed to happen. Rain."

"But you fixed the roof like you said?"

"Of course."

"And it won't leak tonight?"

"How could it? When I fix a leak, it stays fixed."

"But the roofing compound is up there, on the roof?"

"Yeaaaah ..." I said cautiously. "What do you have in mind? Is there some conspiracy to steal my roofing compound?"

"So if it leaks, I'll just go up and fix it myself."

Theoretically he could do that; the ladder to the roof was in a hallway niche a few steps from his apartment.

"I don't want you going up there. If it leaks, call me," I said. "Don't go up there yourself. That stuff won't stick in the rain."

"You don't understand, or you don't remember. The leak," he said with a watchmaker's precision, "is over my bed."

"Well, this'll be a good test of it," I said. "It couldn't possibly leak without you noticing it."

He laughed.

"Kids," he said. "It's kids go up there and break the flashing. I hear them. Don't you know?"

"Yeah, I tell them to stay off. I think they do, most of the time. I don't want you going up there."

He shook his head as if I was a foreigner who would never catch on.

"It isn't me," he said. "I'm an old man. I can't catch those kids."

"So it might be them stealing my roofing compound."

He looked at me closely. A physician's look. What he would give to a new patient with a strange complaint.

"How have you been, Milo? You look a little peaked. Sit down. Don't mind my things. Push that aside."

I slid a pile of medical magazines off a cushioned armchair and reclined.

"Women, I guess."

He nodded. It was a common disease, difficult to treat. Doubtful prognosis.

"I heard you with Miranda. I know you like her. But you have a girlfriend. Do you need two?"

I liked Tartakauer. He was much more tolerant than Sam. Whatever disease you had, he didn't blame you. I shrugged with my hands.

"I'm a flake. We were close at one time. At least I thought so."

"Ah. You want to make up for the past."

"Well, I still like her, if that's what you mean."

"You want to change the past. We all do. No one will say that, of course. But watch people. I can see it in their faces. And in the way they act. Changing the past is a great human occupation. Many men spend their lives in that pursuit."

We were silent while he nodded and played with the drawings on his desk.

"She's seeing me tonight," I said. "At least she says so. She's pretty unpredictable."

"You're a fool for beauty. I too, even I ..."

Tartakauer, "Doc" to his friends, had once (he told it so sadly it seemed like a legend now) been a doctor with a thriving practice and many trusting patients. He had a house, and a devoted wife and at least one daughter, all lost to him now. They had somehow swindled him, as he told it, and they never made contact any more. For his wife, especially, I knew, he had no forgiveness. I saw on his desk the astrological drawings he sometimes tried to explain to me.

"What do you have here?" I asked.

"Ah," he said, as if I'd hit the nail on the head. "I have just worked this part out. You know, Milo, it is so obvious I don't know why I didn't see it before. It is just the story of Samson and Delilah all over again. You see? It is the woman who secretly, without his knowledge, enslaves the man. She takes away his hair, meaning his solar aspect and thus deprives him of light, meaning he can't see. That is very important. I have experienced that first hand many times, so it is not mere conjecture. She dilutes elemental sulfur, which is in his blood, so it can never become gold, just as Venus thwarts Mercury regardless of the trine, which is tonight, and so effervesces the essential solar aspect, the rational mind of man."

He breathed hard. "It's all so simple now, when Vega is high in the sky every night. It's the Lyre that cannot be tuned. That's why the woman is so arrogant. The whole world rises and sets around her. It's a feminine debility. You see, Milo, that's why there is only one female planet: Venus. I think sometimes there should be none. Look at yourself. The woman has crippled your judgment."

He ran his hand through the silver and gray hair on his head. He was really German, he told me once, but had immigrated here at an early age. He was fiercely loyal to the United States. I looked around at the dust and detritus of his front room. A breeze touched the tasseled curtain by the window where the clouds made a pillowed sky.

"It happened to the man across the hall," he said, pointing. I knew he meant Follett. "He was like you. Now they don't speak to each other. I could have predicted that. I am simply a grumbling old man; I have no use for her so I let her be."

I made to leave but he motioned me back like the Ancient Mariner.

"Because you see," he said, "when that woman passes me, I, well, I am like other men. She knows she is so beautiful. We men are crazy for beauty. Half our brains is in our dicks. And in my case ..." He helplessly spread his hands out from his pants. "I'm stupider than most, you see. I could never act on my desires. Ah, let me read you."

He pulled a book from his crowded shelves and opened almost instantly to the passage he wanted. He read:

> "An aged man is but a paltry thing,
> A tattered coat upon a stick, unless
> Soul clap its hands and sing, and louder sing
> For every tatter in its mortal dress,
> Nor is there singing school but studying
> Monuments of its own magnificence...."

"There you have it," he said, waving his arm and closing the book.

"Um ...Yeah?"

"Yeats," he said. "You can find everything in Yeats. Even with my accent. Ah, but with no sex, what have I got left? A good drink perhaps. But that hardly suffices, and I have no desire to become addicted to a thing that might shorten my life."

He tapped the drawings with his middle finger.

"This is the better way. It lets me know where I stand with great clarity, great accuracy. And sometimes it even tells me what is going to happen. Oh, Milo, you can come to me with a question, any question, if you are troubled or depressed. I'd be happy to talk with you. Just let me know. You don't have to bring your chart. Just come and we'll talk."

"I will. Of course."

"You see I am an old man. I open myself up to you. Some people would call me crazy for delving into such things, but isn't that better than pretending to be somebody I'm not?" He shrugged, open eyed.

"Of course." I said.

I fingered the heap of old medical journals harbored on the floor.

"You ever going to read these?"

"Ah, Milo, don't expect me to make sense any more than you do. I might. We all have intentions we can't explain."

As I turned to the door, I saw his rheumy eyes offering understanding and at the same time hoping for some untouchable something that you could never guess. He was self-sufficient and at the same time deeply lonely. He was a true hermit, hailing me from afar on his rock. He was an isolate, even though he lived in this limitless city. I knew a lot of hermits.

5. A Night In The Cellar

I went down to my place and sat with my cat. The sky, which had been so clear earlier, began to darken. The rain came as promised not long after that. Belatedly I remembered I had no money. I got my umbrella and ran out huddled in my tee shirt to get money to replenish what I lent to Miranda. I would give her more if she needed it. By the time I got back the rain was coming down in long gray veils. I got a beer and sat by the window again and looked out and let it get dark. Rain like that doesn't last long, I thought, but then it wouldn't stop, it just changed. Before long it was coming down in a steady drone, and I heard Manuel's sisters in the hall giggling after a hard run to shelter. Akbar coiled near my arm, nuzzled and looked at me strangely when the thunder came, as if it might be something I had done without giving it the cautious circumspection cats expect. Then he bit my hand. This is a kind of kiss for a cat. For him, love and murder are pretty much the same thing. Silly cat.

Leonard called.

"Hey, you gonna be in your shop?"

I knew he would bring over something to drink, which was good, and I wanted to get out of the house too. Especially if Holly showed up. Or called. I wasn't going to carry my cell. It was just that if people gathered and there was a long confab, I was going to have to leave them there in the cellar around midnight. I wouldn't throw them out. And the Widow wouldn't like that if she ever found out. Well, she probably wouldn't. Right then I didn't care.

"I guess. I can't stay late."

"Man, I gotta get away from here, you know what I mean?" I could hear kids yelling in the background. His wife was calling to him even while he was on the phone, asking who he was talking to.

"Come on over," I said.

I went downstairs to the basement. It was dingy down there, but I kept it mostly cleaned up. There was a table and chairs and space for my power tools. I picked up some shelves I was making and recommenced where I had left off last time. I would make some progress with that until Leonard came over.

Sam dropped by.

"I figured you'd be down here. Wanta get up a game?"

"No."

Sometimes we played poker there. Besides the table saw and drill press, and useless bits of machinery stacked around, there was a lot of space, and we had a card table somebody had donated for the purpose. Others showed up. Perhaps the rain had driven us all underground. Follett and one of the kids, Gerald, showed up. This kid was shy and brainy and tagged along behind Follett like a trailing dinghy. Follett had a sailor's build, and an arrogant swarthiness that went with his squinted left eye and his general quietness; he rarely had anything to say. He and the kid broke out some boxes and started playing chess in a space along the wall.

I sometimes invited people down to the cellar, and by now they came of their own accord if they thought I'd be there. There were a couple of stuffed chairs that had been ornate luxuries when they were new, and a cot in front of the TV on a shelf, and when we had nothing better to do, we watched that. But I was intent on my ruled lines and my circle saw. Maybe that's why I didn't notice Beremy when he came in. He was a lanky and harmless nut who never bothered anybody, except by boring them. In a way, for a rainy night, it was too cozy a gathering.

Leonard showed up. He was heavy set and athletic, with hands, you could tell, that had more strength than you needed to be a locksmith. Manuel followed after Leonard had knocked on his window. Leonard didn't live in the building, but he liked to show up with a six-pack when I was working there. He let on how he had gotten Manuel to buy the beer and a bottle of tequila "just in case," as they explained, thinking that all nights should be open ended. Leonard turned on the TV and sprawled out on the cot. He had the rotund face of a cherub who owned stock in some successful electronics company. By his own description, he was the black sheep of a sprawling Hispanic family where everybody liked to cook.

"If I brought a carjack into the house," he used to say, "it would go in the soup. Everything goes in the soup. I think she puts babies' diapers in there when I'm not looking. Noodles, cat food, dead pigeons, I can't guess. Everything is food. My youngest kid will be diabetic before he learns to smoke. And that's a crime. It's like a religion, man. Like being Catholic, which is for the dogs. I already got a Pope, she fixes dinner and goes to sleep in front of the TV. Plus she's fat. I mean, I'm not saying I don't love her. But she fixes a chili meatloaf and expects me to eat it all. Why I'm so fat, you know? It's the Pope feeding you wafers all your life. Thank God for you, you let me come here and don't care, Milo. I know you got your own woman troubles. At least I don't got to go to some grimy social club to get outta the house. Sit with a bunch of old men and punk teenagers who all have five brothers ready to kick your ass for you."

To hear him tell it, being a family man was a religion he would never leave, but would ceaselessly undermine from the inside. He hated Catholics, but he was one himself. "It's born into you, man; they get you when you're young, and what hope is there after that? You never have an original thought the rest of your life without wondering if it contradicts some pious oath taken by some saint God knows how many centuries ago who didn't know nothing, he was so out of it, never had sex except with himself, busy being pious his whole life."

He liked the horses and his friends, and was meticulous about his lock business, which he had built from a mail-order course out of some magazine into his own shop around on the avenue, selling not just keys, but smoking receptacles, chains, and leather accessories with eagles, eight balls, and pentagram medallions.

Manuel, who lived with his mother and an aunt on the first floor, sat by Leonard on a sofa cushion. Manuel had lost his father a year or so ago. Since then, he worked with Leonard on construction contracts Leonard sometimes got. Sam (known sometimes as Possible Sam, a nickname he had gotten from some marathon poker game they still talked about) propped his foot on a milk crate and looked mournfully at the TV on the shelf. In his hands was a deck of cards he continually shuffled like kneading a wad of dough. Beneath the TV, Gerald and Follett, his hair still wet, looked like they could handle any eventuality as long as it didn't take away from their chess game.

And there was Beremy, whom everybody knew, though nobody had any idea where he lived. Beremy wore his trademark vintage Victorian p-jacket with braids and high collar and a tee-shirt underneath with its bold emblem: a skull with Coors Forever across the forehead. The thing with Beremy was that, though he was certifiably crazy, you could have a kind of conversation with him, as long as you kept nodding and saying yes to all his criticism of the city, the mayor, gold prices, the Chinese, Blacks, whatever ... it all began to sound the same the more he talked about it, as he did now he had gotten Manuel and Leonard to listen. But if you didn't continue to at least passively participate in conversation with Beremy, he turned out to be entirely self-sufficient; he would go off on his own, singing little bits and whistling lyrically when birds were around. Or as now, when they weren't. For then Beremy would whistle and twitter out of hope some bird might come and join him in conversation. Beremy was in his own world, with his oily hair and his mouth that gaped when he laughed to disclose a whole cemetery of nicotine red teeth. He was smoking now. He was one of the neighborhood dysfunctionals everybody accepted as a character without knowing more than that. Probably it's truer to say we didn't want to know. Manuel was listening to him tell some story about drugs.

Soon, spread out on stacked newspapers by the wall, I had had a few beers myself. I joined with the others who all contributed to buying more beer—if Manuel (who said now he didn't have money) would run out in the rain and get it.

"The poor work for the rich, man," Leonard said with undisguised cruelty and laughter. "That's the way it is everywhere, not just America."

Before long I didn't care if I was listening to Beremy, or if I was watching hockey on TV. The others seemed to divide their attention in much the same way. I began to feel at home more than I'd felt all day. It was like weathering a hurricane on some Pacific atoll. The walls were thick and old, could withstand any storm. I didn't even have to be alone: I had friends. Why shouldn't I have a few drinks, hen-pecked as I was?

In the back of my mind was the certain dangerous thought that I didn't want to bring into full focus: because the fact was that Holly had a key to my place—which I didn't ever once regret, mind you—but somehow I just didn't want to be around if she showed up again. And it would be just like her to show up then: shove me out the car door with her foot so I nearly got killed, and an hour later come around like I should be able to take a joke. I didn't want to be there when she would "like some help" to unpack the groceries while we "merged" in some corny tête-à-tête where we were supposed to be honest and vulnerable and reconstitute our relationship after we'd had a little spat. I just couldn't be that generous, the way I was feeling—because, now I think about it, there was a strange atmosphere that night, some meanness and recoil in the air, despite our rained-on camaraderie.

Weren't we all fleeing women in one way or another? Manuel was fleeing his mother, who talked in staccato Spanish that seemed to never require a pause for breath. Leonard sure as Hell was escaping his wife; he made no secret of that. Sam I never saw with a woman, but he was so neat in his habits that nothing seemed to get in his way. He was really smart, Sam, and I liked the way he talked to me, even if it hurt sometimes. I saw him dress up sometimes, but he never said where he went. If a woman was in his life she would have a definite place and no vagueness. Follett, if you listened to others tell it, was always fleeing some woman, or else letting her fall into his arms. And Gerald, the kid, I knew was hiding out from his mother. The kid, like all kids, needed a father and sometimes he enjoyed coming down to the shop and helping me glue and clamp stuff, or work on the lathe. It was summer and kids had nothing to do. And me, well, I was filled with irritated ticked-off-ness that needed a few beers to wear off. I could believe the theory that that's why young men went to war: get away from women. Hell, yes: Get. It. Out., why don't we? It can't be hearts and flowers all the time. A little honesty. A man needs some space.

Tommy showed up and began pawing through the blocks and scrap on the other side of the table saw. I didn't care if he played there, if he just kept away from the saw and other tools. But no sooner had I turned my head than he had turned on the circle saw and thrown a two-by-four block on the blade so it flew through the air. I batted it down with my hand.

"Turn that thing off."

I ran around and pushed him away, and turned the saw off myself.

"Where's your mother?"

He giggled and scampered over a stack of boards.

"You don't know."

He wasn't afraid of me, which made me afraid I might hit him.

What? Was he possessed? Play with my table saw. Did these women lock their children in closets with only slasher videos to watch?

"Here she comes," he said sadly. There was a step on the stair and directly Paula came in, smiling broadly. Paula had plenty of common sense; why couldn't she instill it in her kid?

"Is this where my boy ran to? My little man. You rascal," she said as she tickled and embraced him all at once. He laughed and broke away from her and jetted up the stair.

"You don't mind him coming down here, do you?" she asked.

"No, if he stays away from the tools," I said.

"Yeah, he's not that smart sometimes. Just smack him one. Or tell me and I'll smack him."

"Well, he turned on the circle saw just now. He was in here like a ferret and I didn't even see him."

"I'll talk to him," she said seriously. "He's grown enough to have more sense. Don't let him down here till I tell you, okay?"

"Okay."

That would be easy; now I had a reason to throw him out. You always knew where you stood with Paula. She was a fisherman's ex-wife and she used to get up at three AM to go out on the trawlers and day boats. She was a tough broad that took no guff from anybody. With a curious air, she checked the TV to see if it was something she would like, and looked at each of the upturned faces. She went out the door.

"Tom likes hockey," she called from the stair. "Don't you little boy? That's what we'll be watching. Well, tomorrow's Friday, so how bad can it get?"

Follett hunched in a legless chair by the lumber shelves. His attention was only partly on the game. He had a kind of wild, hard-eyed alertness, and he held a coil of clothesline that he picked up nearby and twisted it in his hands as if he were wringing it out. It was a kind of nervous gesture. Add to that he had a tick in his left eye that made him wink when he wasn't looking at anything in particular. He had a charmed smile and a dimpled chin that was probably why women, if you could believe the stories, found him irresistible. He moved the chess pieces with large fingers that were still whitened from the plaster dust of whatever job he had. I knew he was smarter than the work he got. He was a misfit, a guy who fell through the cracks somehow. He stayed with Bernice sometimes, in a kind of sporadic relationship they didn't about. There must have been something there, if you could believe Tartakauer, but I wouldn't join in. I always think gossip is its own reward.

Gerald said: "Check," and Follett started to move and then his hand threw up the clothesline in disgust. He paused and his eyes wandered over the board like he'd never seen it before.

"I resign," Follett said and laughed a gap-toothed laugh like he'd had an obscene joke pulled on him, maybe something more important than a chess game but still easily given away. Gerald intently went about setting up the pieces for another game. The kid was known to be bright, and because his mother worked late, he sometimes played chess till late in the night. In recognition of his victory he licked his lips and shyly wiped his hands on his jeans.

With lazy ease Leonard relaxed back on his cot, a can poised before his mouth. He pointed out the fan that purred by the door. Some relative had given it to him at a special price, and he could get another one if anyone wanted it. He could get air conditioners too. Very good price. Manuel, turning aside from Beremy, said the air conditioners were really good and he'd let Beremy in on a deal.

"Best time now," Leonard said. He shook his head seriously. "My aunt works for a guy—he gets them right off the truck."

Beremy turned to the wall and started making bird sounds.

"Whose truck?" said Manuel. "That guy with the potatoes?"

"The hot potatoes," Follett said.

"Yeah, I bet I know who—it was his truck."

"That guy you seen the other day, with the tattoo here, you know?" Leonard said to Sam.

"I'm watching TV," Sam said.

Beremy somehow started a polemic about who had got the most drunk the Saturday night before, when he and some friends had all closed the Convent Bar. He went on about Tompkins Square, summers long ago—when it was "the park", before they cleaned it up and ruined it—and legendary binges he had been on. I watched him out of the corner of my eye, not wanting him to focus on me for his monologue. Like all predatory talkers, he needed little encouragement. You just had to glance in his direction and he would move closer, talk more incessantly, more emphatically. Maybe he had had a good mind once and had just damaged it with drugs and booze, you wouldn't know. You still meet people like that. Between moves, Follett listened to Beremy rattle on, and you could tell he thought Beremy was an interesting case, not just a fool.

"Gerald, are you down there?" a voice called. It was his mother, but all I could see of her was her high heels and a little bit of her calf on the stairs. She obviously thought it beneath her to come down to the subterranean world of menfolk. She had only scorn for our reptilian side; if we were going to be irresponsible, how low into the swamp could we sink? Or maybe her feet were just tired.

"Hi, Bernice," Follett called. She made no reply. Her child went to the bottom of the stair and there was some kind of intense conversation which they didn't want us to overhear. Apparently the kid hadn't had all the chess playing he wanted, and she wanted him to get to bed. Mother and child stuff.

"Come along, Gerald … where were you? Don't you know I worry? I live my whole life for you and tonight we can be together."

She went on with her cooing, things all mothers say. There was a tone of shushed anger in her voice, even when I couldn't understand what she said. After a minute of intense whispering, the kid came back and picked up his chess pieces and went to the stair. She was so insistent the way she gathered him in. Wasn't it good for a kid with no father to hang out with us? She would probably say we were a bunch of lushes.

Leonard stopped watching TV long enough to sip his beer and make a frown when the kid was gone.

"She does everything for that kid, always giving him gifts."

"Don't gossip," Sam said, eyes never leaving the TV.

Well, you know it may seem strange, but as I watched the kid dejectedly follow her ankles up the stair, I couldn't help thinking about something entirely different: baseball. I looked around and there they were, Leonard, Manuel, and Sam all in a row watching the game. Now I have to think: why was it that I didn't like baseball? What was wrong with me? It had to be a bad childhood. I couldn't make any sense of the game: there seemed to be all this waiting around. Then a crucial moment when the pitcher finally threw the ball, which seemed a mere accessory till then; then some action, which got replayed God knows how many times; it was a Rashomon kind of a game. You got to see certain plays from different angles, as though that would get you closer to the lives of the men who played the game. Then there would be more standing around and they would go through the whole thing again. I was sure the game was designed for automobile commercials.

But at bottom, I think I was rationalizing, wasn't I? Why couldn't I be just one of the guys? The fact was I had no idea where my dislike of baseball came from; probably it was something hidden in the past, the breaks I didn't get that other kids took for granted. That was why I was a misfit and was always getting into disagreements with people. That had to be it. I tried to make up for it by feigning an interest sometimes, but it was no good: baseball was like sex: a great truth serum—you just couldn't sit through all that horsing around without betraying impatience, if that was what you felt. A sensitive guy like Sam would pick it up right away.

Yvette came down. She was known to be Follett's main squeeze and she was something of a dish: she was thin and peppery and always walked with a sexy slink. She stood at the door with her wet raincoat, fingering his hair with her long, pointed skin color nails.

"This is where I shoulda come," she said, chewing her gum. "This is where the guys are."

Follett tried to fondle her hand without getting up, but she moved out of reach with her independent stride and sat on some boards watching TV. The curious thing was she shut Beremy up right away. He wouldn't say a word while she sat there. She seemed to enjoy the game but eventually Follett had had enough of just looking at her. He tossed down the clothesline and got up and said: "Let's go."

"I just started watching," she said.

He held out his hand to her. It was as if he spoke no English and wanted to coax her with no awkward words.

Well, she had demonstrated her superiority at least for that moment, and after a coy sneer out of the corner of her mouth she got up lazily and led him up the stair.

"That's love, man," Leonard said. "If you wanted to know what it looked like you couldn't do better than those guys."

Beremy made an obscene gesture with his fingers.

"You got to wait till the woman's in a good mood or you never going to get any time with her," Beremy said, leering. "Like Follett. He's cool. He don't say much, but he won't stop till he gets what he wants."

"What's that have to do with it?" said Leonard. "He's handsome and the rest of us just look ordinary. 'Cept Milo."

Manuel looked disgusted.

"... But that girl on the top floor, that's one I'd like to get," Beremy said waxing his palm.

"How do you know that's where she lives?" I said.

Leonard laughed.

"Her?"

"She always wears a bandana," Manuel said. "Babushka. You see her today? Like she's some spy hiding out."

Beremy seemed to like that he'd found something to talk about that we'd listen to.

"I know her," he said wide-eyed. "I know that tall lady with the babushka."

"She's too high-class for any of us, man. You're crazy, I ain't listening to you anymore," Leonard said.

"What you mean is you seen her. That's all you did."

"I tell you. I'd just like to be alone with her for two minutes. No, I say two hours. I wouldn't be out of control. I'd be in control, in control."

"Yeah, like you know women. Outta your head, man," Leonard said. "You never get close to that gal." He had lit a cigarette and limply held it away from his lips.

Beremy was undeterred. "I seen her all right. Oh, but she's nice." His lips were wet and he wiped them on the back of his hand. He smiled broadly at us. He said it again.

I suddenly hated him. I got up. Just getting up suddenly made all the drink whoosh to my head and the oxygen whoosh out and I had to steady myself.

"What do you know about it?" I said with more venom than I ever would have sober. "Someone just has to turn their back and you got a lot of talk. Easy talk."

"Not talk. Y-You don't understand. I know her," Beremy said nodding like a child.

I stepped on the cord that ran to the TV. It went dead and they all sat there like dummies. There was a silence, with only the moth-wing whir of the fan. I threw the beer can against the wall.

It happened not to be empty and spewed out as it slapped back on the floor.

"What about Miranda? What about her?" I asked him. "You ever even get her to say hello to you? Huh? Huh? It's all talk. Nice talk!"

"That's what he's saying, man," Leonard mumbled with a shrug and motioned with his beer. They all seemed embarrassed, all except me.

"I just came in to get out of the rain. I only local crazy person. Guy who take no shit from you," Beremy said. All of a sudden he didn't seem like a crazy person.

"Hey, don't get so upset, Milo. Nobody said nothing," Leonard said.

"Yeah, what are you anyway, her brother?" Sam said. I could feel him glaring at me with his depthless impatient eyes. He got up and plugged the TV in. Then he strode back and sat down and watched it. The sides of their faces loomed up at me like moons.

"What's up, Milo? Heh. Ease off, man."

Beremy was glassy and sweating now.

"She's sweet stuff," he said with wispy breath and his leering smile. He had finally got my attention. He was inching up in front of me. His hand looked like he would poke me in the eye. All his fingers splayed out from his hand and his eyes got big like I was changing before his eyes. I wanted him out of there. "What's it to you, Milo?" he said with a leer and then a laugh. He was laughing at me.

Maybe he thought I was going to hit him, and he swung out at me. I batted it away. There wasn't room to fight like that, and I was inside his long arms. The others were up. Sam pushed a chair between us. There was a crazy moment of scuffling back and forth and shoulders and hands and the ceiling flying, and somehow I slipped on something that rolled and I went back against the pile of newspapers. My head hit the wall and pain and confluent colors of a prism bright light on oil on water appeared in the blackness and then the blackness became everything as I slipped down the wall and could think of nothing I wanted more than sleep.

6. The Anti-Communist

I woke up in a hospital and I knew immediately what had happened. I looked around at the white sheets and the white ceiling and the white floors and finally found a human face. Nurses were standing at a counter talking earnestly. Everybody seemed to have a very precious stethoscope. The first real thought I had rushed into my mind like a hot rain: this is going to cost a mint! A hospital! Didn't anyone have better sense than to get me taken to a hospital? Those were my friends! All I did was hit my head. That's why you have a skull, so you can hit your head and get away with it and still go on thinking the way you always did before.

I looked at the faces of the nurses. Nobody seemed particularly excited, but nobody looked bored either. Well, it was just a Thursday, wasn't it? Saturday was their big night.

I looked around at the black woman on the bed next to mine. She was moaning softly, and she was really beat up. Her face was swollen and discolored, and I felt ashamed just lying there taking up a bed instead of somebody who was really hurt. How I was shamed! Not only didn't I want to be there, I had no right to be there. Then I tried to speak and the words just burbled out. I tried to move my head and stopped that pretty quickly: it was like moving a concrete mixer. It was several seconds before I knew I was making sense. Out of the corner of my eye there were gray spiders with green legs crawling out from under the separating sash.

Get a grip, kid.

But there was a needle in my arm and I pulled off the tape and pulled that out. It squirted all over me till I found the valve.

A tall black man in a white coat came over to me.

"You shouldn't do that. Lie back and relax."

"I feel fine." I touched the back of my head; there was a big swollen lump and some blood solidified in my hair. "I feel fine. I have to go."

"You need an X-ray to make sure you don't have a concussion."

"Well, it didn't break my skull, did it?"

"It's impossible to say. There's too much swelling. I advise you to stay the night, for observation. The X-ray lab will be open in the morning."

"I'm not staying." There was a brown-red stain on the pillow.

You could tell from the way he paused while I looked around for my shoes. He didn't want to say the wrong thing.

"Well, this isn't a prison," he said. "But I advise you to stay for observation."

My shoes were on the floor and I got down and put them on. I was still dressed. It hurt to move my neck, but my head hurt less, so I knew that was all right. I made for the door.

A nurse rushed past me and stopped at the door. I knew it was up then.

"I'm afraid you can't leave, sir."

"Why not? I'm not sticking around here."

"Oh, that's very bad. You got fourteen stitches in your scalp. You should stay for tests. You should stay at least overnight till the lab opens in the morning."

"Oh yeah? What would that cost?"

"I have no idea. How're you feeling?"

"I'm clearing out."

She seemed at first like she would lose her cool. The look in her eyes was unfavorable, like she made a habit of being angry and looking polite. I knew I was up against a professional.

"All right, if you want to go. This isn't a prison, Mr. Fyrish. But if you want to go, you have to sign this."

"I'm fine and I ain't signing nothing."

"I'm afraid I'll have to ask you."

"What's it say?"

"That you're refusing to stay against the advice of a physician. You could die."

"I am refusing. What physician?"

"Dr. Makuola. It's written right here, sir."

I signed. Her manner changed entirely.

"I'm glad you're feeling better."

She was all smiles and couldn't get out of my way fast enough.

The rain had tapered down to a soft drizzle. The streets were wet like in a noir movie. I walked down a long ramp and saw Sam waiting for me on the sidewalk, his raincoat wet on the shoulders. I thanked him for coming to check up on me. He nodded.

"What time is it?" I said.

He looked at his watch. "About three-thirty. You have a concussion?"

"No."

"Guy who took you away thought maybe ..."

"How about you?"

"I didn't hit my head against a concrete wall," he said.

We stood and breathed in the wet air. I felt relieved to get out in the wet.

"You know how many people die each year from diseases you can only get in hospitals?" I asked.

"No. Are you delusional?"

"Sixty thousand. That's how many. And that's what they admit to. They're probably sweeping a lot of stuff under the rug. You know if you die you lose all your first amendment rights. And then only the hospital gets to say what you died of. Think about that. And it's full of a lot of people just pretending to be sick, don't forget about them. Insurance freeloaders. I was in there with a bunch of disease-prone, dying freeloaders. People with dirty hands who don't mind their own business and don't take care of themselves."

"Listen, I know you're pissed. Leonard called the cops. You coulda been dying; we had no way of knowing."

"And that's not counting the ones that contract the disease in the hospital and then go someplace else to die...."

Sam looked at me sadly. Why didn't he tell me to fuck off if I wasn't grateful to my friends who tried to save my life? It looked like the idea passed through his mind but he didn't want to be the kind of person who would say that.

"Look, Milo," he said, "there's no way we coulda kept you out of that hospital. It was an act of God."

"And that's another thing: God knows how much this is going to cost me. You know how much? Do you?"

"Don't you have insurance?"

"Insurance is a communist plot."

"You don't have any," Sam said with tight focus in his voice. "You kidding?"

"No. It's against my religion. Insurance is a scam to make people think they're getting something for nothing. When you really need them they don't pay. They have statisticians working day and night to make sure it's unfair. It's communist, like I said."

"Gonna cost you a bundle, man," Sam said kicking his toe

against the curb.

"Yeah, I know."

"Maybe you can get the Widow to pay for it. Line of duty, know what I mean? You were keeping disagreeable types away from her property. It might get her to cough up a little."

I wished he was right.

"You don't know the widow," I said. "I better not tell her about this."

"She'll listen to reason. Wasn't her got clonked on the head."

"Yeah, I can tell her that, it's worth a try. She should be providing insurance. Hazardous work. That kind of thing."

He shrugged.

"A bundle." He sighed. "It's a pisser. And you weren't really that beat up. At least I don't think you were. But you didn't come around right away, and Leonard called the cops. I couldn't stop him. If you'd been okay when the ambulance came I would've talked them out of it. But they said it could be a concussion and you had to be looked at by a doctor. They said they couldn't leave you like that."

"Don't you think I could have done that? On my own time?"

"I know you could, Milo. It's a pisser, like I said. But I didn't give them nothing, or tell them nothing. I was just a bystander. Nobody's stopping you, although I wouldn't give you much of a chance once they get your social security number. They already know your address and your name. I had to give them that."

"What? Why?"

I felt the back of my head. It hurt but it was a hurt you could put up with. I picked at the pieces of dried blood. The bone wasn't pliant, at least there was that. I looked down and there was blood on my shirt.

"Well, the blood and all," said Sam.

And that was a pisser for sure, because if anybody looked at me they would have a clear impression that I was helpless, drunk, and badly beaten up. Every claim I made for my health would be taken as the desperate defense of a weakened individual unable to gauge his own state.

"You're saying I looked pathetic, aren't you?"

"Well, not that."

"That I looked like I couldn't take care of myself."

Sam gave an exhausted look around at the street lights.

"Y'see, Milo, the way you looked. I mean the way you appeared after this accident.… I mean when you hit your head.… Well, it didn't inspire confidence. No. It didn't. That's what I'm saying. When the guys in the green coats came around and checked your pulse, there wasn't a lot I could say, you know? What was I going to say, that you'll wake up soon? I mean you really got clocked."

"And you think any of that's going to be paid by Beremy?"

"Beremy's an idiot, Milo. You got clonked on the head getting in a fight with an idiot."

"Doesn't mean he didn't insult me," I said. "And insult Miranda too. I had a right to get in a fight with him. He's an idiot. I hate idiots. Oughta be locked up. Few nights in the slammer and he'd get smarter, you'd see. It ain't right they let him out like that."

"Well you scared the shit out of him, I'll say that. You won't see his face around there for a while. He lit out like his tail was on fire."

"Serves him right."

Sam looked at me like he wasn't sure who he was talking to. That's the thing about my way of communicating sometimes: I say some pretty stupid things, but then I enjoy watching the look in other people's faces: you can tell so much. Sometimes they feel sorry for you. Others just want to get away. Most want to straighten you out. It's an experiment in human relations. And it's all true; nobody lies at times like that. Sometimes they tell the truth just because they think you're not listening. Or you're an idiot.

Sam looked down the street.

"Come on, I'll get us a cab."

"I ain't paying for no cab."

"I'll pay. You gotta get home and get some sleep and hope you remember half the bullshit you been saying."

But when we got back to Termite Street I was feeling so grateful to Sam I insisted on paying the cab and even threw in a ten dollar tip.

I didn't want to go in right away. I was too angry and not collected at all. I waited by the stoop. Sam moved away.

"Thanks," I said. "You came around when I least expected it." It seemed too little to say for as much as I felt because he didn't desert me, and went to the trouble of coming to see how I was.

"I'm going in," Sam said finally. "I gotta get some sleep." He trudged up the steps and went in.

I stood there for a minute, breathing in the moment of solitude and strangeness. I looked up and down the street, seeing not even an idle carouser like myself. Then from down the street I saw a solitary pedestrian coming closer. I didn't recognize her till she got close.

"Hello, Bernice."

"Hi, Milo. Bagging work tomorrow?"

"Yeah maybe. I got a little too drunk. How about you? You just get off work?"

She looked around distractedly, like she was nervous about being with me, but didn't want to seem in a hurry to go. But she did go.

"That's right. Get myself some sleep. See you later, Milo."

And just as she passed, I realized I was standing there putting off something. It had never left my head. I was too late to be on time for my rendezvous with Miranda, but I had already made a promise to myself while all this was going on: that I would go and wake her up and make her serve me some tea like she had before. We would recommence our conversation, she owed me at least that even if it was four in the morning.

I went in and started to go to my apartment, but something stopped me: she might have left a message on my machine, or maybe Holly had. Or Holly was there, and there would be a long story we would have to go through. I didn't want anything to deflect me. I heard no sound above me. I went up the stairs.

When I got up to her place I knocked softly even though she said not to. I had the key. I fished it out. There were two locks on her door that took the same key. You had to turn one one way, the other the other way. Both were locked. The first clicked back. The bolt of the second rolled aside like dice clicking. The door parted and I slipped inside. Her reading lamp was aimed at the door, so all I could see was bright white light shining right in my eyes. It was one of those super bright halogen lamps and must have been a hundred watts. But it was shaded so it wouldn't start a fire.

I closed the door and waited. There was no sound. I couldn't see a thing. I reached across the bed for the lamp. My foot touched something soft, and I balanced on one foot to reach the lamp and turn it off. I fumbled around in the dark till I found another switch.

Miranda was on the floor beside her bed, lying face down on several layers of blankets. Her arms were tied behind her to the board of the bed. Her feet were tied together and hung from the post of the bed so that her knees were just off the floor. Her head was lying flat on the blankets facing my feet. There was a plastic sack hung loosely over her head and some water in it. A towel under her head was wet. Her mouth was covered in a layer of padding and tape running in long strips back to below her ear.

I knelt down beside her. It was as if she had been tied there purposely so she would be in the way, be seen. And now, again, I was seeing green spiders crawl out of the spots in front of my eyes. I thought: this is impossible. Impossible. And so I couldn't help looking at her.

Right away I was getting nauseous, as though my stomach knew something I didn't yet know. I hadn't even seen a dead person since my father died. The movies never prepare you for real death. If they did, you would value human life differently: it would make you live in other ways.

I pulled the sack off her head and lifted her limp head. I touched her eyelid. It flipped back with the lightest touch, like nobody would let you do if they were alive. I could see the white. It was still as glass. The pupil was glassy black and totally empty. It didn't look at me. It wasn't a face anymore.

She was tied in some elaborate way, with more than enough rope to keep her from getting away. But nothing seemed that messed up. And it was so natural those blankets under her: it looked like she had wanted to stretch out on the floor to get cool, because she didn't user her air conditioner and she left a lot of windows open. She was sort of half-dressed in the same bathrobe I had seen her in before.

I had to get the police, but I was starting to shake. I looked around for the phone, but I didn't see it, and it felt like soon I was going to throw up. My head pulsed with pain with each heartbeat.

I felt the inside of her palms; they were as soft as I had felt them earlier that evening. A little springy. I moved her fingers, and they flipped back like thin dead fish. The walls were starting to swim. I walked out, locked the door, and I went back downstairs, three steps at a time, and threw up in the sink.

"What is it?" Holly asked, her face floating sidewise into my view. I fell down, I was so glad to see her.

"Oh, Holly. You're so wonderful to come here."

I must have looked like a mess. She looked horrified; she already knew something was wrong. I was fumbling with the phone, like it was a strange instrument I had never seen before. I felt very sleepy, as if the most pleasant thing that could happen to me was to slide down the wall right there. Holly would help me, I was sure. I gave up on the phone. The buttons were moving around under my fingers. Everything seemed to be in pools of weird colors that receded away from me and wanted strangely to gather speed.

"Call 911," I said with a furry echo in my sinus that rang through my whole skull. It hurt to talk.

"Tell them to come because Miranda's dead," I said.

Then a great black mountain centered over my skull and descended and kept descending until the thin line of light at the horizon was crowded, pressed down and consented to turn black.

7. A Rash Visit

I must have slept some because I woke up with blankets under me and over my feet. Woke up suddenly, with the buzzer sounding like a hoard of locusts winding up from the tunnels of some subterranean Hell where all the really big locusts wait to be let out.

It woke me up but I took a second to think if I had really heard it. It came again. I disliked using the intercom when I could just look out and see who it was, but I was feeling groggy. I pressed the button and asked:

"Who is it?"

There was no answer. The buzzer sounded again, longer this time. Holly stirred in the next room. I repeated the question and waited. The buzzer sounded again, then stopped. A voice came back crackling through the cavern of the bad microphone.

"Police. Open up."

In a flash it came to me. Of course. What took them so long?

I stuck my head out the door and saw a short wiry cop in a black raincoat. It was drizzling rain still. I went and opened the door.

The cop poked his badge in my face, then flipped it shut, two other cops in black raincoats were behind him.

"You have a Miranda Dauphine living here?"

"Yes. 5C."

The cop seemed to know that. He nodded and pushed past me. His face was bluish from his thick beard, and maybe he hadn't shaved for a few hours. His eyes caught me: they were yellow hued on the whites and pure black in the centers with fine gray irises. There was an oily blue ring under one eye and that contracted in a little wince as he stared at me, waiting. He stood in the little corridor there before the stair as if an awful chance of fate had blown him there and had left him all alone.

"Who are you?" he said.

"Super," I said.

"You the super?"

"Yeah."

"You know Miranda Dauphine?"

"5C. I told you ..."

"We got a call from her," he said blinking kindly.

He didn't care what I said.

"We got word there's a violation in her apartment. We'd like to see."

I stared at him. The whole horrible scene of her death rolled in upon me, as if it would take charge of my mind right now. I had been all right till I remembered that. He watched me with hungry curiosity, as though he had never seen my kind before and he was devouring every detail as fast as he could.

"Did you hear or see somebody go into her apartment last night?" he said like he was cutting into a can with his bare hands. "Because if you did, you'd better tell me now."

He leaned against the wall. While we were talking his left hand was shaking out a cigarette out of a pack and almost put it in his lips. The cigarette fell down in front of him, but instead of picking it up, he shook out another one. He got that one lit and breathed it.

"You let some men in here last night," he said. "How many? Where are they? Are they in her apartment?"

"I didn't let anyone in. Neither did she ... I don't think ..."

"You don't think."

"I don't know what she did."

The other two cops had crowded in by now; they were both big men with cop hats and rain gear.

"You didn't let no guys in?"

"No. Listen, I think you should go up there."

"All night?"

"What?"

"You didn't let nobody into her apartment? All night? You sure?"

"No, I didn't. If she did, I don't know."

He grinned at me and moved closer. He was steaming with impatience, but his thin fingers picked at the cigarette like he could wait like a reptile on a rock if that's what it took.

"It's good not to lie," he said with a kindly tone and a big grin. "It can be unpleasant if you get found out. Know what I mean?"

We all seemed crowded and steamy in the little hallway.

"Let's go up." said one, who had a block-like face and large lascivious fat lips. He was a heavy guy and his eyes were folded in creases of flesh that glistened with rain. The third guy was taller and thinner and wore a black hat with plastic over it. He had a misty sleepy look in his eyes and a stove-pipe neck that seemed to break at the Adam's apple. The sides of his cheeks were incised with deep acne scars. His head where you could see under the hat had been recently shaved almost clean.

The short cop grunted to them: "Up. Five flights."

"Hey, Leo, it could be nothing. Could be a piece of cake."

"Downstairs."

"Billy, you do that."

The guy with the fat lips crowded past.

"How big is the cellar? You, I mean."

I couldn't think for a minute.

"It's a cellar. It's as big as the house."

"Can anybody get down there from the front?"

"Yeah ... if they have a key. What's going on?"

"How many people live here?"

I shrugged.

"Thirty, maybe. Counting kids."

Billy crowded past me and went down.

The tall cop followed him and waited at the top of the stair. Holly, dressed in her pink robe that she kept hung in my bathroom, came out the door and stood between us, looking from one end to the other.

"What's going on?" she asked me, blinking.

"I think you should go," I said. Everyone was still. I didn't feel like saying anything more, and Holly acted like whatever I said it wasn't right. She looked at each of the cops and back at me. Billy came up to our level three steps at a time.

"Nothing there," he said. He heaved a single breath and planted his feet.

I turned around to Holly.

"Holly, why don't you get on out of here? I need to take care of this alone."

"You sure?"

"I'm real sure."

"Yeah, okay. I have to go to my place first. I don't want to be late." She ducked back in the apartment. She took her job seriously and liked to be there early every day.

The short cop turned to me. "She doesn't answer her bell. You got a key to her place?"

I still had the one in my pocket. I nodded to him.

"Come along."

The men strode up the stairs, the short cop first, craning his neck to watch above him. I went with them.

At the top of the next landing the other two were waiting for us. Then Billy went ahead. It looked like they had planned to trade off who went first and who waited behind. It was like a little dance that they did. Without really thinking about it I began to hang back.

On the third landing Victor's sister appeared with her bag to go out. She stopped when she saw us and her eyes narrowed.

"Milo," she said, as if I had just dropped through a window. I shrugged at her and pointed to the cops.

"Ah. I see," she said. She nodded and folded her keys in her purse. She disappeared down the stair.

We made the next two landings without a word.

"Which one is hers?" the short one asked, but he was looking up the stair to the roof when I pointed.

"We gotta check the roof," he said.

"I'll do it," Billy said.

The other two stood staring at Miranda's door until he came back.

"Can you get to her apartment from the roof?" Leo wanted to know.

"Yeah," said the other. He shrugged. "You can if you want to bad enough."

"Nothing on the fire escape?"

"Uh ... I didn't look there."

"You shit ..."

"Forget it. It don't matter."

Then they stood there looking at the door. They huddled together. Billy was muttering something but the other two were speaking too quickly to hear him.

"No, I ..."

"Whyn't he ..."

"Do it."

"Now?"

"Why not now?"

"... not enough time ..."

"... a setup ..."

"Fuckin' do it," the tall one said.

"Fuck you guys," Leo said in his quick tight voice. He didn't want to listen.

"All right. We'll flip for it."

"Hell with that."

"I'll do it but I gotta get extra."

"Extra?" said Billy.

"Yeah," the tall cop smiled with a slack jaw. Like it was obvious but still simple enough to be true. "Oughta be worth more. I oughta get extra."

The other man laughed.

"Your ass."

"Bullshit. Same as before. You're not changing the deal now."

"Half from each of you guys. You want me to do it? I'll fucking do it."

"Who says you shouldn't do it for nothing?"

"I did the skylight."

"Big fuckin' deal."

"Fuck if I care."

"Fuck you guys."

In one motion the short man swung away. The others parted from him as if they were doing a dance and he had the lit-up circle in the center. He went over to the door and knocked on it. He waited to the side, but he didn't have his gun out. Nothing. Then he knocked again. He waited and then he came over to me. I was standing out of the way as much as possible.

"Gimme the key." He grabbed it out of my hand.

"Whyn't you make him do it? He's the super."

"Why don't you fucking shut up?"

The short one walked to the door and put the key in the lock with his left hand. He turned it. The bolt made a sound, but the door didn't open. The same key fit two locks on her door and you had to turn one one way and the other the other way. But why was it locked anyway? I didn't remember locking it, but maybe I had. In as low and calm a voice as I could manage I started telling him how to do this, but he acted like he didn't hear me. With a tight-lipped grimace he was jiggling the key, but he was doing no good. The man in the hat moved around to be clear of him. Billy hung back. The short man was getting more angry but he was getting clumsier along with it. He dropped the cigarette out of his lips. Then he dropped the key. It clinked on the floor like a pixie laughing at us gopher giants. He picked it up and pushed it in the second lock. It turned all right but he couldn't open the door. He jiggled the key some more and it came back and flipped out again with a metallic ting onto the floor.

"Fuck it," he grunted with absolute fury.

He backed away from the door and raised a pump shotgun from under his coat. The blast made the dust come off the wall in an even layer along its length. It was enough noise to wake up Plato. But the worst of it was that he had missed; he only made a hole in the door, and not a big one at that. Mostly he had just splintered the panel. The tall cop opened his raincoat then. Same thing, a pump shotgun. He knelt slightly and fired at the door. He didn't wince. Then they both fired. Then Billy came up with a small machinegun (an Uzi, I guess) and he shot too. The door broke away from the frame, then with another shot came loose from the top hinge.

I didn't think these guys were cops. I got more scared when I thought they might be on drugs.

There was a ringing silence and pieces of plaster pecked down all around. Now Miranda's door was open, for the second or third shot had torn off the strikes. There was dust everywhere. Nitrogenous smells. The tall one went in through the dust, angrily pushed the door all the way open. He leaped over something. Leo looked in through the dust. He kicked the door.

"Hey!" he yelped. "I'm coming in."

"Come in," the other said from inside. "Nothing here. Tell Opov. We gotta go."

Billy went to the side of the door. He hung back and then he saw more clearly. The tall cop came out and walked to the stair.

"Damn," he said and went down.

"What's making noise?" a voice came up the stair.

Follett came out of the apartment next to Miranda's. He was putting on his shirt. He had a cigarette poked in his lip. He took one look at the raincoats and guns and ducked back into his apartment.

"Was that down there?" some voice said.

"No, up there," someone called up.

"Go back in your apartments," the tall cop said from below. "The trouble's over."

There was a shuffling noise from below.

Tartakauer came out in his robe and stared from under his bushy eyebrows at the men. He stood in his doorway stock still. Then he walked back in and shut the door.

Leo came out of Miranda's. He leaned over the stairwell and grinned down.

"Police. Stay back," he called down. "Woman had a prowler. The police are here. Everything's under control."

Their murmuring slowed, at least for the moment. "Calm down," he said simply. "The trouble's over. Go back to your apartments."

It was like a veil had been dropped over them. The shouting stopped. They were calm for the moment.

I went in Miranda's door. She was lying face up on the blankets by the bed. She looked as if she'd sprawled out there to cool off and had slipped into a nice sleep. There were no ropes, no plastic, no gag and no water anywhere I could see. I had a wonderful hopeful thought for a moment that it was a different person. Or that she was okay. But no, it was Miranda. She wasn't okay. She had the same scratches on her thigh, which I remembered. Dust and particles of plaster were everywhere.

"Holy shit," I said without having to fake much. Her eyes were half open just the way I had left them. There were bits of plaster stuck to her eyes that took away the glisten. She had bruises on her face as if she'd been hit there. Her legs stretched out and crossed in a knobby way at the toes like a child's. There were bruises on her ankles. She was still wearing the same robe, though it was bunched up and twisted under her. Her lips seemed oddly drawn apart and the sides drawn together, as if she had been stopped and frozen to death while singing a single sustained note. The skin of her lips was crinkled and over that too there were little chalky flecks of dust. Her arms lay still at her side, and looking at them, I thought stupidly: now she's free.

The wall opposite the door had several small holes in it running up over head-high. And there was one hole you could put your fist in.

Where were the real police? Had they shown up and left while I was conked out? Everything was upside down.

The tall "cop" appeared in the doorway.

"Wait a minute," he said. "Close the door." I went and pushed the door so it was closer to being closed. He stayed outside. A child's voice warbled up from the stairway but no one came up. I took a quick look around the apartment, but everything was the same, as far as I could see. Then I noticed something odd: the picture of Miranda on the beach was gone from the wall where she had placed it. It was far from the door, so how had it been blown away? The only other thing new was the way Miranda lay there, and the debris from where they had broken in. The mirror by the door was cracked. Cracks ran out from the molding in the wall where whole pieces of plaster had come out.

Someone came up the steps and the door pushed open with an aching scrape. Leo came in and after him came a very fat man with a head like an inverted shot glass. He had totally white hair cut bushy short. He was obviously not a cop: he had no pretense of a uniform. He was wearing an open flowery shirt that might have been intended for a casual morning stroll. It was sopping wet and gray with sweat now. In one hand he held a half-open brown briefcase. He kneeled down over Miranda and didn't say a thing. Someone ran noisily across the level below. Other voices floated up. The fat man was looking at the dead woman with intense eyes that glazed as if he was looking into a fire. In another second his face came apart and darkened and stiffened into a mask of pain.

"This is what she wanted me to see," he said sarcastically. He nodded pensively, as if he had all the time in the world. He had a Russian accent or something like it. He wiped his face all over and tried to dry his hand on his chest. Then his eyes got bigger as he looked at her face. The others stood around making antsy movements.

"There's no one else here?" he said in a shaky voice.

"No. Whole place is empty."

"Who's he?" he said without looking at me.

"Super," the short one muttered.

Fatty grabbed Miranda's hand. Then he set it down as if he didn't know what to do with it. He reached over and put his hand under her throat. He had short fingers for a man, not as long as hers.

"We gotta get outta here," the short man said.

There was more shuffling on the floor below. Somebody called up and voices echoed from further down. Someone was explaining something to somebody. That might keep them busy for another minute.

"We gotta go," the tall one said. His gun was out of sight now. His coat was buttoned again and his right arm was again in his pocket. He was feverish, waiting by the door.

The fat man was having trouble tearing himself away from Miranda. The others were standing around as if they had marbles under their feet. Billy strode through the dust and looked grimly down the stairwell. The short man kicked a shard of plaster. The fat one looked like he was going to touch Miranda's arm again, but then he backed away. Each time he made a movement he would withdraw like he wanted to do something else. His face was dripping with sweat. He looked around at the other room.

"She live here alone?" he asked me, his eyes bulging at me.

"Yeah."

"How long?"

I shrugged. "Since I've been here. At least two years."

"We got no time for this," the short one said, going finally to the top of the stair. The fat man didn't seem to hear. His glance for an instant fell on me, and he had dark, large, almost liquid eyes. His eyes were hung out like globes of white around angry lead-colored button ingots.

"Did you look around?"

"Yeah, there's no one."

"I mean did you look ..."

"There's no time for any more of this."

"Cover that gun," he said. Billy had an extra gun and he tossed it to the short guy, who put it under his raincoat.

"... filthy hole," the fourth man cursed, looking around. He hefted himself down the stairs and was gone.

"We going?" Billy asked.

"Whatta you think?" the short one said. Then he turned angrily to me. His eyes were mean little gray cartwheels with the devil knows what craziness in back of them. He spoke each word as if he was lightly touching a cigarette to my face: "The more you forget, the better off you'll be."

Then he turned and was gone.

I went and looked down the stairwell. Murmuring voices stopped on the floor below. They were all four of them running, running hard, the fat man faster than all of them. And nobody jumped up to get in their way.

8. Police Procedural

I called 911, but other people had already called.

The real police soon arrived. Two of the streets they might have taken were blocked by stalled vans, a curious coincidence I thought. They started out by keeping everybody off the top floor. A woman cop and a male cop in uniform came first. On their way up the stairs they got various accounts of what had happened. But it seemed that the cops wanted to work their way down from the top floor. They would get to me last, with any luck. And maybe they would be too tired by then to hear the same story reported over and over. They would want just the facts, which I could tell them in thirty seconds.

Ms. Clamper, across the hall from me, stood in her doorway washing her hands with invisible soap and uncomfortably watching each person who passed as if she hoped she would be asked some question.

"They talk to everyone else," she complained, "but me they don't talk to. I was knocked out of bed by those men. It was like chaos. Absolute chaos. Someone should do something about the police in this town."

Children stared and were serious for once. On the landing above I heard Ms. Fancher and Ms. Tierney trying to talk above the racket of the Fancher's two Pekinese dogs that yapped and snapped at anyone who passed. Ms. Tierney confessed she wasn't up when it happened and hadn't heard anything until the dogs started barking.

"... he said it. They must have jimmied the lock. No sane person in their right mind would let in those men," Ms. Fancher was saying with a snippy edge in her voice. "It was then they said they were cops ..."

"Which men are you talking about ma'am?"

"Those men. The men that did it. They had guns. They walked right in and walked right out.... They could have shot anyone. Anyone."

Victor's wife and sister were out in the hall, apparently, like Ms. Clamper, just standing around hoping to get asked about their version of what had happened. I heard doors opening and closing everywhere.

What was I to do in this situation? I'd probably tell the truth, if they asked me. But wouldn't it be better if they just ignored me altogether? Was that too much to ask? I figured if I hid in my apartment and didn't answer the door, then maybe they would go away. Otherwise they were going to start thinking I was responsible for letting in these fake cops when in fact anyone else would have done the same thing, wouldn't they? They couldn't blame me for that. I began to think I was a fool to hang around in the hallway just waiting for someone to invade my privacy.

I went back in my apartment and closed the door. I sat by the window, looking out at the morning in the backyard. The world was really a very peaceful place, if you looked at it in the right light, but now it seemed slanted, discolored and pretty grim. I could have, at one time, imagined going to the beach on a day like this, but that idea seemed pointless now. The more I looked at the day, the more I could see I was just trying to forget something that was totally beyond me, that had a life of its own that counted me out. Well, depending on what they heard and saw, maybe they wouldn't need to talk to me, after all. Maybe they would get enough of whatever they needed from everybody else. But some things they could get only from me.

What I wanted was to go back to sleep, and I felt the tug of it coming back. And then I remembered the black mountain that descended on me before, spreading out to cover all the blue corners of the sky. And the black mountain said something awful: that if I had made my midnight date with Miranda, she would be alive right now. I sat up and shook my whole body really hard. I stood up. I would ordinarily have grabbed a beer right then, but that seemed silly now, not just undesirable, but repulsive and irrelevant. I needed to connect more with the world, not less. Akbar stared at me and then ran into the other room, taking time to look back before he disappeared. I scared my own cat. I did some jogging and deep breathing exercises and that helped; the more I could get myself physical and awake, the better I felt.

I grabbed the phone and called the glassworks and told Sue I wouldn't be in that day.

"Hold on a minute, Milo, I'll let you speak to Patrice," she said. She was like that. You could never make things simple with Sue.

Patrice came on with a warm Caribbean smile in his voice.

"What's this strange tale I'm hearing about you saying you're not coming in?"

"Something's come up, Patrice. Structural problem in the building. I can't make it today."

"Huh," he said, and took a breath. In the Caribbean, as he says, they have lots of time to think, and he seemed to regard that as a personal necessity.

"Got a lot of things to get out today, man," he went on. We really hurting for your subtle hand and your delicate way of handling these situations."

I began to think the right way to beg off with Patrice was to declare I was dead. I could hear in his voice that he still resented that I had taken off a month ago to go driving down on the shore with Holly. And I had made the mistake of telling him I hadn't really been sick.

"What, is the building falling around you, man? You know you gotta be careful with them bricks falling."

"I'll watch it."

"Okay," he said finally. "I'll tell Lindel. I don't know ... what, are you sick, man? You doing drugs now?"

"I've got a lot on my hands."

"Man, you a flake, you know that?"

"I've heard it said."

"So you gonna have your cell where he can call you if he needs you?"

"Well, sure, he can always leave a message."

I got off the phone and stared again out the window. That was no good. I was afraid of getting morbid. I stood and stared at the wall for maybe fifteen minutes. It became important that I stare at the same spot and clear my brain of all thoughts no matter where they would lead. Then I sat down on the couch. Akbar came back out. I stared again at the wall and kept staring. Then after less than an hour there was a knock on the door. Again my old thoughts came to me: I could just as well lay low. Not answer the door at all, because it was just routine that they knocked on all the doors.

I waited.

Again the knock. Maybe there was a law against what I was doing, withholding evidence, obstruction of justice, or something like that. What about a law to be let alone when you were feeling terrible? I'd vote for that.

They knocked again and then I heard Ms. Clamper's frustrated warble echo through the hall.

"Oh, he's there," she called. "You just keep knocking. He sleeps most of the time."

I suddenly realized that like a gracious gift, it was the gracious thing to open the door before they had a chance to knock more times. Opening quickly would not only convince them that I wanted to help, it would open the possibility that they'd see how little I could help.

There were two men at the door, both in plain clothes. One was a tall man with heavy-lidded eyes that seemed always to be forcing themselves to peer at me over his long-arched nose. He had a morose expression that fitted well with homicide, I thought. His name was Valencio. The other man was shorter and heavy and had thick incised creases running every which way in his forehead. He had a broad over-open smile that showed all his teeth. He told me his name was Spollick. Valencio looked vaguely around the place as though he might be thinking how nice it was he wasn't renting here. I invited them in and Spollick settled into the chair by the door. Valencio just stood in the doorway, watching each person come and go. Two people in green coats carried equipment up the stair.

"Hear you're the super," Spollick said.

I said I was. He noted that in his book. He got my phone number here and at work.

"And these gentlemen who entered this morning jimmied the lock to get in?"

"No, I let them in."

"Any reason why?"

"They said they were cops and they heard there was some trouble up in Miranda's place."

"That's the deceased woman?"

"Yes."

Tommy hung by the door, admiring Valencio's cool sense of weary power. Louis whispered to him to leave but Tommy stayed where he was. He smiled when I greeted him but his eyes would not stay on any one thing for more than a few seconds. He glanced in my direction but then his foxlike eyes wandered over the room, up at Valencio and then at Spollick.

Spollick examined his notes for a minute of deep study.

"Fyrish," he said pensively. "What kind of name is that?"

"Welsh," I said, without a trace of uncertainty. I really didn't know, since both my parents were orphans. He wrote it down.

"You don't sound like you're from around here," Spollick said.

"New Mexico," I said.

He nodded.

"I came here four years ago."

"You married?"

"No."

Spollick wheezed sadly. There was no ring on his annular finger, and maybe there had been once. He looked uncomfortable in the chair. Like a lot of heavy men, he seemed to fit anywhere. You got the feeling all the world around him was made up of little objects, a lot of things that got in the way, but he never minded; he was at home in his skin.

A uniformed cop with a sad sunken look came, stood in the doorway and adjusted the weight of his belt. He had been standing in the hall speaking with each of the people who passed by, only there were none now. By then most of the people who were going to work had already gone.

Spollick took time to explain that what we were going to talk over were only some preliminaries, that he'd want to talk again before he wrote up his report and he wanted to hear from other people that might know anything about what had happened that morning. He consulted again his paper pad. He gestured with his pen like an artist going over a little sketch.

"Ah ... Mr. Fyrish, ah ... maybe you could just give us a ... little quick rundown on what happened this ... morning ... from your point of view. Details you remember. We'd just like to get the feel of it firsthand. Then maybe we'll have some more questions for you later ... if you don't mind ... okay?"

While I talked, Spollick didn't write a word. He just stared at me with eyes full of absolute indifference.

"Well," I said, "this morning these three guys came to the door and said they were cops. They showed me a badge. They pushed her buzzer, but she didn't answer and they wanted to see if she was all right, they said. They seemed to think someone else might be in her apartment or that she might be in some kind of trouble. We went up to her apartment and one guy knocked on the door. No answer. He knocked some more and no answer and then all of a sudden he got excited and pulled out a shotgun and shot the door. It opened and she was lying there inside. He ran out and got another guy, who came in and looked at the woman and then they all left.”

“Did you know the dead woman?”

“Yes. We dated a few times when I moved in.”

“Were you still dating as of last night?”

“No. But she wanted to meet with me to have some tea.”

“Tea,” he said and tilted an eyebrow at me as he carefully wrote it down. “And when did you meet?”

“Well, it was supposed to be at midnight. But I was late. I didn’t get to her place till four AM.”

“You were four hours late?”

“Yeah, I got into an altercation and I got my head split open. I had to go to the hospital.”

“And what hospital was that?”

“I don’t remember.”

“Who took you to the hospital?”

“Emergency medical people, I guess. Someone called them when I didn’t wake up right away. They thought I was dead.”

I expected him to say: “And were you dead?” but he only cocked one eye in my direction and stared me down. I got the impression he did that all the time. He had a steady stare of steel grey eyes.

“So you were too late to visit the dead woman when you had a rendezvous, but you visited her early in the morning. Why’d you do that?”

“Well, I figured better to visit her late than not at all. I should tell you I had a crush on her at one time, and she still seemed to encourage it from time to time.”

“And so when you talked at four AM, what did you talk about?”

“We didn’t talk. She was dead and tied up on the floor.”

He sat back and sighed.

“Mr. Fyrish have you ever had hallucinations?”

“Oh, no. Never.”

“Any memory lapse?”

“None that I recall.”

“Do you sometimes find yourself in a place and not know why you went there?”

“In the morning. Sometimes when I wake up.”

He watched me now with growing curiosity, no longer to stare me down and tell if I was lying. I was a specimen for him, an example of something.

"You say you got hit on the head and you went to the hospital. But you don't seem to be wounded anywhere."

I bent over so they could see the back of my head. I could sense them both leaning closer. I even fingered the stitches and the place around it where I had been shaved. I looked up and they both leaned back the way they were. Spollick seemed to go off in a dreamy state looking at the most distant object in my living room.

"Hmm."

He paused.

"Mr. Fyrish, what made you enter her apartment at four AM when she couldn't open the door herself?"

"She had asked me to. She didn't want to wake the neighbors when she said she might be asleep."

"Sounds like you were on intimate terms with her."

"Sometimes. She was kind of changeable."

"Changeable. You mean sometimes she'd wanted to see you and sometimes not?"

"Exactly. Yesterday she at first slammed the door in my face, and then she invited me back to tea."

"Tea. So how did that affect you, this changeability?"

"Oh, I'm used to it. I change my own mind a lot, I guess, so I understand where she's coming from. Sometimes you just need to be alone, and other times you get lonely. Kind of like that."

"So you used a key to open her door?"

"Yes, I had it in my pocket because I'd gotten one made for her that evening. She lost her purse and got locked out."

They both watched me now and Valencio closed the door behind him and leaned back on it with his hands in his pockets. Four eyes looked at me like I might be some kind of reptile they rarely saw but had read about somewhere. Finally Spollick spoke.

"Sooo, when you discovered the dead woman at four AM, you didn't call the police."

"No. I felt kind of nauseous, so I went back down to my apartment and I wanted to call 911, but I fainted."

They were still for several seconds. They both didn't move a muscle. It felt like I had made a social faux pas and ought to be embarrassed.

"You fainted," Spollick said.

"Yeah, he fainted," Valencio said. "I heard him say that."

"I was kind of upset," I put in.

"And when you fainted, what woke you up?"

"The guys that came in saying they were cops."

"So there were four guys altogether?"

"Yeah. Only three, then another one came."

"So the three guys were making way for the fourth guy."

"I guess. He mighta been waiting somewhere. He got here pretty quick."

"You never saw these guys before?"

"No."

"None of them?"

I shook my head.

Spollick grimaced. His long wide mouth pinched like he was having to make some hard decisions that he hadn't planned on.

He got me to describe the visitors in as much detail as I could give. He wrote it all down.

"And then a fourth guy came, right?"

I described the fat man as well as I could.

"And you say he came up and saw the dead woman.... Did he seem happy to see she was dead, sad ... what would you say?"

"Unhappy. He nudged her to see if she would wake up. He almost couldn't let go of her."

That made him pause. He wrote it down.

"Unhappy," he said. "So then what?"

"Then they left."

"Did they stroll out? Did they run out ...?"

"Ran."

"Ran?"

"Yeah, I think they were afraid somebody was going to call the cops."

"And so they ran all the way down from the top floor in front of a people in the hall?"

"Practically everybody in the building."

This was going to be the easy part now because I knew they were going to get so many versions of what happened next that Jim Dandy couldn't figure it out. Everybody was going to say the same thing entirely for most of it, but then they would all differ just a little, in little ways. And then even that, even the ones who were so sure of what they saw, it was going to become muddied or exaggerated in their minds the more they talked about it. After a time only the vaguest outline of the four visitors would be definite.

They particularly wanted to know about the big guy who came in last, and I did the best I could on him. Apparently he had kept his head down when he passed the other people, the ones they had talked to, so that hardly anyone could say anything constructive about what he looked like. And he had moved pretty fast.

"What did he come up for?" asked Valencio.

"I don't know." I took a long pause, letting them stare at me. "To help her if she was in some kind of trouble, I guess."

Valencio took advantage of the silence. For a while Spollick let Valencio ask the questions.

"So you let in these men," he said. "So a woman got killed."

I didn't want to tell them that they hadn't been listening. I wasn't sure if they believed anything I was telling them.

"And when they came in, did you go up to the apartment with them?"

"Yes. They wanted me to."

"Why?"

"I don't know. They said to bring the key."

"But you went along anyway? I mean you could have gone back to sleep."

"It seemed like the thing to do. They were cops, they said to come along."

"So you went up with them and then they shot the door down."

"No, they knocked first," I said. "Then they tried the key, but they couldn't get it to work."

"Knocked first. But there was no answer. So why didn't they just go away?"

"I think they expected somebody to be there. I think they were afraid there was somebody who might be waiting for them. They were kind of nervous. That's when I thought maybe they weren't cops."

"Why's that?"

"Well, they looked scared. And they didn't try to protect me, even though I was just an innocent bystander."

"And so you saw the dead woman again, when they shot the door down?"

"Yeah, I did."

"And did she look like she did at four AM?"

"No. She was covered with dust. She wasn't tied up. And there was no blood, as far as I could see. So clearly they couldn't have killed her by gunfire."

Spollick I could tell was getting impatient. His look told me he felt he was going around in circles. He completely ignored the fact that Miranda wasn't tied up. They both acted like I was hallucinating.

"No blood doesn't mean a thing," he muttered to Valencio. "Concussion alone from guns like that could kill a man. The way it broke off that door, it might have been bigger than an ordinary shotgun. Had to be to do all that damage. They thought there was another party involved. Who may have been there, for all we know. It's just that somehow those guys thought that somebody was waiting for them in her apartment. Why they came here, God knows. But they came loaded for bear. That's the way it looks to me. Weirdest thing I ever heard."

Spollick smiled at me. It was the condescending smile you give to a drunk who is drinking to ward off depression.

"I hear it made quite a racket. Thing like that."

"Yeah, it did."

Valencio made a broad happy smile.

"Not your unassuming quiet types," he said.

We all smiled. Especially Valencio, who seemed to never smile, he had such a sad face.

There was some noise in the hallway and Valencio went out. When he came back, he leaned his head around the door and said there were some people out there that wanted to talk to Spollick. Reporters. Spollick nodded.

"Tell him I'll talk to him later," Spollick grunted. He motioned him away and looked back at me. He formed a question in his mind with his mouth open a full three seconds before he spoke.

"What about this woman's routine? What did she do each day?"

"She didn't have a routine, as far as I could see. She was a model. I guess she didn't work regularly."

"Tell me, Fyrish, to your knowledge was there anyone in the building she might have confided in? Somebody, say, she talked to every now and then?"

"Might be. But not that I know of. See, from what I could see, you know, she kind of kept to herself. Frankly, I doubt if she spoke to another soul."

"Who were her friends? Did you know any of her friends, anyone she talked to?"

"I can't say I did."

Valencio spread his legs and rocked on his heels. He was getting bored now, and I thought that was a good sign.

"Did you at any time see anything unusual or out of the ordinary recently? Any people coming or going that you didn't expect to see?"

"Well, there was this guy Beremy last night when we were drinking in the cellar. I got into a fight with him and he coldcocked me. Somebody said he wasn't from around here."

I gave them a brief description of Beremy.

"Anything else?"

I paused as if thinking. I really didn't want to think about Beremy.

"Nothing at all unusual happened, say, last night?" Valencio said.

I told them about the key and how I had gotten her a new one and she told me she had gotten mugged. I told them all she had told me. They seemed to be interested in that, and wanted to know more about it, when just at that minute, Ms. Clamper stuck her head in the door. She was wearing her bathrobe and slippers and her hair was tied up with a strip of cloth.

"Please," she said to Spollick, "I just need to speak to this man. Just a few words. A very few words."

She had an air of simple importunity, as if she were in pain and could not be denied. She came over and put her face in my face. Her face took on a pleading, terribly sorrowful look.

"Mr. Fyrish, I wonder if you know how many times I have asked you to fix my faucet. Four times. Each time you put it off. Since you have obviously taken the day off, could you please give your attention to this now? I know this is terribly important, what you men are talking about now, isn't it? A woman died, I heard. But you have the day off, because of all this distraction. Please. My needs are important too. I have been waiting for weeks. Weeks."

She strode back to the door as if she had just finished an audience with a particularly lowly commoner. Spollick watched her warily as she went toward the door.

Then suddenly she turned and said to me: "I don't know why you are talking so much to the police. Wasting their time. You sleep most of the time, while I saw the whole thing. Those terrible men ... I would have thrown them out without thinking about it.... I am not so easily bullied. I saw it all. Everyone else was asleep. Killing an innocent woman ... we should have better police in this town."

She made to leave but again stopped and this time addressed us all, as if we were all equally guilty of ignoring her suffering.

"You want to know what happened.... I live on this floor, where they came in this morning. I have to live with that the rest of my life. But did you ask me any questions?"

She bored down on Spollick, who was chunky enough to slap her spinning, but he only glanced up at her as if afraid she might go on even while he was looking down at his notes.

In fact Ms. Clamper began again.

"Does it ever occur to you men, that the real trouble is with the woman herself, the awful company she kept? Bad company. Very suspicious men. At all hours of the night and day. I have a view of the street from my living room and so I see a lot of comings and goings that you all know nothing about ... nothing ... "

Spollick stood up. He was antsy to get out.

"Mr. Fyrish, you're free to fix her spigot," he said pointedly. "We'll be getting in touch if we need any more information."

He pushed the lady aside as he made his exit. He and Valencio conferred in the hallway. I was left alone with Ms. Clamper.

9. The Woman Who Worked For The IRS

The cops were deserting me just when I needed them. Ms. Clamper was even in my apartment, which I couldn't prevent, and her acidic accusations were only going to get worse as she went on. And on. I bounded up and happily smiled in her face.

"You know, it just occurred to me. Now would be just the right time," I piped up like Mr. Clean, "to fix that pesky faucet that's been causing so much trouble."

I got my tool box and placed myself in front of her to make damned sure she didn't occupy my home while I was in hers. She crowded into the hall flapping her slippers and led the way across to her apartment.

"I've been waiting ... and waiting ..." she moaned sadly.

"Now which one is it?" I asked in the manner of knee surgeon. She put her finger on the spout at the kitchen sink. It was indeed dripping.

"That's the worst one," she said.

I began work in earnest. I quickly saw that I wouldn't even have to shut off the water on her floor. As I worked, as I expected, she went on talking incessantly. About the shock of the crime that had occurred, but more about the shock that it had subjected her to. I had developed, over the years, an unusual ability I sometimes could use: I could listen to English as though it were a completely foreign language, only a stream of odd sounds to which I could connect no meaning. It was truly a great gift. But this ability deserted me as she went on.

"You didn't go to work today," she asked me.

"No," I said, "it's too important that I stay here."

"Yes. Yes, yes. On a day like today I also called in sick. I am sick, after what those men did. I heard it all the way down here. I am sick. Sick to my heart. I have a heart condition you know. And I worry that people may find out ..."

She paused meaningfully, but I said nothing.

"Find out about the kind of work I do. It worries me, Milo. It worries me no end. I tell no one, but still there are ways people can find out if you work, as I do, for the ... Internal Revenue Service. Do you think anyone will find out?"

"I don't see how they could."

"Oh, they examine your mail sometimes when it gets put in the wrong box. People have ways of finding out things. And I'm so afraid, if they found out, I would be exorcised, scorned, a cast out woman. Could you believe such a thing could happen? Blamed for things I never thought of doing just because I do the only work I know how. And I'm old enough to worry about such things. I know what people think of people like me. I know they harbor unkind thoughts. At first they are afraid I will turn them in. As if I was a Nazi. I am not a Nazi. I am a good person. I just have to make a living like everyone else, and I happen to be involved in ... you know ... the IRS. What if people talk? They'd all hate me. I couldn't show my face. What if I lose my apartment because of this? The first thing they think of when you do the work I do, is getting rid of you. Out of sight out of mind. A pariah on the streets. So I live a secret life. Do you think anyone else knows?"

"Not if you don't tell them," I said, struggling to loosen a screw that seemed welded in place.

"I wring my hands, Milo. You see me wringing my hands? I wring my hands when I think about it. And you won't tell them, will you?" she implored.

"Not a word," I said. "I can sympathize. It's a terrible thing to have to bear. I can imagine how you hate yourself."

"Hate myself, yes. No. Not so much. But it would be worse if others hate me. And it could be happening now. With everyone out in the hall talking, talking. I can tell they're all very excited. No one can believe it, it's such a shock. But I know she had visitors. I know that. They came and went. But I work hard. Extra hours. Except for today, when I need rest. Just thinking about what happened to that poor woman. Because you see I know people. From my window I see them, but they don't know that. You can tell. It's an unguarded moment."

She didn't stop there, in fact she didn't stop at all. But when the new gasket was in place and the seat polished down, the water flowed and then stopped as dry as a kettle on the moon. I said I had to hurry to attend another spigot right now, which had been begging attention for too long. I was going to use the day to fix spigots wherever they dripped. I knew if I moved intrepidly, she would not get between me and the door. I knew also she would occupy the hall, and I planned how I would duck back in and slam the door so loud it would be heard by the deaf.

But just outside my apartment there was Spollick, who seemed to be just passing by from the news wagon parked on the street.

"I think, Fyrish, there's something else we ought to look at. I think we all ought to go upstairs and look it over again," he said. "You can give us a run through of what happened. That all right with you?"

"Sure," I said gratefully. I put away my tools and slammed the door as loud as I could. But even as we were turning to go, Ms. Clamper lightly touched my arm.

"You won't tell anyone, Milo?"

"No. No, not a soul," I said.

As I looked back from the stair, I saw her standing there in her floral housedress, forlorn and disquieted as if with some secret knowledge.

We got up to Miranda's. Two medical people were there, a youth with auburn hair and a rotund woman in a white smock. Someone had draped a sheet over Miranda's body, but the rotund lady had a delicate look of cheerful inquisitiveness as she partially withdrew the sheet. Miranda's face looked bruised and oily now. Before, it was her beauty you noticed, and she could have just been asleep, you would think, but not now. Her nose poked up to a peak as I could never imagine it would have done in life. Spollick followed each step I made, asking questions and making notes. Valencio stood back, indifferent, skeptical, like he had before. He took no notes.

Spollick stopped me after the business with the key.

"And where were you when they first started shooting?" he asked.

"Right ... here. About here."

"And where were they?"

I pointed it out.

Step by step he wanted to go through it, and step by step we went. He wanted to be precise and not miss any details, and in fact we repeated everything.

"Then they shot through the door," he said.

"Yeah," I said. "Like I said, I think they were expecting somebody to be in there besides her. I don't know, but that's the way it looked to me."

"What sounds did you hear coming from her apartment?"

"Well ... I didn't ... can't really say. It was pretty loud. I don't know ... and then people started coming out on the other floors and yelled up at us. It all happened pretty fast."

"Did he yell before he shot? Did he bang on the door?"

"He knocked on it pretty hard."

"And then what happened?"

"Uh ... well, he tried the key and got impatient with it 'cause he couldn't make it work and then he shot a couple times, and then a couple times more and the door gave way. Then he ran in. The other guys went in too."

"And did the woman scream?"

"No."

"And when the door went down where was the woman?"

"She was right there."

"You could see her?"

"Partly. Yeah. I could see all of her when I went in."

Spollick nodded and his pencil went back to the pad. Then he stopped. He looked as though he had just raised his eyes from The Racing Form and was trying to translate a cryptic past performance into the probabilities of today's race. Valencio came around and stood square in front of me. It was like we were sparing partners and he was trying to set up a tricky move.

"Now you're there, and he's here, right? And you don't expect him to do anything, am I right? You think he's just going to knock on the door and ask her how she is polite like, you know? And all of a sudden the guy pulls out a shotgun and blasts the door. How come you didn't run, when he did that?"

"Well, they were between me and the stair."

"So that's why you didn't make a break for the stair when he started shooting?"

"It was over too fast. I wasn't going to run in front of them."

Valencio laughed. Spollick looked at me and didn't say a word, just grinned. They both grinned.

"You know, Fyrish, you could've been in the middle of something really weird. You know that? He could've shot in there and somebody else shot back. What a party that would've been."

"Yeah," I said. "Guess I was just lucky."

The crisp auburn-haired youth stepped over the sheet by the rotund lady. He was holding a camera and he moved gingerly, taking in everything. Beside the woman was a portable

Dictaphone she addressed with short and sporadic sentences. She noted purplish markings on Miranda's stomach, the odd shape of Miranda's open mouth, the temperature she read from a thermometer, the time, the layout of the clothing and bedding. All as if she were talking to an operator on the phone.

In a way it made me relax seeing how competent they were. They would make it all work out, I thought. Let them find whatever they found, I doubted if it would mean much to me. Nothing could change what I had done. She moved the sheet so it exposed Miranda's big toe, obstinately pointed up. Even on the tip of her toe there was still a little sprinkling of grainy white dust.

The auburn-haired kid looked around at us and grinned shyly and then muttered to the woman as if it was a private joke.

"Great apartment," he said.

She looked up and grinned, but said nothing. She went back to her notes.

She tore open a small white package by biting the corner. It made a little zipping noise. Spollick stared at the ceiling, Valencio at the floor. My thoughts just wandered away to what a sorry end it was for Miranda.

"I got a good score on my SAT," the medical kid went on. "Ninety-seventh percentile. Tomorrow I'll send my application to Cornell."

"That was your first choice, wasn't it?" the woman said.

"Yep," he nodded, snapping his head to get the hair out of his eye. "Sure was."

10. The Trailing Sash

Things took a while to cool off. Eventually Miranda's body was carried out. The police deliberated about whether I could fix the door.

"Yeah, you better," said one. "But we'll be coming back."

"Nah, we won't be coming back," said another. Then the police departed, leaving one lone officer to question each of the people who came or went. They tied yellow strips across the door of the apartment which might keep people out till I got to work. Not long after, the cop they had left got called away; there were other things going on in Brooklyn.

All day people talked in the halls. They gathered by the stairwells. A continually changing coterie on the stoop talked all afternoon and showed no sign of stopping. People talked from their doorways and invited others to enter their apartments for coffee and cake. Each new arrival had the story recounted again. Doors were left open and people stood in stupefaction listening to the news of something they actually witnessed.

Leonard remarked, sad as it was, that getting killed was the best thing Miranda could have done for the social life in our building. People who had avoided one another's glances for a decade, who could hardly muster a cheery word on the brightest day in spring, were chatting with animation now, happily going over the details of what each knew about the murdered woman, what the cops asked or said, didn't ask or didn't say, and the things they could do to prevent it from happening to them. Each time some person came by who didn't know the whole story, or hadn't heard some particular angle of it, the event was gone over once more in loving detail.

Ms. Peretti in particular seemed better prepared than the rest of us to deal with the immediacy of death.

"To imagine it happening here," she called aloud. "A murder right in our building. It's like ... what? Like television, that's what it's like. You always think it will happen somewhere else. But here. Here. Right under our noses. I told the children a woman died. I had to tell them, what could I say? They're gonna find out anyway. They were dumfounded, of course. How do they know how to take such things, with their little hearts? But I feel so sorry for the poor woman. She had so much to live for. She was so pretty, although I can't say too much about that because she always wore sunglasses. Oh, but her lips, her lips were beautiful, that I grant you. Pretty women get in the most trouble, though I had no idea before. But it isn't just me; no one seems to know about her. What did she do with her time? Didn't she talk to people? She came and went without speaking to a soul, so far as I can tell. Like a shadow in the night."

Ms. Peretti brought cookies out in the hall, fresh from her oven and offered me one as I was passing by.

"I just tried them out on my grandson and he loved them. It's so sad. You need a little relief."

Ms. Kissich's face rose up beside me. You can feel when you're being lain in wait for: this was the way with Ms. Kissich. She was another person whose messages I hadn't gotten around to returning.

"Oh, Ms. Kissich, I've been meaning to get back to you about that ... what was it?"

"I told you, my window sill is falling off," she said precisely. "Can't you hear? I wish you would just let me know when can I expect you."

From her tone you could feel she was speaking to me as a servant; it's a particular inflection I'd grown familiar with. As far as I was concerned, it insured that her window sill would inexorably descend, hopefully by slow agonizing degrees, beneath all other things on her floor.

"Well, I can't get to it today," I said with sadness. "Little emergency. But tomorrow ... oh, that's a Saturday. Are you home then?"

"Come at eight, sharp. Ronald will let you in."

Her husband, a fellow servant.

And then I had the perverse revenge of all servants: I made a promise I intended to forget; I said I would get to it definitely, eight o'clock, no question, I was so glad she asked because it was my one desire in all the world to give her satisfaction and nothing meant so much to me as her window sill. And then I walked away chewing one of Ms. Peretti's cookies.

"And concerning the deceased woman," Ms. Kissich said to anyone in hearing, as if to draw me back. "She never spoke to a soul, so I don't know how anyone can say anything useful about her. I tried to talk to her and she just ignored me."

I said I couldn't imagine Miranda being rude.

"Well," said Ms. Kissich, "I'm sure you knew her better than we did."

I moved on up the stair.

The door was not salvageable; its left brace was broken. But I had other doors and I could hopefully make one of them fit. Leonard came over to help, which I was grateful for, but he could only stay long enough to salvage Miranda's lock. I had others on other doors. He might have been able to do more, but I wanted it done that day, so I did it myself.

As I passed up and down the stairs for wood and tools or things I forgot, people asked questions and told me their theories. Particularly since I was supposed to be more knowledgeable, an authority even, on the four visitors. Everyone said they were Mafia, and that it was safest not to know any more than you knew. But in the absence of any certain facts, the four assumed larger and larger proportions. It was said they drove up in a huge white stretch limousine like no one had ever seen before. That they carried M16 assault rifles as well as shotguns and automatic pistols. They wore studded boots and carried walkie-talkies to communicate with a network of comrades waiting outside. They had grenades under their clothing. That the police would not have dared to come around until the four were well out of sight. There was even doubt about how many there were, since some said others waited outside, and that another two had come in at the last moment.

I was even partially exonerated for believing they were cops. No one could stop those men and at least I had prevented anyone else from getting shot like Miranda. How was I to know they weren't who they said they were? I came close to being killed myself, I let them know. Ms. Fancher even said as much, proclaiming now that it was hardly my fault. Next to those four hoods I was a happy flower-picking ingénue who survived by good fortune and naiveté. It was whispered knowingly that those men would never be caught.

As I set to work on the door Tommy and Louis came up to look around. Tommy asked if it was all right for them to stay and watch me. I said fine.

"You guys haven't been up on the roof, have you?"

Tommy shook his head.

"No," he said with a lingering lilt to his voice, it was the tone he liked to use with his mother. Everyone, including children, went up on the roof whenever they wanted. I had tried to stop them because it hurt the roof, but eventually I gave up. Louis sat down by the stairway. I was just getting to pulling out the hinge pins.

"Can we look inside?" he asked.

The cops had told me not to let anyone in till the next of kin arrived. I should have shooed the kids out, but I knew I would have to leave it now and then, and there would be no stopping them. So I struck a balance by telling them not to touch anything.

"What's that room, Milo? Can I look?"

"Look but don't touch."

"Come on," Tommy said.

"Nah, you go," Louis said.

"Come on. Don't be a dweeb."

Louis paused over that. Then he went with his friend. I could hear their high-pitched chatter echoing in the empty room.

"This is where they fought it out," Tommy said with positive glee. "See, here's the marks on the wall. Pow!"

"Pow back!"

"Pow! OH! You got me," Tommy cried.

"You're supposed to lie down dead. Lie down."

"Here's where the bullet went in."

"Aw, where ...?"

There were four apartments on that floor: Follett's, Tartakauer's, and Miranda's—and another apartment diagonally opposite hers that I had nicknamed Salty's place, even though it was empty and Salty never lived there. He was the previous super and he must have known every stick and paint spot on every floor. He had shown it all to me. Salty's place had been gutted by some tenants before I came, rumored to have numbered more than twelve, and they had taken all the plumbing fixtures, the commode, the stove, sinks, the light fixtures—even linoleum right off the floor. Now I had boarded up the windows and used the place for storage, unwanted furniture and odd wood that was easier to carry down when I needed it. Of course, this was another missed chance at income that the Widow would hound me for if

I reminded her, but in fact I doubted that she knew. Ever since she bought the place that apartment had lain empty and too costly to repair, and she had, as far as I could tell, forgotten about it. Or so I assumed; I never brought it up. The apartment still had no fixtures. The water was closed off. It had been a big deal to run enough wire so some of the lights worked.

As I was cutting down the new door, Tartakauer came out in the hall. He peered into Miranda's apartment and then around at me.

"That's a pretty piece of work, isn't it?" he said.

"Well, it could've been worse," I said philosophically.

"What can't?" he said pushing a stick with his toe.

"I mean, you must have heard something before this morning, coming from her apartment."

"Nah. Well, you talked with her. I heard nothing after that. Not a sound. Ah, she kept to herself most of the time," he said. "Well, what's this?"

He squatted down and picked out a key from under the molding on the floor. He handed it to me. It was probably the key I had given Leo and he'd dropped.

"Oh, yeah, I been looking for that," I said.

"It probably belonged to that poor woman," he said.

"Yeah ..."

"God, it bounced me out of bed when that happened. I thought it was the toot of doom. Everyone felt it as much as heard it. I felt it in bed. Mean bastards in this city. Mean thugs. You ought to do something to keep that element out of here, Milo."

"Yeah, you know, a thought just occurred to me, Doc."

"Yeah, what's that?"

I walked over and pointed at the jamb right beside him.

"You see that?"

"Yeah?"

"It's the strike for the lock."

"Yeah, it is, Milo. I can see that."

"So if a shotgun blast was necessary to open this door, why is that strike still bolted in the jamb?"

Tartakauer backed up and laughed.

"Oh, Milo, I gotta tell you the funniest thing. It was on TV last night. There was this guy trying to walk through this door. And each time he would get close to it, it would open without him doing a thing. Just ... opened. It was like magic, you know?

Without him doing a thing…. And then when he would back away the door would close. And they would go through it all again. 'Cause he was trying to catch it so he could open it himself. God, how I laughed…."

"What made you think of that?" I asked.

"Well, you just sitting here talking to me about this door. It's pretty obvious …"

"Yes, it is," I said, "but that's exactly what happened to this door."

"What's that?" he said. "I heard all about it from the police, Milo. It's my floor, and I live here. So they couldn't keep me out."

"Well, what did they say about this lock?" I asked.

"Lock?"

"Yeah. What'd they say?"

He looked disgusted.

"Didn't say anything. There wasn't anything to say. A man with a shotgun blew down the door and killed the woman that lived here. 'S the worst thing I ever saw."

"Yeah, but why did he use a shotgun?"

"I don't know. You were there, weren't you?"

"You were there, Milo?" Tommy said, coming up from behind me. Louis hung behind, rubbing his sneaker into a spot on the floor.

"Hmm," I said.

"Oh, I see what you mean about the strike," Tartakauer said, pointing at a place where the wood had splintered out. "This strike is the one that broke."

It was the one for the doorknob latch.

"That's right. And the others didn't," I said.

"Well, you got a split up this board half an inch wide. Something did that."

"But it's different. See this one is bent, for the doorknob latch. But in addition to that she had these two deadbolts, and they were both untouched. So this here is the only thing that kept the door from opening. The guy used a shotgun to open a door where he could have turned the knob and walked right in."

"Nahhhh," Tommy said backing away. "He couldn't get in if he didn't use the shotgun. That's crazy. My mom always keeps her door locked. Especially at night." His brow furrowed and he stuck his finger in the crack, feeling the splintery wood. Tartakauer laughed with glee muffled by his raw throat.

"You gonna play detective, Milo? Everyone else is. Like there's a mystery what killed her. Well, you can think that about the door if you want to. You go ahead and play detective. Maybe the police need your help. Ha!"

I looked at Tartakauer and thought: so maybe the shotgun cowboy did get nervous and make a mistake. What did that prove? Nothing that I could see. Tartakauer turned away disgusted and went back to his apartment. A few minutes later he came back out and waved on his way down the stairs.

Whatever was going on with the locks, there was something more important to me at the moment. For it had dawned on me that rather than replace the jamb, a few good nails in the right places would hold it well enough for today. Why not do that? I drilled through the molding and then placed the nails at odd angles. I nailed it like that while Tommy inspected my toolbox. Louis came up. He had found a lampshade tassel and he showed us.

"Can I keep it?" he asked. I said no, it went with the apartment. By now they were both getting pretty bored. All their toys were down in their apartments.

"Why don't you kids go outside now and play in the street?"

Tommy looked sullen. Louis looked at Tommy.

"I bet you I know something you don't," Tommy said.

"Yeah, what's that?"

"I know where Miranda went." He paused, looking to see the effect on me, waiting to see if I would come for the bait. I looked quizzically down at my work.

"Oh, yeah?" I said. "How do you know that?"

"Cause I heard her," Louis said.

"I heard her," Tommy corrected.

"Heard her what?"

"Heard her say she was looking for you."

"Oh, yeah?" I said.

"Yeah, only she didn't find you," Tommy said with an impish smile.

"Why not?"

"Cause she went to Hell first."

He spun away and laughed. Louis grinned as though he didn't know whether to laugh or not. I couldn't watch Tommy anymore and told him to get out. Whirling as if that was to be their last foray, Tommy made a run down the stairs.

"Come on," he cried brazenly.

After some hesitation Louis went too.

I was intent that one way or the other this door was going to be fixed that day if I had to nail it shut. I wanted to be done with it. And now with the kids gone, I was just getting up to speed when the phone rang. I looked around. Where was the phone anyway? I followed the sound, and there it was stuck in the oven, with the cord leading out under her bed. That's why I couldn't find it when I was here and got nauseous. In the oven. I opened it and picked up the phone.

"Hello."

There was no voice on the other end. I said nothing else. After about ten seconds, the line went to a dial tone. So I hung up and went back to my work. But in about five minutes the phone rang again.

"Hello."

"Is Miranda there?" a man asked.

"Miranda's not here," I said. "You want to leave a message?" I waited.

A kind of crackle hung on the line and I could hear someone breathing.

"When do you expect her back?" There was a husky pipe and a little twang to the voice. I waited three beats.

"Well, I don't know. She left and didn't say. Why don't you call back in a couple of hours? Okay?" But now it was he who didn't want me to hang up.

"Who are you?"

"Super. She had a problem with the door. She said someone might call, though. Want me to have her call you back?"

"No, I'll call back."

"Okay, Vincent."

My voice said I was slipping away, but my hand told the truth and didn't move. I held onto the silence like a man holding onto a cliff face. No matter how crazy and incongruous it felt. And it went on for several seconds like slow drops of water.

"Hi." He took a long breath. He didn't remember my name and he might've even felt a little silly. "But she's okay?" he said finally.

"Yeah, far as I know. You want me to tell her you called?"

"Yeah. Tell her I called."

"Okay, if I see her I will."

There was silence again. Longer and heavier this time.

"Thanks." He hung up. I dialed *69 to see what number he called from but it wasn't available.

By midafternoon I had the new door in place. I had to move the hinges which is why it took so long. I had fixed it with only one lock now but it closed and opened and was serviceable. I spackled the broken plaster and swept up. If you didn't know about the shooting you wouldn't think twice about it. I started returning what I had moved out of Salty's place. The broken door, for one thing, since I didn't feel like carrying it all the way down the stairs just then....

A shot!

"Hah!"

Louis and Tommy leaped out of the corner behind the door to Salty's, laughing exultantly. They had snuck back up when I wasn't looking. With a lusty leer Tommy showed me the shreds of the balloon he had just punctured for my benefit.

"Hey, come on. Help me," I said. Louis would help; he helped with the broken door and some of my tools. He was a little more mature, but then he dropped into taking the lead from Tommy. They played at shooting one another while I swept up the rest of the mess in Miranda's apartment. As I shooed them down the stairs an idea came to me and I stopped stock still on the next landing: These kids could probably get into Salty's apartment. Because I knew the fire escape on that side could be reached from the roof and went right in front of one of the plywood windows, which I had seen needed fixing weeks ago and never gotten around to it. There wasn't much worth stealing in there; my tools had their own lock. But they might hurt themselves or start a fire and so I really ought to do something about it.

I locked Miranda's door and went into Salty's room. The plywood sheet had sure enough been broken inward just enough for a child to get past it. I drilled some more holes and drove in deck screws at odd angles. Then it was pretty solid. They sure couldn't get through it without making a hell of a racket.

While I was deciding what to take back down, Yvette showed up. She didn't seem that happy to see me but she must have felt we ought to be polite. Obviously I was going to know she was there. Her face was glistening and bright, as if she had just been swimming. Her neck muscles came out and gave crazy curves to her collar bones. She seemed to be experimenting with moving her shoulders. She gave off heat like a python. It was part of her eroticism, I suppose, the way she wrenched and squeezed each word in her lips like her chewing gum, showing you all the spots where the crimson of her lipstick faded into the visceral pink on the inside of her mouth.

"You're a long way from Queens," I said.

"Don't tell anyone," she said. But she obviously had to tell me something or I would imagine something underhanded. "Follett wanted me to get some of his stuff, because he's staying over at my place till this blows over."

She was in a hurry.

"I don't care," I said.

"I gotta get out of here and get to my job." She went into his apartment and I heard her rummaging around. I was in process of moving some of my tools downstairs, one flight at a time, so I never left them out where kids could steal them. When she came out of Follett's I looked up and saw her at the top of the stair, and instead of having a shopping bag full of stuff, she had bundled it all into a robe and wrapped that up and was going to carry it out to her car. But a long sash of the robe dangled down behind her onto the floor. You could tell, she had to think of so many things at once, she wasn't at her most organized. As she descended the stair the sash dragged back and wouldn't you know it? Tommy was right there and put his foot on it. Well, the bundle came undone like thrown laundry and in her scrambling to get it back in her grip, on her high heels, she almost fell on the stair and had to catch herself on the banister.

"You little bastard," she yelled. But Tommy could easily outrun her, especially if she didn't take off those high heels.

"It was an accident," he called, perched at the top of the stair, and looked around hoping someone else had seen—and then he smiled.

"It was not!" Louis said, but that only made Tommy beam more.

I was on the floor below her looking up, and while she was getting back on her feet, I picked up a picture that had blown out from the scattered debris of clothes, razor blades, belts, shoes and whatnot. It was a mate for the picture I had already seen in Miranda's apartment. In this picture, Miranda was still at the beach, with a child at her feet in the surf. She had the same flamboyant hat. But now the man who had taken the other photograph was beside her: it was Follett, with his arm around Miranda. That would be a photo taken by Simone, whoever she was.

I paused, not caring if Yvette noticed my stare. By the looks of it, Miranda had known Follett before she knew me. Big deal. But something made me want to keep the photo. I stuffed it in my shirt with Yvette plainly watching me as she picked up the scattered garments. I helped her gather them up. When she was near to me on the stair, she whispered to me:

"That picture, I woulda destroyed it because he didn't want the police searching his apartment and finding it. But he wouldn't let me destroy it. Some sentimental kooky thing. Come on up here. I want to talk to you."

I grabbed the tools Tommy could lift and took them into Miranda's apartment and threw them on the bed. When the door was closed behind her, Yvette, pointing at the picture under my shirt, seemed like she was coming all undone, that there were too many facts pulling on her from different directions.

"He doesn't want it destroyed," she said. "Well, how you think that makes me feel? He said their affair ended a long time ago. So why does he want the photo? It's dead, buried. Let alone that she's dead, what I heard. That's probably what made him so sentimental. He can't stop his self-pitying long enough to just love me, what it amounts to. Keep the thing. Get rid of it."

"It's all right," I said. "I'll do what you say. I'll give it back to him when he comes around for it, if that's all right. And I won't show it to the police. My guess, he's just sentimental, like you say. The important thing is he cares about you now."

"Yeah, right. His errand girl. Oh, Milo, if I knew he was mixed up with her when she got killed ... he wouldn't last two seconds with me. He'd be history. Even having me do this: isn't it a bitch? Let him get his own laundry."

"Why didn't he? He was here when it all happened."

"Was he? He was scared, he said. But what's there to be afraid of now? The cops have cleared out. They're off on some other thing, probably. I feel sick doing this."

"Well," I said, looking around like the air was filled with strange tropical fish, "That's love."

I was a little piqued to find such a memento of what Follett had meant to Miranda, and some jealousy tinged my otherwise clear objectivity. But what was I so surprised about? That she had other guys in her life? I knew that, didn't I? But I had probably lied to myself about it. Secretly, probably, I wanted to believe I was the only one. No doubt a lot of guys thought they were the only one. And Follett was a stud in his working-class way, hardly beneath me. In fact, she had probably treated him the way she treated me, and there they were living on the same floor.

"Running away makes it look bad," I said.

"Yeah, why doesn't he think of that? Instead all he wants to do is hole up at my place. He won't even go to work. Says he'll go to Mexico with what he's saved. But does he offer to take me with him? Yeah right. But I never thought this would happen. Never in a million years. I didn't know she had enemies. If I'da known that I would have kept the hell away from this place, you better believe it. I spent last night here. Didn't hear a thing until those ballerinas with the shotguns showed up. Then I snuck out after Follett. Now he's like a scared puppy. I got a feeling he knows something he ain't saying."

Yvette strolled around in the open space of the second room. You could tell she'd never been here and didn't like the décor or something.

"Because you know she was not making it as a model anymore," Yvette went on. "She's not sixteen you know. So how was she making it? Huh? Selling? Or was it drugs? Could've been a lot of stuff she was into.... Because it's been bothering me now. And because Follett seemed to pity her. I know they came and got her because what, she was a threat to them. She stole from people, Milo, and that's why they killed her. And that's why she kept to herself in this apartment so much of the time. When she was staying here. Most people don't have her phone number. She wouldn't give it to me. She'd say she'd call me when I spoke to her. But she never did. She's secretive."

"Well, if you had conversations with her, you're one of the few. She really kept to herself, as far as I can tell."

"I know," Yvette nodded like a drunk. "But I'm aggressive. I go out to people and give a lot of myself and I expect them to be up front with me. But you don't get that from her. I know people that are secretive like that and I don't like them. No."

She paused to take a new stick of gum. And the moment seemed to make her pensive.

"I'm so bummed," she said. "You think he loves me, Milo? I don't think he loves me. I think he mighta left last night when I was asleep and mighta got in bed with Miranda. He coulda, 'cause I'm a sound sleeper. And he woulda got killed too, but you know what? He's too fast for them. He snuck out just before they closed in on her. He's not a macho like will stand up for a girl. He left and then they came and finished her off."

"Well, that's pretty strong, Yvette ..."

She was like a cat in a bag; you wanted to give her her freedom (whatever that would mean), but you didn't want to be in her way when she got it. She sat down on the bed and twisted her hands around each other. Her shoulders were still curled up like she couldn't uncoil. I wanted to console her, but it seemed impossible.

"So what did you take?" she asked me out of the corner of her eye as she sucked on a new stick of gum. "When people die, somebody's going to get it. Might as well be you. Maybe you think I'm dumb. But I know she hid stuff. What do you say?"

I made her shut up for a second. Answering her was like kicking a wind-up toy; you think it's run down and it takes off after you again.

"The cops told me not to let anybody in here except her relatives."

"I bet you look around and you find stuff the police didn't find. Wanna bet?"

I explained it to her slowly and simply, but each time I did she took off on another tangent. About Miranda, about Follett ... the more she talked the less it seemed like she knew. She asked again about "looking around" and I could imagine what a circus that would be, with each of us going off in different directions and her filling her pockets with God knows what. Finally I told her flatly I wouldn't let her look around and I told her to get out. She shrugged like getting her suggestion rejected was like not getting a seat on the subway. She packed up her laundry and left.

I got my tools and put them away where they belonged.

Downstairs, I got a beer and settled down and fell asleep before it was finished.

11. The Bashful Private Eye

Toward evening a man paid me a visit. He had a round shiny forehead, a shy smile, and the softest brown hair I've ever seen. He introduced himself as Frank Wyent and said he was a private detective. Then he showed me a card that looked legal enough and said he was working for his "employer" who wanted him to check into the matter of the death on the fifth floor. I let him in on the strength of that, and he stood in the center of my living room like a berry on a white plate. Akbar came over and gave a sniff to the unfamiliar shoe. Then he turned away scornfully, leaped back onto the couch and stood looking at Wyent as if he was seeing a tasteless fish.

Wyent had eyes with that burnt-out blue you sometimes see in people who spend all their time on the beach and have wonderful tans. Yet he was too protected to have a wonderful tan. His cheeks were rounded and kind of peachy, like they needed a lot of stroking, and you felt he would be disappointed if they didn't get it. They were slack now, and he needed a shave. I had a vague impression that if I let a silence between us go on for too long, he was going to ask me for money.

"Who's your client?" I said.

"A friend of hers. He doesn't want to make a fuss, just wants to find out a few things." He looked around, as though making sure there would be enough space for his vermillion wingtips on the thin rug of my floor. "And the police will do their job. They always do. I'll just be going over the same ground, most likely. Families sometimes do this sort of thing. Think of it as family, that's all."

"Okay. But I don't know that much. I can tell it all in two minutes."

But the next thing he wondered was if he could visit the apartment where "the Dauphine woman" had died.

"Well," I said, "I guess so. If the police have no objection." I actually could have prevented it, but I wanted to see what he would find of interest in her place.

"Of course," he said in a businesslike manner.

"You want to call Lieutenant Spollick, or should I?"

Wyent seemed irritated. "I'd rather you spoke to Lieutenant Sallen. I can call him up."

"No, that's all right," I said.

I dug out Spollick's number and I dialed it. He wasn't there, but I was given his home number and I called that. I got him and he asked to speak to Wyent. Right then I knew it was pointless; they obviously knew each other. Wyent was all Yessir, and Fine and We'll get back to you and so on ... until finally he gave the phone back to me.

"Listen, Fyrish," said Spollick. "This guy works for various attorneys around town. He's valuable to us, but you don't owe him a thing. However, in the interest of keeping other people interested, let him poke around if he wants to. Make sure he doesn't steal anything. He shouldn't bother any of your tenants and he knows that. I don't think he'll find anything. If he tries to take anything from her rooms just give me a call. All right?"

I said fine and hung up. I went and got the key and went to the door.

"I think it would be best if I went alone," Wyent said.

"Nonsense," I said. "You might get lost by yourself."

"Please," he said, holding his fingers to grasp the key.

"Heyyyy, I'll show you around. I don't want you to miss any clues."

He looked a little hurt and he didn't move.

"Be nice if you let me have a look by myself," he said with a worried expression on his face. He was so ... sticky. Like he didn't want to move unless you shoved him. And he seemed so gentle. I felt like I was being a bad sport not hauling out a motorized dolly and wheeling this potato up the stairs. I stared into his flat button eyes till he looked away.

"Oh, well. If you want to come I'm sure there'll be questions I'll have," he went on. "Things I'd like to ask you anyway. It won't take much of your time."

I squared off on that.

"Listen, enough people have told me how to use my time. You're getting a look and that's all you're getting."

"Well, let's work together on this. Okay?"

He was so unruffled. You got the feeling nobody had ever given him a hard time in his life; he just wouldn't let it happen. He'd be too nice.

I locked my place and took him up to Miranda's. I shut the door behind us.

"Good enough," he said cheerily and added, "We found a lot in the other apartment."

"What other apartment?"

"She didn't tell you she had another apartment? Well, you must have picked it up, I would guess. She couldn't have spent all her time here."

"No. No, I imagine not."

I should have been smart enough to figure that.

"Yeah," said Wyent. "Apparently she just used this apartment here as a getaway and conducted all of her business from the other place. Pretty nice, if you can afford it. What'd she tell you?"

I spread my fingers in the air.

"I never asked."

"Funny," he said. "She was a strange lady, Miranda. Did you get to know her, Mr. Fyrish? I mean to any level of intimacy? In the course of your business?"

"You can call me Milo," I said.

"How well did you know her, Milo?"

"We talked. Not all that much. So what did you find? In the other apartment."

"Not much. She kept stuff with her. Not even any phone numbers."

When he just stepped into the place I noticed his manner changed. He just stood by the door and took in the rooms. He was doing that now. He looked over every inch as slowly as if he expected to see small messages penciled on the wall.

"Interesting," he intoned as he floated around the dancing room. Maybe he admired himself in the mirror.

"That's where it would be," he said. He talked as though he didn't care if I were there to hear or not—he would say the same thing if he were alone.

"She furnish it all herself?" he asked.

"Yeah," I said. "It's rented unfurnished."

"That's always wisest. You get better people if they can buy their own things. But you're just the super so why would you care?"

"Well, I have to clean up."

"Say, this is nice," he said in the end room. It was nice. The sun was setting like the night before. It caught the burnished dinginess of an heirloom candlestick with initials carved in the base. The room was filled with the same orange glow it had had at about this time the day before. Only now it seemed gaseous and not pastel. Wyent knelt in front of the hope chest and opened it up. It was the same jumble of clothes and boxes and jewelry. You had to pile things on the floor if you wanted to dig in and look around. The police had been through it of course, and now Wyent was doing the same thing, piling things out on the floor. I picked up the Bible and thumbed through it.

"Hmm. It should have been here," he said in a matter-of-fact way.

"What's that?" I said.

He stopped and put his arm on his knee and looked at me thoughtfully then looked away.

"You were here when those men came in here this morning, weren't you?"

"Yes, I was."

"And they took something, right?"

"Maybe. I didn't see it if they did. They didn't seem like they came in to rob her. Didn't stick around."

He smiled but said nothing.

He looked back in the chest. He held a huge jewelry box in one hand and opened it. He pulled up a string of gold links and held them dripping in the air. It looked like it might be worth something. Why hadn't the police taken it?

"Maybe yes, maybe no," he said. "She could have been vain. Vain women are different. See, thing about a bauble like this is where do you wear it? If you're the kind of gal that has one of these in the first place, then maybe you do wear it around the house. Can't say. But she didn't keep it in a vault. She kept it here." He pointed into the chest as if it were a steaming well of treasure. "A lot of people would take notice of a necklace like that."

I stretched my back. I sat in the lounge chair and stared out at the sky while he rambled on. He poked through everything, but out of the corner of my eye I watched him. He moved nothing that he didn't put back.

When he finished with the hope chest he went to the desk and went through that bit by little bit. I tipped one of the slats of the venetian blind. It seemed so peaceful up here. Through a gap in the buildings you could see the next street, where the suntanned man with the torn yellow shirt walked backwards and forwards. Behind him an old man walked with tiny steps. After the longest time Wyent gave a little sigh and shoved the drawer back in place. He got up and slammed the chest shut.

He took a careful tour around the rooms, peered under the bed and in the closet, where she must have had thirty pairs of shoes. He pulled each one out of its pocket and put it back. The cops had left the garbage, he noted rather critically. Probably there was nothing in it that would interest them, but he checked through it himself. Finally, with a chipper smile he admitted that was enough and we walked back down.

On the second-floor landing Ms. Peretti was standing next to a suitcase that was so big it came up to her heavy thigh. She was obviously out of breath and had just stopped on the landing for a rest. I offered to help, but then from right behind her emerged a little figure dressed in the purest red dress I had ever seen. The little girl's hair was dark and her eyes were big and brilliant brown like little underwater caves you could dive in forever. She was not as tall as the suitcase that apparently went with her.

"This is Alla," declared Ms. Peretti proudly. "I was out at the airport to pick her up. Isn't she beautiful? Hey? What do you say to the gentlemen?"

"Hi," the child piped and grinned up at each of us. She was taking us in; we weren't intruders to her.

"Her parents in England taught her to say hi. When I saw her at the gate that's what she said to me. Hi. Her father has to stay in London because of business, and her mother is sick, so I said, fine, I can be mamma to one more, what's the difference? They said you'll see her because she'll be dressed in red. See? Heh, what do you say? Heh?"

Ms. Peretti made encouraging motions to the child, who was indeed adorable, and not all that shy. She stood there gaping up at us, her eyes filled with a sort of serenely contained excitement.

I heaved the suitcase up the next flight of stairs. The woman followed behind me, stroking the child with comforting words about the new place, while at the same time telling me how she had found the little girl at the airport and how she liked the ride in, and how she was already excited about New York. Wyent stood expectantly on the landing for a moment and then followed us up.

I set the suitcase on her bed and came back out. She was

effusively grateful and she motioned me back. Her look was serious, though she didn't say a word. When she saw she had my attention, she disappeared inside for a second and came back with a small tray of cookies. Wyent and I each took one. We munched and Ms. Peretti brightened and pointed across the hall with her corpulent hand.

"From that lady, you know, who makes cookies. Kathrine."

Kathrine was Louis' mother.

"Her little boy came by and sells them. They are good cookies, so I buy them. Eh? I tell my husband I hate to cook in this weather. Oooooh. Heh? You like them? They are good, aren't they?"

Alla came back from her first look inside and stood by the door. Her shiny dark hair was mussed from the trip, and one ribbon, also bright red, was dangling loosely to her shoulder.

"Bye-bye, Mr. Milo," she called as we went down the stair. I was a little relieved that no one mentioned Miranda. When we got to the first floor, I started to say farewell to Wyent too, but he made like he wasn't quite ready to go.

"Is there any place we could talk?" he said.

"Why? Have we got any secrets?"

"I'd just like a word with you where we wouldn't be interrupted."

I let him back in my place. He sat down and crossed his legs and dusted his cuff. There was a little cookie crumb on his upper lip. I sat down and waited for him to say something.

He began by telling me he had talked to the police and he wondered if there was anything I could add to what I had told them that morning. I said no. He stared off, searching somewhere, like he hadn't gotten through to me because he hadn't said it right.

"Is there anything that you might have left out of your account of what happened that you would rather not tell the police?" he said softly. "For … one reason or another."

"Well, if there were, and I told you, wouldn't you tell them?"

"I might be required to if there were litigation … but I suspect there won't be any in this case."

I looked at him open-mouthed. He seemed so in control, so trusting—so why shouldn't I trust him? He was so different from the police, from anybody I had met on that day, that I felt a kind of tug toward helping him.

"You mean you think the killer will never stand trial?" I said. Wyent just smiled his nice boyish smile.

"Well, we don't know that she was killed. Not really. It's still possible that she could have done herself in."

"She could have?" I said. I was sure he was joking but I didn't laugh.

"It always has to be considered as a possibility," he said slowly. "Always. A lot of people do it to themselves and we have no way of knowing without a thorough investigation. Some people even commit suicide and try to make it look like they were murdered. How about that?"

I paused to think about it. If he was laying a trap I couldn't see it.

"I told them all I know," I said. "You want a beer?"

He smiled and waved it away. I got one for myself.

"You sound like you don't care that much, Milo."

"Um ... of course I care. I'd like to know anything I could about something in my building. I'm the super after all."

Wyent shifted around in the chair. It was the same one Spollick had sat in. The Interrogator's chair.

"You know," he said comfortably as he looked around my living room, "I thought most supers lived in the worst apartment, in the basement usually. And the owner has a house in Westchester. No? Well, you're obviously the exception."

"Yeah, I suppose so. I'm just making ends meet."

He leaned back expansively, admiring my sheet-metal ceiling and the orange-stained walls.

"Well, your ship will come in. The future's what you make of it, my way of thinking. There'll be enough for you down the road, I expect. So anyway, if she didn't kill herself, then somebody else had to have done it. Doesn't that stand to reason? But it couldn't have been those men you let in."

"Well ... that's good news for them, I guess. Why not?"

"Well, they came here to protect her, wouldn't you say?"

I stopped in mid-slurp and stared at him.

"I don't know," I said unsteadily. "If they did, they did one hell of a job."

"They came to protect her," he nodded as if he had done his PhD on it and now I had agreed and it was a generally accepted fact.

"So you think she was dead before they came in," I said. He

nodded emphatically. It was the only emphatic thing I had seen him do.

"Oh, had to be. She had to be."

I leaned a little closer so I could get every word, he was so soft-spoken.

"Well, you know," I confided to him, "I ran that by the police this morning and they didn't seem to think so. What you're suggesting is cute but you gotta admit how things look, it's pretty unlikely. A shotgun can kill and leave hardly any blood at all, they told me that."

He didn't like hearing that at all. His brow furrowed. I went on smiling at him. The beer was cheering me up.

"Who's the party that wants you to look into this?" I asked.

He straightened up in his chair. He took on a kindly but confidential tone.

"Would you like to meet him?" he asked. He strained to make a sort of smile, and a sensitive pause. "It could be arranged."

I leaned back with my beer and took a slurp.

No, I didn't want to meet him. Also, Wyent didn't seem all that angry at the shotgun cops, and I wanted nothing to do with them.

"Would he ask me questions like you?"

"Maybe. You might give it a different slant. Depends on what you told him. He could also be a good friend. You might find in this business you could use a friend, Milo. He'd rather not have it known, but he was ... close with the dead woman. It's ... possible that one of his enemies did her in."

I spread my hands and mugged a cheerful smile.

"But that's for him to decide anyway," Wyent said.

Right. You're only the lieutenant. Wait till the big fig plucker comes around.

Well, you know, after taking it all in, nothing about Wyent seemed like a private detective to me. He seemed almost ... well, intellectual. He was like an attorney from upstate, this guy. I couldn't imagine him getting his hands dirty with this kind of a mess. I put down my empty can and got another.

"So what does your client think," I asked. "Does he really think an enemy of his would do what was done to her?"

"Nobody thinks anything yet. Somebody got into her apartment, though. Could have been anybody. Anybody at all."

I looked as blank as I could. Perhaps this was what he was after.

All this buildup so he could watch my face right now. He looked so relaxed. His eyes were little impenetrable dots, passive, completely without will. They were like a child's eyes, the part of him that remained a child after the rest had grown up. Everything was facts to him, and everything was obvious. You would never be able to prove him wrong about anything. No matter what you said, he would always go on to tell you how things were just the way he expected them to be.

"Like who?"

"You tell me. What about Beremy? You didn't tell the cops that your fight with Beremy was over Miranda."

"It never came up."

"No? How well do you know Beremy?"

"Not at all."

"Are you sure? Because that fight you had was a pretty personal thing to happen, and you acted like it was nothing to the police. Nothing at all. It looks funny, that's all."

"Why, Frank? You think I got something to hide?"

"Do you?"

I stared at him. I was going to stare him down. It was that or punch him in the face and I was doing him a favor, all the nice feelings that were in my eyes then. It was a long time, but he looked away and started talking again.

"I mean, I know you didn't do it. I know that. I can swear it, now I've seen you. But there're other people who can't see what I see and have to be convinced. Know what I mean?"

I took a big breath.

"Well, since we're just talking, Frank ... I mean ... what makes you so sure I didn't ... assassinate the deceased party?"

Wyent made a pained expression.

"Well, you could've, of course, but ... you're not the murderer type, Milo. You're the super here, right? Your main concern is holding onto your job, I would imagine. Even getting personal with somebody in your building would be bad policy, no? It would be bad policy. You wouldn't do anything without a plan. I can feel that about you. A plan. Not crazy like this. Not like this lady went out. You see the bruises? She was beaten up. Violent crime. Had to be a sex criminal. You have a steady girlfriend, right? Nah. Doesn't fit. People who are in a satisfying relationship never do a thing like this. People have ways of operating and they almost always fit into some pattern. First thing you learn in criminal work. Now I can tell my client that, but he's going to read the papers like everyone else, see? And he'll have the same questions. Only perhaps a little more so."

He was like a guy with his toy soldiers all spread out on the rug. He was lining them up. You could see it in the little smile on his face as he thought about it.

"It's going to create a furor, you know. This thing. It could be on the front page for weeks. Have you seen the papers? There's going to be a row about this. You could wind up with your picture in the papers."

He went on some more about that. I finished my beer. What a cocky bastard this Wyent was. He wasn't a wimp as I had thought at first. He was a cunning little wheedler. "People who are in a satisfying relationship never do a thing like this," he tells me. Where'd he read that? I had an idea he had a filing cabinet behind his ears chock full of stuff like that.

"So what do you say?" he started again. "You want to meet my client? I think he'd like it if you did. I don't see why you'd mind. Unless of course you have something to hide."

I was beginning to catch on now. It was beginning to dawn on me, this conciliatory chat of his. In another world and in a different age this gentleman and two or three hired thugs would have coldcocked me in the alley and taken me for a ride. They would have put me under a blanket and maybe kicked out a couple of teeth, and then they would have let me talk to the main guy, who would have found out what he wanted in the old style, by torture. That was the way in former times. Now I was getting a different version. Much more modern. I was not even being told what to do. I was being invited. I had shown curiosity about his client after all, hadn't I? And if I refused, then there would be plenty of time for the other stuff.

Suddenly I regretted those last two beers. I felt like I was in a box. I couldn't decide how to make him go away.

"So what do you say?" he repeated. He really wanted to see me say no, I could sense that. That would up the ante. Whatever he wanted, I didn't want to give it, even if it was to tell him to go to Hell. I just sat there staring at him.

There was a soft knock on the door. I waited. A key turned in the lock. We both waited till the door opened.

It was Holly.

As she shut the door behind her it was like a glow had entered the room. She dropped a red shopping bag by the door and took a breath. She seemed to sort of melt into the air around us and infuse it with her warmth. She smiled at me and then at Wyent as though he was a guest at her party whom she didn't know yet but she'd make sure she introduced herself and made him feel comfortable before the hors d'oeuvres came around. Wyent and I didn't say a word. She seemed to be walking on tip-toe as she came closer to me and in a whisper she swelled.

"I got a promotion."

"You did?"

"Ah-huh." She nodded, her big eyes following me. Akbar, who had been in hiding all this time, came out and caressed her feet. He leaped up on the kitchen table and sat looking at us humans.

"They made me manager of a new group and I'm responsible for training and organizing the work and everything. Can you believe it?"

"This just happened today?"

Wyent was looking at her like she just sailed in from Neptune.

"Ah-huh. I mean there've been signs, you know. I've noticed for a while. Things needed being reorganized, but I never expected this. Fred just called me in his office and asked me if I wanted the job. Can you believe it?"

"That's wonderful, Holly."

She went on talking as she circled by the fridge in the next room and got herself some ice water.

Wyent and I were silent. We were like schoolboys waiting to see which one of us would confess to big sister about spilling the jam. For the first time since he had appeared Wyent looked like he actually couldn't muster a smile.

Holly came back, looking at us over the glass as she sipped, spilling a few drops on her blouse. She brushed them off with grazing flicks of her fingers. Her eyes swung as softly as a long pendulum from me to Wyent and back again to me.

"Holly, this is ..." I began, but she had her own cadenza:

"I mean five of the new people, they'll all be reporting to me. Jerry, that guy, remember I told you about? Flies airplanes. And Alphonse. He's okay. And Adrian, oh, she's a dream, Milo. I love Adrian. She comes up to me and plants this big kiss on my cheek. And they were all there congratulating me and standing around. Even Frieda came over and congratulated me. Even her. The Danish iceberg. Can you imagine that? There was a meeting and Fred told them about it and tomorrow we move our desks. And if it works out, in just a month I'll get a raise. Can you believe it? I had to go out for a drink with Carol just to level my head. I must have talked for an hour without shutting up."

"That's wonderful, Holly," I said. "Uh, this is Mr. Wyent, Holly."

"Hi. And then to cap it off, Terrence comes in. He wants to know how we're going to change some layouts with the new computer and stuff. Like maybe Terrence has an idea for how to improve things, right? And Fred just tells him right there. I was so proud of Fred. Right there in front of everybody, he just tells him. I mean Fred has been aching to tell this to Terrence for a year. And you should have seen the look on Terrence's face. He felt like crying, I could tell it. 'Cause I know Terrence pretty well, after all. I know. He wanted to go hide in the supply room and cry for an hour for all the things he's said to me. But then he had to stand there and smile and congratulate me like everyone else, because that's what all the others did. Isn't that something? I couldn't believe it. I told Carol I bet Terrence calls in sick tomorrow. I bet you anything. He's incredible. You guys want me to take you out to dinner tonight?"

"Well, actually, Holly, Mr. Wyent and I were thinking of going to visit a friend of his and maybe talk over a little business."

"Oh," she said, looking mildly stunned. "Can't it wait?"

Some small voice was telling me not to go along with Wyent. Not just then, at least not on his terms. Add to that, it bothered me that maybe I would have to forego an evening with Holly and instead spend it second-guessing Wyent and maybe getting into some unpleasantness with his "employer", whoever that was. While Holly went on more about the new wind that was blowing through her life, I wondered what was Wyent's plan anyway? He wasn't a cop; he couldn't have expected me to drop everything because he had a client with a special interest in Miranda. As Holly went on talking, I watched Wyent out of the corner of my eye. He was becoming more uncomfortable. Holly, in her own special way, had offered me a way out and I didn't think it was so smart to pass it up.

"Holly and I have something to talk over," I said finally. "So I think that thing can probably wait. Why don't we talk again tomorrow, Frank? When we both have more time."

I liked using his first name: familiarity made me feel brotherly and powerful. I waited to see how he would take it. I was ready to throw him out on his ear if that was necessary.

Wyent stood up slowly. He seemed dismayed, his face took on a distant almost dreamy look, as though it was not he who was being put off, but something he respected and thought I ought to respect.

"Well ..." he said, "that's really too bad. I know that he would really like to see you. I think he would like to be your friend. Maybe he could do you a few good turns. He's like that. If you do a good thing for him he remembers it ..."

"Yeah, but you see how it is, Frank. A guy's gotta keep his own gong ringing. You know? Tend his own patio, don't you think? Why don't you give me a call and we can work out a time which is mutually satisfactory to both of us, together, when we see eye to eye on a thing like this?"

He looked more sullen now. He was speaking to the wall.

"I think tonight would be a better time," he said with an unkind edge.

I couldn't believe this guy.

"As you can see, I have a lot of other things to attend to," I said.

"What's going on?" Holly asked with a lot of genuine incredulity.

Wyent didn't want to talk anymore with Holly here. She had ruined his concentration. But he wanted to be graceful.

"Don't make a mistake," he said looking straight at a spot under my right eye.

I just stood and looked at him.

"How about say at ten?" he said. "At the Catalyst Pub on Houston Street. You know where that is?"

"Why would I go there?"

"If you go," he said softly, "then everything. Will. Be. All right."

I felt admiring of the shiny smoothness of his perfect forehead. It was as though, if Wyent softly sweated and remained calm, everything would indeed be all right. I wondered what the world would be like if Wyent ruled, since he seemed to want to. We'd all have particular places to go.

"I'll wait for you there," he said.

"Suit yourself."

"You can make it," he said and walked out the door.

12. A Quiet Dinner

"What a rude guy," Holly said while he was still within earshot. "Where'd you meet him?"

"Friend of the Widow's," I said, hoping that would end the conversation.

Holly became thoughtful. She got a wet towel and daubed the back of my head. One thing I'll say for her: she had the God-given native instinctual intelligence not to ask me how I had got cut up. She knew that would come out if it had to, and she didn't care more about that than helping me feel better and get well. How can you not love a woman like that?

"I worried about you," she said. It was like an angel had spoken. All the good things I had ever felt for her flowed back and more besides and came into me like a warm glow spreading through every muscle and every pore. I glowed at her touch, with her soft voice brushing over me and telling me how I was going to get better. Akbar bounded onto the table and muttered in his guttural whimper about how I could be as healthy as he was if I would just look after myself as well as he looked after himself. And ate the right food. The world was really a simple place, wasn't it? Made up of tuna cans and shredded furniture. Milo's condolatory cat.

Holly stroked me behind the ear. It was lovely: four sympathetic eyes staring hopefully at me, not impressed by my blundering ways. Holly cooed at me again.

"Oh, Milo, I missed you. I couldn't tell you this morning, you were so out of it, I just let you sleep and we could have had breakfast but then those cops showed up. And I had to get to work. I'm sorry I got angry in the car. I regretted it two hours after I left you. An hour, even. But ... I don't know ... I didn't think it was right to come back earlier. Maybe it was a little that I was feeling jealous. I know you had an affair with that woman on the top floor, and I saw her just standing there when we drove by, and I knew something was wrong and I just had this wild idea that you would suddenly ... do something ... oh, I don't know what I thought ... It was crazy, it was the stupidest thing. So I came back last night.... Are you angry with me? I don't blame you if you are. Look at me. Talk to me."

"I'm not angry. I think you're wonderful."

She looked at me for a long time, just taking it in. It was me that was holding something back, and she would guess soon enough.

"Let's go eat," I said finally. "That place we go to. We have to celebrate. Your new job."

Over dinner Holly talked more about her job, the triumph of it, but by the time desert came around, she was growing wary in a way, as though she could feel the different air in the room, in the place I was in.

"You know," she said in a softer tone, "I never told you, but I believe in something you may think is kind of crazy. Have you ever heard of 'supernatural balances'?"

"No."

"Well, it's a term I made up. I haven't told a lot of people about it, but it probably will catch on. But, well, it's like all the good in the world somehow stays the same, more or less, no matter what happens. There's just so much of it, but it's constantly getting, you know, redistributed. So different people have it at different times. You know what I mean?"

She was stirring an imaginary goblet in front of me as though that was the mixing pot where all the good in the world got mixed about, and now she cocked her finger at me as if to give me a taste.

"Now it will be one person. Or a group of persons. And then later it'll be somebody else. So when something good happens, then something bad happens somewhere else."

"Well, something bad happened to Terrence today," I said, "when you got your promotion. You saw it in his face, you said."

"Yeah, only it's more transcendental than that. It's not cause and effect. In fact Terrence probably isn't the one it will happen to, because he was right there. You can't usually see it if you're right there. It kind of happens when you're not looking. It just happens. And so evil people can cause good without even knowing it. And good suffuses into places where you think it won't go. You know, like where people are despairing and they don't think anything will work out, sometimes a bit of goodness is sneaking into their lives and they don't know it yet, but it will work out that the despair caused the good ... you get what I mean? Maybe I'm not explaining it well enough."

"You're explaining it just fine."

"I believe in goodness, but I believe in balance too, if that's any help."

"So will someone suffer because you got a piece of good news today?"

"No, I hope not," she said with a sigh. And then she looked me square in the eye.

"Milo, what is it? You haven't said a word about how your day went. And those men that came in while I was leaving, you never said what they wanted or why they came or anything. And your head got cut up. I saw that last night. I just hope you're all right. Are you all right?"

I thought for a minute how I was going to say this; if I did it wrong it could ruin my relationship with Holly, but if I lied, that would absolutely destroy it, no question. And if I said it and wasn't believed, or she thought I was playing a joke, I doubted we would be able to communicate for weeks to come. I steadied myself so she would be sure, as sure as I could make it.

"Those cops that came in weren't real cops," I said. "And they shot Miranda's door down. They were expecting some kind of fight, looked like to me. But she was dead because somebody strangled her hours before. The police think these guys, who were pretending to be cops, killed her. But I had promised her the night before, that I would go up to her place at midnight for some tea. Only I got into a fight and got my head cut open and had to go to the hospital, so I didn't get to her place till four AM and she was already dead. It's all in the papers, you can check out what I'm telling you. It's all there."

She listened to it without saying a word till I was finished. She never even set down her desert fork except to get a sip of wine. When I finished she just waited.

"That's it? It's all true?"

I said it was. She paused and kept looking back at me to check out that I didn't do something that would tip her off that it was a joke. Pretty quickly she realized it was no joke.

"Milo, if you'd seen her like that, why didn't you just call the police?"

"I did. I mean I tried to, but I was feeling weak. I'd just seen a dead person and I got hit on the head and it affected me. That's why I asked you to call 911, before I fell asleep on the floor."

Her eyes got really big.

"You asked me to call 911? You asked me to call? Is that what you were saying? It was just gibberish. Milo, you were babbling like an idiot—and foaming at the mouth. I never saw you like that. You don't remember any of this?"

We looked at each other like we had never met before and had made a mistake about identities but couldn't bring ourselves to break eye contact. We were talking across an abyss.

"Of course," I said, looking down. "That explains it. I must have been just babbling. And then you took the best care you knew how: you put blankets around me and a pillow under my head, because I must have been immoveable."

"Well, yes," she said. "Slightly so. Moveable like a dumpster. I tried to take care of you. Is that so bad?"

She was obviously baffled. I should have assumed it from the start—of course I must have been babbling, or she would have called 911. How stupid of me to bring it up. As if what happened to Miranda weren't enough to ruin the evening.

She took a long breath and just stopped and grew somber. Her eyes welled with tears. She waved me away when I moved to comfort her. She just sat there with her cheeks red and her face covered with tears. I felt kind of insensitive because I wasn't able to cry like that.

"And you loved her."

I was struck dumb. Of course I could deny it, but that might only make things worse than the way they were already. But to let it sit there without saying anything, I couldn't make myself do that.

"I was infatuated with her a long time ago. I was just distracted, that's all. Besides I felt sorry for her. She had just gotten mugged and she needed money and so I gave her some, and she begged me to come back and see her at midnight and so I promised."

Holly just looked at me through her tears.

"That's love," she said. And another flood of tears went down her cheeks.

"Let's go," I said.

"I'm not going anywhere with you," she said. "And I'm not going back to that house."

"Well, that makes sense, I suppose."

"Call me superstitious. I'm not going back there."

I paused, knowing that with the slightest wrong step from me and she was going to run out of the restaurant, and who knows when I'd see her again? Things were going so well until I told her about Miranda. But what was I going to do, keep it a secret? Let her find out on the news?

"I don't know why you're so upset. You didn't even know her, did you?"

"You idiot!" she cried. People at tables nearby stopped talking. "You think I'm crying for her? I'm crying because you love her. And not me...."

She wiped her face with the napkin. I knew enough to shut up at least.

"And ... and ... It happened to somebody. Isn't that enough? Isn't that enough? And, I don't know. I didn't wish her well. And ... maybe in some way I wanted something bad to happen to her. Getting angry and driving you out of the car and then the next morning leaving like I did when those men came. I ran away at just the moment when she needed help."

"I wanted you to go. I wanted to protect you."

"Oh, I don't know. It just makes me sad, that's all. I'm just ... sad."

"Let's go," I said again.

We didn't say a word all the walk back. She was deep in thought. It had rained while we were inside, but now it had stopped. The wet smell was all around and the cars made a shhhhhh sound in the street and glided past with shiny backs. We were a block away from her place when she stopped.

"Don't walk me any further," she said.

"Okay."

"Milo, there's just one thing."

"What's that?"

She sighed and looked around at the street lights. The tears were still just under the surface, and she was forcing herself to talk.

"Don't go with that man, Milo. Frank, or whatever his name was."

"No. I won't. Of course not."

"I don't trust him."

"No. Neither do I."

"Good night." She turned and I watched her till she got in the door to her apartment.

I stood there, staring at the place where she had gone. I was utterly stunned. I had just experienced a moment I was entirely unworthy of. She had just said the most loving thing she could say to me, outside of outright saying that she loved me. And for what seemed like the first time in my life, I realized it right after it happened. All this time I had been loving the wrong woman. The whole thing was utterly astonishing. It was the tiniest gesture she made with her hand, yet it meant so much to me at that moment. And it meant that our relationship wasn't over, despite what happened with Miranda. Despite all that.

I turned and walked down the street as if I were carrying a pot of gold rubles I had just found, and there was no possibility it was going to get away from me. It seemed that complete. The most precious thing she could have given me, and there it was. I walked home in a haze that I thought nothing could damage. What could possibly bring me down after a moment like that? Go with Wyent? What, was I crazy? I had something to protect, now. Myself. I felt sure and certain like I had never felt before.

13. The Widow's Curse

As I came to the corner of Termite Street, I saw a cab stop down by the playground. Out of fear I waited. A small dark figure got out and paused as the cab took off. It was as though the cab had to disappear first before this person would move. I walked quickly forward. The figure heard me and stopped short. It did not move and then it suddenly darted down the center of the street toward my house.

"Widow," I called. She stopped. She stared at me as if I might be some strange obstruction she was going to have to destroy with her cane. She wore a black hat and a black raincoat, and I caught her smell from ten feet away, as if she'd just come from cooking up something dank and rancid and had left the pot on the stove. I came running up and stopped before her and took one heavy breath. She stepped back and stood in exactly the spot where Miranda had stood the day before. I coughed heavily and drew a fresh breath.

"Milo," she said at the top of her voice. Her eyes narrowed. You always felt with the Widow Kytler that she could see you better with her eyes half shut. "How odd to meet you here, since you're just the person I want to see. You're not inside watching the news."

"Nor you."

"It's all lies anyway."

"It's exaggeration and partial truths, much of the time," I said, since she wanted to talk about TV.

"There's been trouble in my building."

"Well, yeah, there was. But it doesn't concern you."

"Doesn't concern me," she sneered. "A structural failure in my building and I'm not supposed to be concerned?"

The day whizzed by fast forward in my head. "Structural failure?"

"You told Patrice there had been a structural failure. That's why you took the day off."

Patrice? She talked to Patrice? What kind of a witch was she? Was there any place she didn't get to, any bit of confidence that was safe when she was abroad on the night? That Patrice, of all people, would repeat what was only a business matter between him and me, it boggled the mind.

"Aww, Widow, I had to tell him something. I haven't slept two hours in the last two days. And I fixed your door. The building's okay. I swear it. Nothing happened that I can't fix. You must have seen it on TV. They just knocked the door down. Happens all the time in these old buildings. Besides, on a night like this, (I gestured up at the yellow-grey sky now cleared of rain) how could anything really go wrong?"

"Are you on drugs?" she nearly shouted at me. No one was out on the street, but they wouldn't have to be to hear her screech. There was no reason why she'd have to shout, but she didn't care who heard her. "Could anything really be wrong? Where have you been? My building is in the papers, Milo. Listen to me. In the papers."

"Well, I can't help that."

"You could have protected her. If you didn't throttle her yourself. You didn't, did you? I wouldn't like that. Pretty women are always getting into trouble. I shouldn't rent to them. Just that she knew the other woman. Friend of a steady is usually a good bet."

"Who's that?"

She turned an exasperated cheek.

"You're not too smart, Milo. I don't know if I should keep you in this job. Super of a building requires a lot of mental acumen, a certain alertness and awareness of people which I don't think you have. I wonder about you."

"Don't badger me, Widow. Most supers are drugged-out winos addicted to porn and television. Where you gonna find talent like me? Good natured, kind, and do I ever call you for a minor problem? I fix electrical stuff, doesn't cost you a dime. You willing to pay union wages for that?"

I had her there. If the city ever discovered the condition of her electrical system, she'd be out thirty thousand easy. I took another tone.

"A woman just told me she loved me. I guess it kind of affected my mind."

"Love? Loved you? What are you talking about?"

"You've been married. Four times, right? Haven't you ever been in love?"

"No."

"Well, just imagine it, then. You care for someone else. And you put up with their quirks because you see the essential divine humanity in another person, the absolute unfathomable mystery in the way another person experiences the world and even experiences you yourself. Till even the slightest thing they say or the slightest gesture made seems to be rich with meaning. There's no miracle greater than that. So I lied to Patrice so I could take the day off. Is that such a big deal?"

She cocked one wild bloodshot eye up at me and stood stock still for a second.

"Milo, I don't think you've got your head on straight."

"Well, I do well enough by you. Taking care of the building and all. That's totally under control. Totally." I realized one thing she might not know was that I had let in those three crazy non-cops that started the whole thing. Well, almost started it. I wasn't about to tell her. "And I appreciate you're taking care of me the way you do."

"You do? Milo, if I didn't love any of my husbands, I sure as hell don't love you."

She brought up Hell like she might own property there. Molten sulfurous seas beneath trees festooned with the eternally hanged were not impassable to her. Might open a mall.

"Give me one good reason why I don't fire you on the spot."

"Why do that?"

"You let those men in. If it wasn't for you ..."

"They said they were cops, Widow. They pushed their way in. A tank couldn't stop those guys. Cut me some slack. I did the best I could."

"You weren't thinking of my property."

I pointed my finger at the point of her nose.

"Yesss! Yes, I was. Every minute. The whole time. It was the first thing on my mind. Besides, you'd just have to replace me."

"There's forty Puerto Rican winos would love to have your job."

"Now that's racist, Widow. You're not among your snotty whitebread East Side socialite friends out here. This is Brooklyn."

"I'd pick the ugliest one so he'd stay out of trouble like you get into—with women I mean. Talking about love! No wonder you'll never get anywhere."

"It's the Theory of the Loser Class, Widow. People will give up everything for love. Money, freedom, peace of mind ... It's the whole blessed blissful cornucopia of human experience. You name it and somebody will give it up for love. Doesn't that say something to you?"

It seemed oddly appropriate, like a picture all of one piece, that we were standing in the edge of a rain-soaked street where God and everybody could hear us while we talked about love at the top of our voices. Were we up to the subject or did the surroundings make it beyond us? Nothing seemed beyond the Widow.

"Were you seeing that woman who got killed?" she asked and rapped her cane on the pavement.

"Of course not. Don't you think we could talk about this in a more private place?"

"I think you were seeing her. And if you get involved with the police ..."

"No way. Absolutely not. They're off on their busy police stuff. Trust me. They don't care about your building. They won't be coming back."

"What did they tell you?"

"Nothing they didn't tell the news people. Why would they talk to me?"

"They talked to you. What did they say?"

"Cops don't give info, Widow. They take it away."

She snorted in the air. I saw a feather of smoke come out, but it might have been the humid air.

"I don't want to talk to you," she said and tramped up the steps. I was just a disposable inconvenience to her.

She wanted to see the inside. She let on that she would have come earlier except for fear of "appearing on TV", she said in a loud voice. I took her inside and up the stairs to Miranda's place. Bernice walked by us on the floor below Miranda's. With her sidling stride she said hello, but before I could introduce them, she disappeared into her apartment. They should have met, I thought sadly; one witch to another. On the next landing a cross and a candle in an ashtray were set before Miranda's door. There were scattered flowers. Set by whom?

"I replaced the door right away," I said. "You know you can never be sure, and it pays to be cautious."

"Let me in."

The Widow was like a walking stick figure: she had only one

intention for every moment, and that intention was desperate, insistent, imperious—she stared at the door until I unlocked it. And then, as the air from the sealed apartment rushed into my chest, it hit me. When we were inside the apartment, I suddenly felt a welling up of grief as if Miranda's ghost had dropped a veil over my face and nothing would lift it. I felt nauseous and depressed all over again. The place was a fresh tomb with the corpse due back any second. It was immediate, immanent, more absolute than anything we could say, and it struck us both silent.

The Widow, however, was intrigued. She looked everywhere but touched practically nothing. The hope chest caught her eye, and she rubbed the wood with the toe of her boot. It was then I noticed a pensive side to the Widow: she seemed to absorb that piece of furniture as much as she was absorbed by it. Her eyes glinted and concentrated on certain things: the cornice of a wall, the lathe marks on the bedstead, a bit of paper on the floor—all had something else going on with it. You could feel it had some meaning for her even as she was ready to cast it into a fire at the first chance. What did she see, as her eyes darted around? Familiars? Household gods? Revenant ambitions of ancient tenants? I couldn't guess. She steadied herself and backed away. She stepped as if she thought she might implicate herself if she left so much as a footprint too heavily on the floor. She looked everywhere, even in the closets still stacked with clothes. She was thorough, complete, and when she was done, she stepped back at me so directly I felt I ought to back away to let her pass. But she stopped, gathering it all in.

"She left a pall over this place," the Widow said bitterly, poisonously, glaring over her shoulder. You could feel the depth of the way she took it personally, even the people involved as if she knew them, and how much she despised each stitch and stick of what was in Miranda's apartment. And this, I surmised, could be because it reminded her of some crime with which she was all too familiar, in some way it would cost your life to find out. She didn't care that the place couldn't be rented; that seemed the least of what she thought.

She walked out the door unafraid that the candle might singe her hem. I paused for a minute and looked down, hoping the delirium might sink past me all over again. The air was thick in my lungs. I slipped out, locked the door and stepped over the candle. I should have felt relief then, but I only felt the darkness sink into me deeper. I walked the Widow back out to the street. Her building was intact. Nothing had been damaged. She could sleep content.

"That poor girl," she said at last. Then she turned to go down the street, moving her cane as if to push the sidewalk out of the way. It was the way she said, "That poor girl," that felt like it was an icy irony, a parting dart, a little snag in her cynical dark. It was still miserly and harsh, if not dishonest. There was nothing natural about it. It was as if, really, to her, Miranda had finally found her rightful place. And the Widow would let her stay there.

"I'll call you if I need you," she yelled back. I watched her go on her way down the wet pavement: her diminutive form primitive, unstoppable. Her whole dark figure flew like wind of an ineluctable passion for the essence of possession: money. Money and all the strange things it had always gotten her, always and forever promised, like perfume that evaporated in air. Her skirts followed her along, a dark shadow that left a trace wherever she walked. Was she eighty years old? Or a hundred? Why in Hell did she care if she lost one of her buildings to structural failure? I knew she had a dozen more. It was like everything else about her: she was opaque as the smoky glass she coveted. That's how I knew her: her house was filled with all forms and shapes of vials in opalescent glass.

I looked down at the sidewalk and stopped cold. On the grey flags there was the chalk outline of a fallen person and a splatter of something dark red. It was carefully gone over and you could see how he/she lay. Here there was a hand awkwardly bent, there a foot. The rain hadn't washed it away; if anything it was clearer now with the damp. I stood there looking down at it. Crime Scene.

I smiled at the obvious: a child had drawn it. Tommy and Louis and Gerald and their friends. Nearby there were smudges from the colored chalk they had been using the day before. It was their joke. I thought sadly how abstract the death of Miranda had to be to children: could they even care? Was it a heightened reality to them because of the freshness of their minds? Or no more real than murder on TV? How could a kid reach the age of ten and not be cynical like that? Death was the last scene before the credits rolled up.

I sauntered back to the stoop but stopped again. Something was wrong now where everything had been much better before. Sickness was starting to swell in my gut. I had definitely felt better when I was with Holly. I was in a funk now. Now all of a sudden the demon was back with me: who had caused Miranda's death? Not me. But maybe I had let it happen. No, that can't be right. Then the nausea came again.

I was in the lost, obsessed, paralyzed swamp, left over from the Widow. It hadn't gone away, like I thought; it had just gone to sleep in me like a poisonous snake that was waiting for the Widow's kiss to wake it up. Plus I had a strange fear of paralysis. I feared Wyent and his crazy mission and how that might mean more paralysis. Sleep would be under a shadow. The Widow had left her curse on me, even as much as I was guarded against her: nothing could be enough, she could bring down a stouter man with her imperious picking, her niggling contempt, as if I wasn't even human to her. And she never brought me down like now. I had gone through a whole cycle in the space of an hour, from feeling bliss to now feeling so depressed and angry and dark I knew a beer wouldn't help. Some presence in Miranda's room had drawn the veil over my face. It was stupid to think I was free of her: it had only lasted for a few hours, but I was back receding down a funnel again. Back in the pit of that morning when the barbarians ruled. I had seen a ghost.

I walked over to the avenue, hailed a cab and told him to go to the Catalyst Pub.

14. Invisible Swans

The Catalyst Pub is not the kind of place you would take a date you were trying to impress, it's much too homely. I was late, of course, but Wyent was there, sitting at a table by himself with a half full stein of beer. He looked like the loner at the party, the one no one wants to talk to. We left and got in his car. I imagined that we looked like a blind date that had met in the personals: that was cool, I thought—hey, for two minutes I had the cachet of a secret life.

We didn't talk at all for several miles. His mind was obviously on the driving and that was fine with me. We whizzed into the neon and cadmium-lit heartland of New Jersey where the sheets of road spread out like a turntable and the heavy driven obsessive tread of commerce slunk over us like a slowly crawling giant.

"The guy you're going to meet is called Opov," Wyent said. "And don't make fun of his name."

"Wasn't thinking I would."

"In fact you've already met him. This morning."

"The big guy with white hair?"

"That's him."

"Figures."

"He remembers you."

We said nothing for another mile.

"He was very upset by her death. You should respect that."

"Well, I figured they might know each other," I said. "Might've been friends."

Wyent sighed and gave himself time to think that over.

"They were more than friends," he said. "They were ... very close."

"Not surprising, I suppose. She had the looks and he has the money. Meant for each other."

His sleepy eyes glanced away from the road.

"You're pretty cynical, Milo."

"Oh, I dunno. Some of my friends think I'm a sweet kind of guy who writes poems on rainy afternoons and talks to his cat."

"This whole business with the shotguns has been exaggerated and blown out of proportion," Wyent said. "This poor woman was probably feeling bad before they arrived this morning. Could be there was some extraneous cause. I imagine she wasn't really dead when my client arrived. She might've been beaten up later. By a lover probably. Probably the motive was jealous rage and she got killed after my client was long gone."

"She got beat up?"

"Probably."

"That's not the way the cops see it," I said.

"Cops have been wrong before," Wyent said philosophically. For a guy who made his living finding out things, he was so lacking in curiosity I couldn't imagine how he did his job. And what were we going out here for anyway? Not to find out anything. That couldn't be it. I had to strain to keep from chuckling. He hadn't gotten any farther than they were that morning.

"Well, wasn't there a medical report?" I asked innocently.

"Oh, there will be. There's a problem at the medical examiner's office. There're always delays. Seems that the guy who should have done the examination didn't get back from some meeting, and so somebody else did it and screwed it up. Then they were told at first that that didn't matter, and then they changed their mind. I went over there and they put me off about seeing the report. So maybe there is no report, know what I mean? It's not an ordinary situation. A lot of egos. It's a turf war, if you want to know. The bottom line is that the medical examiner's report won't be done for days. Then people have to sign off on it. Could be no one will see it till next week. But I'll get a peek."

I bet you will. The cop's little helper. I tried to take a fraternal tone.

"Tell, me, Frank. How did you get this job? I mean I'm just curious how you get into the detective business in the first place."

"How I got the job is just that he called me up. I'm in the phone book. You can hire me, if you can pay my rates. I started out like most guys in the work, as a cop. Then I quit and worked for some other guys for a while. Now I'm on my own. It's not like Sam Spade anymore."

"No? I thought it was."

"There's a lot of work. You'd be surprised. Lot of real estate investigation. Anyway, getting the conversation back to you, Milo. Maybe you knew Miranda more than you said. Could that be?"

I gazed out at the heavy metal lights that streamed like pinballs on a journey from the nearest star, flung in a headlong whirl to surpass us and go on to another destiny behind us in the past.

"Could be," I said cheerily. "Lots of things could be. She paid the rent. We talked a few times. That was all."

"Well, my client seems to think otherwise. I don't know why. You're just the super after all. Just tell him the truth as you saw it. That's the best thing to do."

That sounded right.

"Okay," I said.

"Then everything will be all right," he said solemnly. "And ... we won't lose sight of our main goal."

I looked around again.

"What's that?"

"To keep my client out of it, of course. And his friends and relatives. That's what we're after. We want to smooth things over. That's why I invited you out here: smooth things over. Until the killer is found. And justice is done."

He settled back like a young exec at a board meeting.

"Oh, that shouldn't be too hard," I said.

We were silent again, and for the rest of the way. Soon we left the freeway and dove through an underpass and on through a sleepy little town with no name. We went out a country road for more miles and swerved on a graveled drive. There was a sign on the fence informing you that this was private land. The road wound in graceful curves over a shallow knoll. Without the moon, you saw only by the headlights: the lawn was broad and calm and spotted with random trees. Soon we topped the knoll and descended down a gentle slope toward a house nestled down from us where the open grass stopped and gave up to trees on one side. Against the discolored sky the forest was dark and withholding and there was a patina of reflected light on the lower leaves. It was a country estate, all right. Tucked back in a corner of the forest, the house glowed like a furnace in a coal chute. Every window was lit up. Cars were parked in rows out front on white gravel. There seemed to be a party going on. Wyent parked up the way on the drive.

One limo was having its doors opened out front, and a sextet was just leaving as we drove up. A man in mauve pants stared into our headlights and then motioned a woman to hurry up. Her cellulitic rotundity fairly bounced within loose white pants. Seeing the place gave me a good feeling, really; I had feared we would meet in some dark and desolate spot, on some unidentifiable country road. That would be dangerous. And then this. Coarse laughter and churning music poured out of the open front door. I got out and walked around.

The main body of the house was stone, with gables and a high slate roof. The top floor seemed to have been lit up mostly for show; the windows were open but no one seemed to be behind them. Extending a little to one side, there was a summer porch and circles of people had gathered there, some dancing, most seated around the edge. Two chauffeurs lounged on the fender of one of the cars. They talked and took no notice of us. Another was reading a paper by the dome light of his stretch limousine. Beside where we walked, rose bushes spread out in thick floriform curves. They had thorns like I couldn't remember seeing on roses, like enlarged needles. By the steps to the front door were two cement urns with a carved shield on each and the letter R over a bar sinister. We walked past them and up the steps.

"I bet the chauffeur did it," I quipped. Wyent's gaze was on the glow of the doorway.

"Don't talk about that here," he said. "You never know who's listening."

Wyent spoke to a man with close-cropped hair as we went in. The man looked at me and then he nodded. I was all right now. Wyent motioned me forward.

It was a party, all right. Some people had come in evening dresses, a few were in dungarees. Down one hall there were hoots and laughter, down another there was disco music. Right in the center there was a table with snacks and drinks and a punch bowl with two men dressed in off-white suits and black bow ties.

A woman in a black evening dress had an orchid corsage dangling from her shoulder. She came running by and spilled her glass in front of Wyent.

"Sorry," she said, and rushed on down the hall where there were people and furniture in clumps of dark places. We went that way.

The place seemed at first to have recently been moved into— there were crates crowded in corners, chairs that didn't match ... but the more you looked the more you got the impression it had been this way for a long time. There was furniture lining the halls and over the chairs heaps of clothing were piled. Some of it must have gotten wet; I got a leaden whiff of mildew. There were fans set up to keep the air moving, but even so, the air seemed to hang on the walls and the people with it.

In one room people sat in semidarkness and looked up suspiciously when we appeared. A man reached over a joint but backed off like a garment in the breeze when I motioned him away. A disco drum made a dull thumping sound here, and a radio squabbled with itself on the shelf. In another room the only light was a floor lamp lying on its side. People lounged on sofas and laughed as a man balanced himself on a ladder that led up through a huge hole cut in the ceiling. Shadowy figures moved to the music and called down from the floor above. We went off down another hall and came to a marble-floored patio. A swimming pool was straight beyond. Brown palm fronds reached up from ceramic urns and stroked the gauze of a lady's gown.

I wondered out loud if Miranda had many friends at this party.

"Miranda was invited of course," Wyent said in the tone of a manhole lid. "Don't talk about her."

It was a cool evening, for that late in summer. A breeze blew across the pool, which made it seem odd there were so many people inside, so much clear air out here. Couples sat in lounge chairs talking and looking up at the sky. Others stood and talked; we wandered among them. We passed a dinner table where people seemed strangely silent and a man with wispy white hair sat at one end with his delicate purple fingers barely moving the glass in front of him. Beside him a woman with equally white hair sat with a shawl over her and a blissful smile on her face. Further on, three women stood apart; a tall woman with downy shoulders that curled toward her collarbones threw back her head and laughed out loud. Then they ran off like three conspirators with an appointment somewhere.

Wyent stopped in front of me.

"Wait here. I'll be back in a minute." He went down past the pool and into another wing of the building that looked like it was a summer guesthouse connected to the main building by a long glassed-in corridor.

The couple with white hair got up and walked arm in arm along the pool. When they came near they smiled politely. The man's smoky eyes drifted up to me. He seemed to pause before speaking as if he knew I was a stranger who would naturally be interested.

"Um ... you may not know ... did you know, that all this is ours?"

"You mean the house?" I said.

"The house and eighty acres besides. It's all ours. All belongs to me and my wife." He said it with a sad thinness to his voice, like it was the saddest fact, and I should be saddened too, even surprised.

"Well," I said, "thanks for inviting me."

"Inviting ...?"

"To your party."

"Oh, no," he said, shaking his head as if a different realm of thought had to be entered now. "This ... all this is not our idea. We don't know any of these people. They're friends of his."

He gestured with his cane at the summer house where Wyent had gone.

"But it's your home. Where do you live?"

"Up there," he said, half turning around to the lit up main house. "That's where he lets us stay. But this is our home. We're Reyndolphs. All of us."

He said it as if I ought to know what that meant. I nodded as if I did. I looked at them more closely. The old man's eyes were filled not with mystery but with misfortune.

"Then Opov is your guest."

The old man would have spat if he could.

"Not our guest. We are his captives. All this luxury. See? We are allowed to creep about here. We stumble and fall but no one picks us up."

"Why don't you call the police?"

"Oh," the old man said weakly, "they are the police. Yes. It's all decided. But it's ours. All this. Our ... home ..."

Before I could ask them any more, they recommenced their slow promenade, arm in arm, as if there was no reason to say any more, looking only a few feet ahead of them. Suddenly I felt like I might be a shadow to which they had pointlessly spoken.

I stepped through a hedge to get away from the light, since from there I could see more clearly. There on the grass in the shadows two feet were sticking out of the ground. I went closer to look. The feet were tied to an ax handle which spanned a hole just big enough for a person to hang in. It didn't move. Impulsively I bent down and heaved up the ax handle, drawing up the body of a man. I spread him on the grass. He was breathing but looked drugged. The dirt still clung to his face and his tattered suit. He mumbled something and the slit of his eyes coursed in my direction. Vaguely he pawed at the rope on his ankles. I saw he could help himself from there.

"Hey, it's the super," a man said behind me. It was Billy from this morning. He was smiling. He nodded at what I had done. "Always getting into stuff that don't concern you. Super."

"Surprised to see you, Billy."

"Whaddayou come out here for?" he said, drawing me back to the pool. He seemed to want to ignore the man who had been suspended in the ground. "Super gonna fix the lights? Ha. Ha. But you're all right. I'm gonna let him hang there the rest of the night. But you're all right. I'll take care of you. You watch your step around here, though. You hear what I'm saying? Most of these people here are real nice. Right to the core, they really are. But there's some people ... they're not as nice as they seem. You get what I mean?"

He nodded and breathed into my face a heavy odor of liquor.

"Yeah. Thanks for the advice."

"The best thing is you don't speak to nobody. It's that simple."

"Okay."

He turned abruptly and walked away. Just like that.

I wandered around the pool. Nobody there was alone, except for a fleshy young gentleman in a cream summer suit and a Panama hat who lounged near the far corner throwing orange peels into the water. No one went near him. It was like there was a large space provided for him to sit there and be alone. It was Vincent. He wore tailored white loafers of thin reptilian skin that looked like they had been bought that afternoon and placed lovingly over the pointy feet of a dancing master now gone to seed. Because of the hat, you could only see his nose and lips, which was how I recognized him: those little mauve pillows that had never known strain. I went over and pulled up a chair nearby.

"Too bad there're no swans," I said. "Pool as big as that ought to have water fowl. Add to the beauty."

"There're swans. You just don't see them," he said. "But swans don't eat orange peels."

He never looked at me. He might have seen me from across the pool. But he clearly didn't welcome my stab at conversation.

"Oh, yeah. Yeah. I guess that's right," I said as though I had made a study of waterfowl and ought to know better. I sat down beside him and watched. His pudgy pointed fingers went on tearing at the orange. There were other oranges. What he had peeled were in a pile between his legs. There were several on the ground he had yet to do. His eyes were glassy but intent, as if he vaguely expected something to come out of this project, this solitary feeding of invisible birds with food they wouldn't eat.

"You lied to me, asshole," he said. I smiled happily.

"Yeah, I guess so. I was delaying the truth. I didn't want to be the one to tell you."

"You didn't tell me she was dead."

"Yeah, well ... I didn't know how you'd take it."

"How'm I supposed to take it? I loved her. Loved ... Now she's ..." He couldn't go on.

"Well, you were pretty believable," I said. "You sounded like you didn't know at all." I wanted to bait him and make him angry at me or somebody. I felt any chance was better than none. "No. You sounded totally ignorant of the whole thing."

"What's that supposed to mean?"

"It was obvious you didn't know she was dead. So you couldn't be the one who ..."

"Get outta my sight," he snarled.

"Okay. I'm not surprised you're moody. You've been through a lot. Oh, well.... It's none of my business. But I never could figure that out," I said. "I wonder what swans do eat."

He seemed to be inert for a moment.

"Is that it?" he said sarcastically. "Is that what you wonder? Wonder wonder wonder ... Wonder, do you? Eat sweet meat Pete. Eatle meatle in the middle. Wonder, who? Wonder hoooo? Whodoo? Who do you do, we do, whoopdidoo. Do, do, oh, please, oh, dooo ... Hoot to the moon, duderoo, like you too, train runs true, salute to you, if in a tiff, sniff, griff ... but don't wake up a stiff ... "

He was cackling like three junkies in the rain. His eyes whirled in his skull as he went on and on like that, for at least a minute. He said every line in some crazy different inflection of his whiney voice, like he had a chorus of bickering old women in his head and they never shut up. I got up to move away and his voice suddenly dropped and was deadly serious.

"I know who sent you," he said with his bulbous eyes glinting at me like telescopic sights from some metal office tower. "Tell them to fuck off. And you do the same, asshole."

"A friend of Simone's sent me. How'd you know?"

"You're fucking with my head, man. Don't fuck with me. I don't care who sent you. Fuck off."

His little purple lips went back to their pout.

"Well," I said. "I imagine swans eat snails and, well ... well, grass, I suppose ... and maybe once in a while they probably have themselves a little fish. Something like that."

"And little babies' eyes," he said with sudden flaring viciousness. A sound of clicking heels came toward us.

"Vincent," the woman's voice called. "He wants to see you. You have to come now." She had that same east European accent.

I turned to see a woman in a lavender dress with a gorgeous shock of ruddy hair. She stood awkwardly there, expecting him to move and when he did not, she sat down with the peevish air of talking to a servant who has to be nagged to do anything.

"He means it," she said.

Vincent grunted.

"Meet the super," he said.

She turned and glanced at me up and down, then stuck out her tongue: there was a gold lizard pierced into the flat of her tongue. I was with the lizard people.

"Hi. So?"

"Talk to him."

She looked at me as if maybe she was supposed to smile, but she couldn't be sure.

"Well ... what should I say?"

He yelled to her: "I don't care what you say. Talk to him. Talk nice."

She shrunk back. It was like watching a flower crushed by a cinderblock.

"Why don't you say what you've got to say, Vincent?" I said.

"Who are you, motherfucker?"

I grinned at him.

"Tell me, Vincent. I've been wondering something about you. Are you afraid of getting a suntan?" I reached over and picked the ridiculous Panama hat off his head. I leaped away and past the insistent woman. His hand snapped up but he was too slow. On the side of his head there was a gauze patch with a brownish coagulation near the center. It covered most of a shaved spot just above his temple. I held the hat with my fingers inside the brim. He leaned over towards me and his lips hardly even parted. People forty feet away stopped talking.

"Gimme my hat."

His arm flashed out for the hat, but he hadn't gotten his balance on the lounge chair before he moved. I easily held it away. I waited, taking him in. He was going to kill me for that. He lunged at me and I backed away. He rolled off the chair and onto the concrete and howled when his elbow hit. The woman reached for him. She touched his cheek.

"What, are you my mother? I don't need you," he hissed. In one explosive motion his arm flailed out and hit her in the stomach. She went back and gave a sickening grunt. Then she cried out. Other voices murmured across the water. Feet were running everywhere over the tiles. I tossed the hat on the ground.

And then, just when he leaped up and I expected him to come at me, he grabbed her by the shoulder and pulled her up. He would have hit her again but I caught his fist and pushed it away. A mistake. It just let him recoil to get a better aim. He spun around and kicked my shin. I went down but I got hold of his foot just above the lizard loafer and pushed it up as far as I could. He was frozen for a second and I twisted it around. He fell unbalanced over the lawn chair. The oranges made a satisfying splash as he sat in them, his feet kicking out. People were crowding around us now. In a blur I saw Wyent's face as he heaved his shoulder into me.

"Back away."

I backed away and pulled the woman with me. She was crying and had her arms crossed stiff in front of her. Across the pool guests were standing watching us and not saying anything. Billy loomed up behind Wyent. Wyent was yelling at Vincent. And he yelled at me, "Get out of here."

"I don't give a rat's ass," Vincent was yelling over and over. He leaped up and one push from Billy put him back in the chair. He kept on cursing me, but he didn't get up after that. I tossed the hat back to him.

"Just kidding," I said.

They stared at me.

"... listen, you don't want everybody to see ... this to turn into ..."

they were saying. Wyent grabbed my arm and bounded away.

"Come on," he said. He was stronger than I would have thought.

"Who's the girl?" I said.

"Some one of them. Who cares?" Wyent doggedly pulled me away. "She's in love with him. Doesn't matter."

"Funny. I could feel that romance was in the air."

"Forget that," Wyent said.

People crowded between us and I didn't see her anymore. I went with Wyent. Faces gawked up and spread around us and then cleared a path and let us pass. Some ran out to the edge of the pool and stood watching, thinking something was going to happen. I began to feel the air again, cool as a mountain breeze. I had a sudden realization; it was like a cool air blowing through me, wiping away the sickness in my gut, I wasn't acting in a prudent way anymore. I felt driven, a feeling that was new to me. I felt a vortex to act against the way I had always done and over my own carelessness and the fact that it seemed to me I had never given anything to anybody, and I didn't care what anyone said; I was going to plow ahead no matter what, even if it involved making some strange people feel displeasure. And what did I matter? For the first time I had the strangest feeling: thinking about my own advantage nauseated me; I couldn't do it now.

"That was a nice move you made," Wyent said.

"Well, the kid's a real charmer," I said. "Maybe he just needs a friend."

We strode past more palms. A young man with a girl in a tie-dyed tee shirt asked us what had happened. We slipped by. They ran back to the far corner of the pool.

"You liked him, huh?" Wyent hollered at me over the din. "Well good. You're going to meet his dad."

15. The Poker and the Gun

We walked down a corridor which was so crowded with furniture you had to go single file. Wistful potted plants were everywhere. Some ferns, still living, unwrapped their spirals in the humid air. There were special grow lamps clamped to the furniture. Who needed so much furniture? But when we passed an open door, usually there was only rubble, with people seated on cushions or rundown sofas. Down another corridor there were pictures spotted on the walls. A sweaty-faced man holding a drink backed up against the wall as we passed. Behind him a woman crouched, as if with some hilarious passion. Other faces were knitted with heavy anger and the pressure of keeping it in. Their eyes fed on us, wondering how we stacked up in some pyramid of envy or power I knew nothing about—and then they looked away. Where the corridor widened there was a large oak chest of drawers with a spray of dry flowers in a crystal vase. A heavy wooden door stood opposite the chest. Wyent tapped on the door and walked in. There issued out the languid sound of dance music like you sometimes hear in restaurants, but then it went off. The room was huge and quite dark. A fan purred in the window. I shut the door behind us.

There was a writing desk set before the opposite wall, and beyond that a latticed window where you could see the lawn and shrubbery illuminated by the subaquatic lamps. A green-shaded brass light sat on the desk, and behind that sat the big man with white hair that I had seen that morning. This was Opov. No trace of recognition shown from his face, which was dark and glistening with sweat. He was on the phone speaking in a foreign language when we entered. He made a ghostly impression, like an incubus sitting on a lily pad. I had a feeling if I sat down the ooze would come up to my eyes.

On the next wall was a large mantled fireplace like a dark hole. Near where we entered there was a fish tank fully eight feet long that let out a subsea glow on the floor around it. All you could hear was the bubbling tank, the dull lilt of a band off somewhere, and the buzz of the fan stuck in front of an open casement window. Opov hung up the phone and looked at us. He belched softly. He ponderously got up and went over to Wyent and touched his head with his ham hand. It was like a father might touch his son. Then he walked over to the mantelpiece and motioned Wyent to follow. It seemed to be a ritual between them.

"You ... come just now?"

"Yes," Wyent said. "I tried to make it sooner."

"You see ... hmm ... when you came in?" Opov said. He didn't speak in sentences, expecting the other person to get what he meant and fill it in. Wyent shook his head. The other picked up a poker from the fireplace.

Wyent said something funny and Opov laughed, and spit flew out over Wyent's head. Then just as quickly the mirth was gone.

"Why's he here?" Opov asked.

"You said ... " Wyent mumbled something.

Opov squinted at me.

"Ah. He's super?"

"Yes."

He nodded, watching me as if he might buy a pound of fish. Then he turned back to something else.

"... or Patterson, or other guy? What was his name ... with truck ... maybe ... hmmm ... call cops if he thinks ... thought they would be ... you know about that? You know about it for sure? I didn't tell them one way or other what it was going to be...."

"I know, I told them," Wyent said. "I brought the guy ..."

"Hmm ... and you took that ... to quiet lady ... yeah ... no, you call her.... Meet 'em on train.... Hit 'im in a sensital—you say sensital?—sensitive area if he would ... couldn't keep them away ... you in town all this time? I ... Opov ... know where to find me ... take look around when we're through here. You could go out there ... "

"Of course, I could," Wyent said. He was nodding at each of the things Opov said. They talked in this kind of dream language for what seemed like twenty minutes and then broke off. I heard a scrape from the other end of the room, which was mostly in dark. I looked around and saw Leo and the others sitting like shadows that never moved.

"Yes," Opov said cheerily. "We waiting for you."

He breathed deeply, like a human bellows. You could tell he was Vincent's father: they had the same kind of dark lips, only the father's were thinner and more artistic.

"So you knew her. Knew the woman. Miranda. You knew her?"

"Yeah. Well, she lived in my building."

"Yeah," he nodded. "That all? Just because she live in building? Not maybe something more?"

"I, well, I went out with her once or twice."

He hummed and spun around, enjoying the poker.

"She dates super. High fashion model dates super. But she lesbian. Why she go out with you?"

He eyed me, staring through me. I looked away before it became a contest.

"She was sometimes confused," I said. "I didn't know all her habits. I'm sure she'd have been happier with other people. In fact, I think she was. It didn't last long."

Opov turned away, taking a different tack.

"You know, I have enemies. Nice guy like me. Would you think? Not police. Police are like weather; they always there. No. But my enemies, not always people I know. Some I know. Some I don't. Maybe you know."

"I ... don't follow you."

He looked away, as if the most interesting object in the room might be anywhere.

"Did she, Miranda, did she talk to you a lot?"

I was getting impatient.

"Listen," I began, "I think we can shorten this whole thing ..."

"I ask questions here," he spat at me.

All of them were still.

"I knew her to speak to," I said.

"Really?" said the fat man.

"We saw each other when she first moved in. That was some time ago. She dropped me like she dropped a lot of other guys, I imagine. It's no big deal."

"Maybe not. Maybe is not big deal. I want to believe you. You came out here, like I asked, and that means you are not afraid. You Americans have a saying: Charge gun, flee knife. Very clever. Americans are smart sometimes. So you come out here, you say you not very involved, am I right? Woman draws us to her, then she dies, and you not involved."

He stuck the poker under his arm and slapped his hands together, showing me how they slapped.

"She had a way of keeping to herself," I said. "A lot of the time

I had no idea whether she was there or not."

"She had a lot of secrets."

"Not from you, I imagine."

"Yes, from me," Opov said factually. But there was a note of sadness that didn't fit with his bluster.

"I didn't mind her other lovers," he said in a morose drone. "But she ... grew distant from me. Withdraw ... from me."

And just then, from a look in his eye, I could tell he loved her, as much as he loved anybody. This strutting miasma was another rival. Opov seemed to accept that.

"We kept it a secret how close she was to me. Our friendship ... wasn't publicized how some are."

He seemed to be floating in the room, in some dream space, like one of his fish.

"So you live in building ... where happened," he said. He swallowed and straightened his pants and seemed to drink me in for the first time. "She had no reason to have that place. None. I gave her apartment. Maids ... everything. Luxury. Palace compared to that hole she rent from you. I assumed she was with ... one of her young men.... I gave it to her. Like that."

His gut rolled and his fat hand cut the air.

"She wasn't the kind to be owned," I said. "Some people like it better if they pay their own way. Not everybody likes being someone's property."

Wyent winced at me and made a little gesture with his hand to shut up.

"I knew guy cracked wise lot," Opov said quickly, looking at the ceiling and still toying with his poker. "He got mouthful of cement and then he never said word after that. Maybe you like to meet him? He don't talk much, but might be lasting friendship. If you like quiet people."

I said nothing to that. I waited to see what he would do next. He turned suddenly in my direction, his slit eyes open wide, and mouthed at me:

"Hm?"

"She was a very independent woman," I said. "That's all I meant."

"It was secret," he went on as before, as though explaining something to a class. "She didn't tell anyone. And she had no reason not to tell me. I wouldn't have minded ... if I had known

... I would have ... You get what I mean?"

"Well," I said, "maybe she had some secret reason for keeping it to herself. I don't think she had lovers that she brought to that building. I think she had her own reasons. I imagine she just wanted to be alone."

He was breathing hard. His mouth hung open like a crevice in a pillow. I had the impression for a second, watching Opov in the subterranean light of the place, that he was really a giant reptile and I was a fly that had wandered into his part of the pond. The party outside was the rest of the jungle, which somehow managed to have its own life separate from any of us. He was huge and powerful maybe. But he was puffy and deeply bruised now. Suddenly he was back at me.

"She had something to hide. She was escaping from me."

He walked over to me. He held the poker cocked on his shoulder so he could scratch his mastoid. He wheezed so the hair blew out his nostrils, and he winced from pain. Slowly he turned away. Now he was like an old man the way he walked. Nothing like the strides I had seen him take that morning.

"You too smart to be super," he said. "Temporary job, yes?"

"Yes. I'm going on to college."

"Don't lie. You not college kid. You think I get to be Opov because I don't know people? You not college kid. You not really super, I think."

"I have another job on the side."

"What kind of job?"

"I work at a glass factory."

"Ah," he said smiling. "You like clear things. Glasnost, Russians say. I like clear things too. Out in the open. Where everyone can see. Is that what you are?"

I took my time answering.

"I had nothing to do with what happened this morning. I knew the woman. I liked her. That was the end of it. And frankly I don't know why you asked me to come out here in the first place. I didn't kill her. She was killed by concussion. Ask the cops."

They all stared at me. There was a slippery movement in the dark part of the room. Opov looked like I had physically hit him. Only his eyes moved. His hands were still, like soft subsea animals that never saw the sun. Wyent, wide eyed, was just a couple of feet behind him and he shook his head slowly just a millimeter to show I should never have said that.

Opov let out just the faintest guttural breath.

"We thought … it seemed …"

"He's crazy," Wyent said.

"Of course," I said. "You probably didn't know. You and the gentlemen who came in with the shotguns."

Leo was up like a flash on that. "You talk entirely too much. No way I'm taking the rap for that."

He came at me like a torpedo and hit me hard in the chest. I bounced backward off the wall.

"What happens to me won't change anything," I said. I spoke very slowly, holding my voice so it didn't tremble much. I chose each word carefully, hoping he would listen in the same way and cool down. I, of course, could be murdered here with no trace whatever; no one knew where I was. Leo pulled out a gun and fired it into the wall over my head.

"Don' kheel super," Opov said viciously. He gently took the gun from Leo's hand. Plaster fell in the next room. Wyent's eyes glistened; he would have enjoyed seeing me get cleared away, but then he would have to worry about himself. Opov pulled out the clip. He drew back the slide and one shell tinkled on the floor. Then he one by one emptied the clip into a drawer and threw the gun into another drawer and slammed it shut.

"Just take it easy," Leo said, turning his shoulder to me. "We'll meet again."

Opov stared wildly at the air around my head. For a minute he said nothing. Then he flashed up. He whirled around holding the poker like a sword.

"There was no blood. No blood at all. She had been bruised. It's very clear in my mind…. But she wasn't cut anywhere."

"Ask the cops," I said. "If she died instantly, she wouldn't bleed. But if it wasn't bullets, it could have been concussion, like I said. There would be enough of a shock to do it, especially if she fell back on her neck. The lead wouldn't have to hit her, necessarily. The blast could do it. That's what they told me, anyway. Could easily kill a person in that narrow space. And she was found lying practically in front of the door."

"Whose idea is this?" Opov blurted. "Is this your idea or cop idea?"

"It's his idea," Wyent said.

"No," I said. "It's what the cops think might have happened. I don't know. I'm not taking sides. I didn't have to tell you."

"It's crazy," Wyent said. But Opov wasn't listening. He whirled on Wyent.

"You fuck! You knew that, didn't you? I pay you for information.... My God ... you shit ..."

Wyent mumbled something about the autopsy not having been done, but Opov was in some other place.

"... it ... oh, God ... oh, no ... can't have been like that.... No, she was off to the side ... off to the side ..."

Seeing an atheist like Opov praying to God warmed me a little, much as I was scared by what he might do next. I shrugged.

"I'm just repeating what the police said. Concussion ... would ... leave no blood."

They were all silent. Nobody looked at anybody but me. The bubbling from the fish tank seemed to grow until it filled the room.

"That so?" Leo said. He didn't mean it as a question.

"It doesn't mean shit," Wyent said. "The autopsy hasn't ..."

"Shut the fuck up," Leo yelled.

"It's just a possibility," Wyent said.

"You weren't there," Leo said. "It's not a possibility. You weren't there. What did the cops tell you?"

Wyent shrugged, too.

"They don't know. If the shotgun blast killed the girl," he said, "it might not have shown right away."

Leo whirled and put his face into Wyent's. Short as he was, he looked big enough now.

"Whaddayou an idiot?" Leo cried.

He stood still where he was and waited till it was obvious Wyent didn't want to pursue it any further. Leo faced each of us.

"Cops say a lot of things," he said slowly. "They like to talk. They like to talk to make you talk. They always do that. It's a cop trick."

"I know ... it's not possible ... is it?" Wyent asked. Leo stared up at him. He was incredulous.

"Whaddayou kidding me?" he said.

"It's just an idea," Wyent went on. "They may have had that idea and dropped it. But ... is it possible?"

"He said that, didn't he?" Leo said sharply, pointing at me. "Did he say that?"

"It was one of the things that came up," I admitted. "Like he said."

While he was standing there Leo had developed a tic in his forehead. Both eyes blinked when the tick flashed. I watched it, wondering if it would pulse regularly now. I wanted to time it. Everybody knew it didn't matter what the cops said that morning. All that mattered was what Opov believed—and if he would go on believing it. Opov grunted softly.

"I hope ... it not happen that way," he said quietly. But his eyes on Leo were red with hatred.

"I know it didn't," Leo called. "The cops love this kind of thing. And who do you think they want to believe did it? Who?" He gestured with his flat palm towards Opov who began again speaking softly, waiting for Leo to shut up.

"... but when I think that maybe, if you hadn't busted in there that way ..."

Leo backed away and blinked from the sweat on his face. He looked like a man who had crawled through a sewer and who was just now looking up at the light, and seeing now the stuff he'd been crawling through. He whirled around and turned his back to Opov. In one step he leaped on top of a table. He stopped still, but you could see he was breathing heavily in little controlled sighs of air.

"Don't make mistake," Opov said, motioning like Leo ought to get off the table. It was like dropping a pebble into a still pond; you kept thinking there would be another sound and there was none. There was just silence.

"Listen," Leo said, squaring off so he had a clear view of each of us. He was talking like he was the biggest guy in the room. Even to Opov.

"I did what you wanted done. You saw what we were doing. You knew. You said so yourself. You knew. You knew what we were up against. You said. I didn't say that. Is that clear? You said what you wanted, and what you would pay for it. Is that clear?"

He waited then, but he waited as though he would trample and kill anyone who spoke up.

"Top of that, the girl was no good. The girl was no good. A dozen times a day you could replace her. Get some other bimbo slut to bleed you like a snake. It's easy. She wanted to set you up, you said."

"I never say that."

Opov's eyes looked glazed; it was all he could do, or wanted to do, to get his voice out. Leo went at him again, each word like a nail he was banging down.

"And you were sitting right there. You remember? You remember? Sitting RIGHT THERE like you sat just now. And you was sweating. You was snorting and you was sweating, 'cause this was something it wouldn't go away. Hm? Could've been lotsa people set you up. You had no idea who. I was a good man for you then. Yeah, I was the best friend you ever had. You called me and I came and I was loyal to you. You was glad to see me coming around. You's afraid for your ASS. For your ASS to walk in that place! You ... you knew what you wanted, though. You could've let it go. And I said so. There was no need for us to go in there. No need. Let her fry. I told you then. Let her fry. There's a bitch like her on every street corner. Why didn't you think of that? Only you couldn't see it wasn't that. It wasn't none of that. It was her wringing you by the dong! THAT's what it was. She did it lotsa times, like she did it again just the other night. Front of everybody. And you took it. Like she was doing you a favor. You smiled. Thank you, oh thank you for pissing in my face, darling, I love you.... Would you shit on me too? And she did the same thing to your kid Vinnie, got him by the dong too ..."

"Keep my son out of this."

"She mighta done it by herself. That cunning bitch. But more likely she had someone in on it with her. Like this guy, the innocent bystander. The too-smart-to-be-super here. And isn't it funny that he gave me the wrong key? Isn't that a laugh? Yeah. If we killed her we was set up to kill her. Huh, Super?"

I said nothing, only watching his eyes.

"And I told you that the other night," Leo went on. "I said that then. It was a ruse. I told you that the other night. And last night. I told you. You didn't listen."

Opov stood stock still, but his voice came out like he was blubbering. He waved for Leo to keep back.

"I didn't say go in there and ... hurt her. I never said that...."

Leo straightened up and looked down at Opov.

"Are you crazy?" he called. He backed away looking around at each of us. He hitched his shoulder so his arm was free. Opov reached out toward him.

"Sh … sh … she may not have done what you say. She may have had no ch … choice," he stuttered.

"You play 'em the thing," Leo snapped. He leaped to the floor and bore down on the big man. Opov wouldn't move.

"Play it. Play 'em the tape," Leo called out. "Play 'em the fuckin' tape. Then we'll see."

"He's right," Wyent said. "I didn't hear it either."

Opov sat still, wheezing at them.

"What difference make?" he said. "… make no … difference."

Nobody moved.

"Come down," Opov motioned morosely.

Leo wouldn't move.

"Let's just see," he said. "Then let's decide." He went to the bookcase and yanked out a phone and pressed some buttons.

"… don't want to hear again …" Opov moaned.

"Which phone is it?"

Leo went to the desk and pecked at another phone.

"I pick up," Opov said and walked around to the desk. The mention of the tape had very much brought him down. He couldn't be angry while thinking about it. He found the right phone and punched it with his baby fist. He spun around so sweat sprayed off his neck. Leo leaned closer, not knowing what button to press.

"No need get touchy," Opov said. "Put here," he said, pointing to the table. Leo moved the speaker to the front of the desk. A box of cigars tumbled onto the floor.

Opov huddled over it.

"Clean up cigars," he said with conscientious patience. He knelt down on the floor and busied himself with each one as if it was some sacred rite. Wyent went to help and picked up what he could. Sweat was dripping off Opov's chin onto his hairy chest. He was staring down at the box. He was in a private space where something he really revered was somewhere in the air before him. He looked up at the desk.

"Press that button."

"You guys are gonna hear something now," Leo said.

He jammed his finger on a button. The first sounds were garbled short syllables. A man's voice, a broken sentence. Then he zipped to another spot. All of a sudden Miranda's voice came out. We all waited like stumps frozen in ice.

"… if you please come and help me. As soon as you can. I … need you. I'm sorry I was mean to you. I tried to play with your feelings. That was stupid. Can you forgive me? I'll be here if you come, in the morning about seven. I'll be ready then. Waiting. I've had secrets from you, that was wrong. Because I loved you, from the first. And I still do. I made mistakes that I see were foolish. I won't do it again. Now … I'm … all right, really. I'm not … not in danger. If you come quickly. If you help me now. There's something I have to tell you. Something I've had to tell you for a long time. We have to settle up on some things. Just come here and I'll … be waiting. I'm all alone. You must promise me to come alone. I'll be all right. I'll be waiting…. I'll be waiting for you …"

She gave her address on Termite Street. Even described which apartment she lived in. She said each phrase and then took a breath, like a few words was all she could say before she had to gulp for air. And there were pauses when the message seemed to break and then come up again. And she repeated herself as if she hadn't said it right the first time. She might have had to memorize the whole thing, but she said it as slowly as if she were reading one word at a time in a bad light. In my imagination I could see her mouth forming each word.

"… no one will hurt me … not with you to protect me … if you come … Please come, come quickly … please … I need you … I'm sorry … what I said … I need to tell you now … "

It was a voice to make you melt inside.

Over our heads her voice sailed between the walls, into every dank corner and every unswept molding, so thin, so still, her voice, even blurred by the recording, reaching us over reefs and barriers, it floated among us. That disembodied voice seemed to touch every speck of dust in the room, and every hair on my skin—and maybe at the last, the voice couldn't help but blame you for the greatest sin you had being there: you were alive.

After it ended Leo went back to the start and the cut it off. Opov went to his chair sat down like Buddha with his eyes down, not making any face.

Now we were all as silent as sculpture at a mausoleum. There were no threats to make and there was nothing to say. Opov sat slumped, his putty hand wrapped around the poker on the desk, his gaze somewhere on the floor. Wyent looked straight ahead. His fingers felt over the collar of his shirt, as if thinking about the next place he had to be. Leo was watching all of us. In fact, Leo was growing impatient. Playing the recording hadn't had the effect he had thought.

"That's a great acting job she did," Leo called viciously at all of us, but his voice was dry and a little hollow. It was the voice of a man who wanted to be believed. But we were all impassive. Not listening. The ghost of Miranda's voice still hung in the air, passing through everyone, clinging to us.

"Great acting job," Leo went on. "You don't think so? She set you up. You don't want to see it. You don't and so you don't. I know. You think I don't know? I know. She was in on it. Yeah. Maybe not all the way. Maybe she thought she was smarter than she was, and maybe she paid for it. All right. She paid, okay? But she was in on it. She knew what she was doing and she was using you."

Opov just sat there in a gelatinous slump. Only his eyes made any reaction to Leo, following him with the smallest motion. Leo held where he was and turned to me.

"You heard it now, but maybe you heard it before. Hm? 'Cause you were there last night."

"How do you know that?" I said. "Must've been somebody said so."

"Yeah," Leo said, striding around. "Somebody said so."

Then he made the slightest motion to the other men and his mouth hardly moved.

"Get the kid."

"No," Opov moaned. "I don't want him in here."

"Go get him. He knows stuff. We ain't leaving him out."

The two men hesitated, looking at Opov, who slowly nodded. The men left the room.

As if out of genteel politeness we were all silent till they came back.

Presently the men walked in and one held the door for Vincent. He came in and saw us waiting and stood stock still, as drunks do. He was still wearing that crazy Panama hat. In his hand was a revolver that wavered slightly from side to side.

"Get the fuck away," Vincent yelled. "I got some business with this guy." He raised the gun and pointed it at me. Everything moved. I pushed a card table at him and threw it up and came at him. I thought it was my only chance. He pulled the trigger but it just clicked. He stayed where he was, or he moved too slowly to see. I swung at the gun and hit it, but he craned back and cocked it. Hands reached out around me, I batted them away. Opov's was large and heavy, I didn't move that. Everyone pushed. I reeled back on a chair that toppled behind me.

"Why is he here?" Vincent screamed, holding gun with both hands. "Why didn't you kill him?"

Vincent pointed the gun at my nose.

Then with not even a breath to back it up, Opov flashed out with the poker and sliced down on Vincent's arm. The gun clattered on the floor like a can of marbles. Opov made a quick strike off the floor and Vincent went down on his knees with a caterwaul of pain.

"I didn't mean it," he cried. His face was open and inflamed. "It was blanks. I just wanted to pay him back."

Opov's eyes bulged. He picked up the gun and furiously fired it into the floor. Sure enough, blanks.

"You pisshead," Opov said, and threw the gun in a drawer. Vincent lay there with his arms bent and rigid in the air to fend off more blows. Without any warning Opov heaved back and spat on him.

"You little twat," the big man screamed. "Where were you? In the bathroom with your boyfriend? Hm?"

He hovered over his son calling him names like that till Vincent just sat there frozen and couldn't move at all. Tears were streaming over his swollen cheeks.

Finally, he just lay there trembling.

Opov tramped away from him, done with unfit people around him, his manner said. He had had enough of this one. Vincent groaned on the floor.

"Now let him hear it," Leo said, as if he was orchestrating a show. He pressed the button on the phone.

Miranda slipped into the room again. Nobody protested. None of us had the guts to make her stop talking now. Each tone of her voice hung in the air, reaching in to touch you and then dancing away. Very clearly she gave her address again. She was saying it so carefully, it made me think more of a painful but desired confession than of a woman with some vicious bully holding a gun to her head. But she would say it all the right way, just the way he wanted. No extra words. No hints. And no mistakes.

"… I'll be all right. I'll be waiting for you …"

This time when the recording ended Leo let it run and there was a high wailing squeal. Leo walked away from it and stood over Vincent, whose face was open and red. Opov let the wail go on, as if it were a relief to his ears. It was like a stainless-steel golf ball sailing a thousand yards through your brain. Finally Wyent walked over and turned it off.

From his crouch on the floor Vincent managed to point at me. "He's the super. He did it. He ..."

Leo turned away.

"And made her call? She didn't know to call that. Only you knew the number."

"I didn't. I didn't," Vincent yelled.

"Yeah," Leo said, strutting around. "Did she sound scared? What? She sounded like she was reciting something, didn't she? Or reading it. Yeah. Like that. Didn't she?"

I couldn't help thinking how I liked Leo just then, and what a pity if they fried him for something I knew he hadn't done.

"He's was in it," Leo went on. "The super doesn't mean shit. If she didn't think this thing up herself, your son got her to do it. Because he's like that. Yeah. Just crazy enough to impress his father. Yeah. You look at that."

Vincent's face was open and covered with tears.

"I didn't mean to," Vincent exclaimed. "I didn't mean it to happen that way." Then he looked at us wanting to take back the words. Leo homed in.

"So daddy's trust fund Don Juan wanted to impress. Wanted to be a big shot. Is that it? Is it?"

I expected Opov to react to this attack on his son cringing below Leo—but Leo knew the father too well.

"You made her make that tape. Huh? And then you throttled her just to show what a big big shot you are. You little shit."

Leo backed away and Vincent only lay there whimpering, from his wound and humiliation, you couldn't tell what was worse. Opov came over and stared at his son.

"You kill her? Did you?"

"I left her alive."

"Did you?"

Vincent could not even speak. He only vaguely shook his head, as if he didn't even know he was fighting for his life.

Opov paced in the open space. It didn't matter what anyone

said. He had to think. Finally he turned to me.

"You saw my son last night," he said. "When you saw her. Did you tell police about my son?"

"No."

"Hm. Why not?"

"I thought it might not be a good idea."

"Why? Why leave him out? He's a shithead. You leave a shithead out? That was very smart, what you did. Very, very smart. Didn't do. That all I want from you. You keep my son out of it. Just forget that part of evening. It could easily not have happened, you know? Just coincidence. That's all I want from you. Can you assure me that police will not hear about my son?"

"Won't hear from me, if that's the way you want it. But he may have been seen by someone else. The cops talk to everybody you know. If they're happy with their story about concussion, why rock the boat?"

"So the police will not question my little shit son," Opov said, nodding down at Vincent.

"Why should they?" I asked happily.

Opov strode away again.

"Impress his father. It is American disease, no? Man shot president Reagan to impress movie star. American disease. Way Americans think. Don't like teacher, shoot teacher. Impress movie star. He grows up here in America so he thinks like you do. In Russia, *tak*, and then is done."

He said *"tak"* as he aimed an imaginary gun at the floor. Then he held the poker under his arm and dusted his hands to show the matter was all wrapped up like a piece of meat.

"She was alive," Vincent whimpered. "When I left her."

"Who else saw you besides super? Eh? Quit whining."

"I don't know ... I don't know," Vincent cried.

There was silence for a few seconds. Finally Opov sat down again, silently brooding. Somehow I wanted to talk, to invade that great husk of his hatred and grief, but I was waiting in hopes Vincent would finally break down and confess that he knew Miranda was dead before Leo and the rest arrived. He knew because he killed her.

"I didn't ... I didn't," Vincent kept saying through tears all over his face. "I wanted ... to show you ... and ... to make you happy, proud of me ..." he said raising his hand to his father. "I wanted you to see ... I could ... I did ... I made her say ... that ... but I didn't want her to die.... For God's sake believe me. This one time ... see I'm telling the truth ..."

His voice trailed off. His hand was upraised to his father. With a snap the poker flashed out and struck the hand like a sprig of wheat. Then Opov turned on all of us.

"Get out. Get out! All of you. Get him out of here," he said, pointing at me. "He knows what to say. Get him out."

I was out and down the hall before Wyent came running after me. I passed a hundred faces without seeing one. When Wyent didn't keep up with me, I got behind him and pushed him like a grade school wimp. I couldn't make it to the car fast enough.

As we got out on the road all I could think of was how grateful I was I had gotten out of there alive, how close I had come, and how, even though I had gotten out what I came to say, I was still struck dumb by Miranda's voice, her confession it was, whether or not she meant the words made no difference. I opened the window and let the flush of air blast my face. And finally, after miles of silence, when we finally hit the Parkway, I thought about Holly, and I knew she was safe now, the dread and the wrongs were behind me, and wouldn't surface now. Might never surface again, I had so abashed them. She was safe asleep, right then, and when would I get to talk to her again? I thought of Holly all the way home.

And when we got to my house, I got out and said something meaningless to Wyent and slammed the door. And then the car was just a pyramidal streak of lights gone off to their apex up the block.

Inside, I fed Akbar an egg and went to bed. And then, as if my head were a pound of uncleavable stone, I cast it out as far as I could over a beautiful blue lake, and I didn't even see it fall.

16. The Mortician

Late morning I wakened to Akbar insistently nudging my cheek. I got up to find there was only one egg, no coffee, and no cat food. But the egg was good enough for Akbar right now. He loved them. He would want more but that would hold him while I got dressed and out the door; I could pick up cat food on my way back.

It was Saturday and Holly was away today, I remembered, so there was no calling her up for brunch. I decided to go to the Creation Cafe around the corner. When I got out into the splashing light on the street, kids were playing, tearing open boxes they'd found on the street. I joked with them; you could feel their energy. Treasure hunters they were. Plundering captains on hot tar seas. Privateers opening intriguing mysteries: why people throw out the things they do: books and dilapidated furniture, boxes of bottles, kitchen gadgets, broken radios.

On the way I passed a newsstand where the papers had: "Slain Model May Have Been Involved With Organized Crime: Cops." You couldn't force me to read it. I didn't want to know what they thought, wrong or right.

I got breakfast and wandered around by Klondyke's Funeral Home. A boy in black with a black skull cap greeted me at the door, but when I said I wanted to speak to Klondyke himself, he merely led me back to the office and effortlessly walked away. Klondyke was in, talking on the phone. He hailed me into his office where there were comfortable chairs, rows of books on shelves, a menorah on the top shelf flanked by way too many flowers. Apparently he had no place else to put them. They were lilies in baskets and their sweet smell combined with the mustiness of the old book bindings to give the over-furnished room an air of medieval scholarship. Framed icons in gold lettering were crowded on the wall. All seemed artfully appointed so the bereaved could mull the cost, in all senses, of sendoff to another world.

Klondyke was soon off the phone.

With the thoughtfulness of one used to understanding the intolerable pain of others, his papery fingers felt over the fold of a newspaper on his desk before he looked at me.

"That ... that woman was in your building?" he said softly.

"Yeah, she was," I said. He nodded and looked at me with quiet inquiry. No astonishment.

"Terrible thing."

"Yeah, it was."

"My wife read it to me last night. I couldn't believe it. Did you see the papers?"

"Well, um ... actually, I didn't get a chance ..."

He nodded and drew me along with his glance. What I got from his motioning to me was that really I wouldn't find out anything from the papers I might get; he had the one I needed. He had the story of something more human than the other media would expend energy on. He flopped over the paper from the night before. The headline screamed out:

MODEL SLAIN IN MYSTERY APT

Under the giant type there was a picture of Miranda that looked like a something from a shampoo ad—the effect they aimed for was to make her look so happy, so perfect the way she held her head and smiled.

"Did you see her picture?"

He turned to the story inside. He held it up to me as if he were proselytizing for a new belief, a conviction that was just profound enough and strong enough that it would be possible for even me to believe it. There on the page was another picture of Miranda, and that one, even in sepia, was striking.

"She did a lot of work," he went on, slowly choosing his words. "And it says here, she was 'highly paid.'" He looked at me to see if I had any reaction to that.

I had come around to Klondyke's seeking comfort, a friendly face, a few kind words which I knew he had in abundance within him, but now I was forcing myself to sit there.

"Well, you see," I said, "I was in a way involved with her and it's not a pleasant memory, what happened."

"Ooooh," he said gently. "Of course it's not a pleasant memory, for anyone." He patted the paper down. It was still valuable text, but he could set it aside to listen to me. "Did you tell the police?"

"Yeah, I did, but I don't know if they believed me."

His forehead became furrowed, his eyes large with compassion. "What didn't they believe?"

"Well, I went to her apartment and found her at four AM, before those guys broke in, and she was already dead. I was going to call the cops, but I fainted. I slept for three hours."

"You fainted before calling the cops? But that's entirely understandable," he said. "They can do nothing at all to you for that. Don't let them bully you."

"No. Of course not."

He settled back in his armchair. He nodded slowly.

"'Gangland-style,'" Klondyke murmured with the slightest edge of scorn in his voice as he pointed out a certain passage. "They are entirely too confident. The mob would not like to go in an apartment house and wake everybody up like that." His old flattened finger ran across the columns as if the letters might ball up beneath his skin and flake away. "Strange gangland-style ...", he read in another paragraph. "No, I don't think so."

"It wasn't the mob really," I said. "They're Estonians, I heard."

"Ah." He nodded. "The Russians are the worst. You cannot predict what they will do."

I glanced down the article.

"That's not much about what the police are saying," I commented.

"Oh, the police," he sniffed. "They won't say anything right away about something so ... sensational. They will want to keep their cards up their sleeve because some people will confess to a crime they have not done. It's a peculiar fact of human psychology." He paused thoughtfully. "Was anyone else hurt?"

"No."

"They like crowds sometimes, granted. Better that way because of all the confusing stories. And they think no one will talk about anything mob-related. But people will talk today. It's not like it used to be."

His voice came out thin and slow like audible twine. Then he read more of the article to me. It was like he was reciting a famous story, one that every honest person should know—and if they didn't, well, he would step into the breach and define every detail till it could not be ignored. There were names of people she was supposed to have known well, other models, agents, club people.

They had interviewed Ms. Fancher, who created the impression that Miranda lived a pretty secretive life, and had no friends in the building. There were addresses, mine and her other address, in the east sixties. Two people had been interviewed up there who were on speaking terms with her. She was older than I had thought.

Twenty-nine.

I could feel myself go dry inside. Twenty-nine. When he stopped I took a breath. I wanted none of this. If Klondyke hadn't dragged me to it, I would never have known what was in the article.

"People not safe in their homes." Klondyke nodded sadly. His tired eyes looked out at me. They seemed to hold the greatest pain, far more than anything he could say. The way he said "homes" was the saddest cut.

"Well, it's not as bad as all that," I said. "You don't know what she was into. It says it's thought to be mob-related. She had to do something strange to get people like that angry at her, I would guess. Anyway, the cops wouldn't say it was a mob killing, and I kind of agree with them. The mob won't kill women."

Klondyke smiled. His old eyes seemed to contain a story like a deep mist he was staring through. His lips parted so softly.

"You think they won't," he said. "They have."

He sat back thoughtfully. His curiosity never died.

"So when you found her dead, did she seem to be the same person as later, when the police came?"

"No. She was tied up when I first saw her. And there was a sack beside her head. All that was gone when the visitors came."

"Tied up," he said, nodding. He showed little astonishment. "So you think she died when she was tied up and the killer went back and untied her."

"Yeah. Only stands to reason."

"To cover his tracks."

"Or at least obscure them."

"Hm. But there is no mention of her being tied up," he said, delicately feeling the newsprint like it was canon law. Canon law for one day.

"No. Because I guess they couldn't tell."

He leaned back and grinned at me. It was a grin of deep sadness, not mirthless, but as if there were comedy and sadness together everywhere: in the air even, in flowers meant to honor the dead or appease the living, in mounds of books.

"Milo, they know. And they're keeping it a secret, and you should too. A man died not long ago, and his body was handled here. He had been holding a key in his hand and pressing it against the other hand when he died. It was a red indentation in the back of his thumb. The rest of his skin was grey. I was worried that it would be seen since his hands had to be visible when the mourners came. I wanted it off. But the impression never went away. Rubbing too much might abrade the skin, so I made them stop with that. We could discolor it to make it look more natural, but the key was there, for all to see. When his sister saw it she asked the rabbi, where had the key been found? No one knew ... They were quite upset."

He said this last as if alluding to something completely beyond words. No matter how carefully he formed his sentences, reality would still be more than words could bear.

"It meant a lot to them and I was unable to make it go away. I still have not heard the last of that story. So, you see, Milo, if the woman was tied up when she died, the impressions would remain and the police could not help but know. They'll believe that part of what you say."

He sat back slowly as if contemplating the amazing miracle of death. I watched him for a moment, struck as I was by his calm completeness—it was so wonderful to be around him: nothing seemed too strange to him. I felt better now; it had done me good to talk with him after all.

I looked down at her picture, tried to imagine her actually taking that pose. That beautiful smile with the air of blithe confidence. I knew some of that was good acting. But some, the best, was really her.

"A beautiful woman," he said tapping the page.

I folded the paper back and pushed it back on his desk under a bobbing fern. I was about to go when he stopped me.

"Oh, wait."

He extended a brace of lilies.

"Put them at her door," he said. "I have too many. I get them all the time."

I thanked him, feeling a little sheepish that I had not thought of so simple a tribute, and took them with me.

I stopped by a deli, got the usual sundries and a microwaveable dinner or two, and headed back to the apartment. It was a warm sunny day under a nearly cloudless sky.

"Hold up!" a voice called from behind me as I opened the front door. It was Tommy, carrying a cardboard box that looked bigger than he was. Gerald followed behind him, and Louis, heaving an empty suitcase back on the garbage, came running after. Tommy's face was gripped in self-important seriousness. Of course I would hold the door for him. I opened the next one too.

"Thanks, Milo," he called as if I were close to being an honorary treasure hunter now. The others called after him and he led them back and down the stair into the yard. I went in my place and heard them out the window. Like a little caravan they trooped out into the yard, and they were already starting to squabble.

"Let me see," Louis cried and tried to open the box before Tommy set it down. Tommy pushed him away and took his time. When he opened it, the treasure was the richest you could find on earth: comic books. Someone had thrown away a whole hoard, it looked like.

I took the flowers and put them in a vase with water and took it up to the top floor. There were sprays of flowers now, and a new candle, all arranged in solemn symmetry. There was a cross drawn in chalk with a Celtic circle. I placed the vase next to the door. Then I went back down.

Downstairs, the phone rang. It was Spollick. He wanted me to "come down for a talk" and he gave me directions. I wondered if he always worked on Saturdays.

"We get days off like everyone else," he said. "Just not today. Today is special."

17. The Cop

When I got there, I was led into a room with Sgt. Valencio, who looked at me over his ruefully long nose and seemed to be trying to give me the benefit of the doubt with his dark, romantic eyes. He said there would be others who would be along soon. He swatted his folder and newspaper on the door as he closed it. There were several chairs and a single table before the wall. In one wall there was a large mirror. Tin ashtrays were everywhere. A pitcher and glasses but no water. Valencio sat down at the table. I took a chair across from him.

"We thought this was all wrapped up," he said opening his folder. "I could have taken the weekend off, spent some time with my nephew and my sister's family ... you know, a nice summer day."

He spread out some notes.

I just watched, wondering who we were waiting for. He seemed not to care if anyone else showed up.

"You know, Fyrish," he said in a confidential tone. "If I could break this one, I'd make lieutenant next time I got reviewed. I would. Because it's made a big impression. It's made a splash. Some crimes make a big splash. The News had it on the front page yesterday."

"Yeah, I saw it," I said thinking of Klondyke and his lilies. "But then they seemed to have downplayed it today because of ... some other scandal."

Valencio gave a mugged smile and shook his finger in the air.

"Nooo. That's not why they downplayed it. Nooo." Valencio pointed his finger at me and then walked across to the window and closed it.

"That's not why they cut the story to just hearsay from the neighbors. Why they dropped it is because we don't have anything to give them. See what I mean? News is a commodity. Like shoes and milk shakes. But we don't have any news to give them. You see this?"

He came back and opened the newspaper several pages in. There was a headline in the middle of the page: "Slain Model Tied to Possible Drug Dealing". I looked at it. It detailed some of the work the police had done. But a police spokesperson had been unwilling to speculate about the mysterious death, other than to say it might be drug related. No drugs were found in Miranda's body, but there were some in her apartment uptown.

"Drug related," he nodded to the window. "What isn't drug-related? You scratch deep enough in any dirty business you find drugs."

He was silent for a moment. He sat back and fidgeted with his pencil. It was as though there was a vacuum in the room, just crying to be filled with words. The air between us got hotter and staler the more we sat and said nothing.

"You rent the apartment yet?" he asked for something to say.

"Well, as a matter of fact a few people expressed an interest." No one had.

He chuckled.

"No sooner is she out the door, right?"

He wanted to be right in his cynical opinion, but I wouldn't nod. That was the Widow talking through this ... stand-in.

"Oh, by the way," he said, "her sister called. I imagine she'll be getting in touch with you. She'll probably want to talk to you about the things in that apartment."

I didn't say anything and pretty soon he got up. "Just a minute, let me check on those guys. They were supposed to be here." He walked out.

I began to think Valencio would never make lieutenant. Not in ten years. He had left his folder open on the desk, and I could look at it if I wanted. Wasn't that an open invitation? But I thought about it a moment. That was what the big mirror was for, wasn't it? The more I wanted to look at the folder the more I just sat there and tried to look bored. Finally I got up and went over to the window just when the door opened.

Valencio came in. Behind him was Spollick, who wore a short-sleeved white shirt with blue pinstripes. The shirt looked like he just bought it, clean and smart-looking. Then another man came in, tall, with a weathered face and large eyes, and cheeks sculpted with lines that looked like they didn't change if he smiled. I learned he was connected with the District Attorney's office, and his name was Profumo. He didn't smile at me. Valencio waited and shut the door and came around to the desk. Profumo sat in back of me, and out of the side of one eye I saw him put his legs up on a chair. Spollick tapped the manila folder on the table like he might smear it, and then he stepped back lightly. He watched me and clasped his hands. He had a smile that went back to the cleft of his jaw. He was instantly in control; he didn't have to say so or edge himself in.

"So you're the super," he said in his clipped way. I nodded.

He came around the table and sat on it, looking at me. Valencio sat behind him and jotted stuff down. Spollick began gently.

"Mr. Fyrish, the reason we asked you here is because we're trying to clear up some questions we have. You may be able to help us. If you're willing to do that."

"Sure. If I can."

"You know Fyrish," he went on, dreamily for the moment. "That makes me suspicious right away, I gotta tell you, you don't look like a super. I mean just to look at you ..."

"I know," I said. "A lot of people tell me that. It's really not a job I can keep forever. In fact this whole thing has got the landlord so shook up I could lose my job from just being there. Know what I mean?"

"No. How could you lose your job?"

"Well, she's like, kind of superstitious, and she might fire me just because I was the super when this thing happened. Forty winos could replace me."

But Spollick didn't care about my future. He went around to Valencio's notes and picked up the edge of a page.

I held steady on the grey circles of Spollick's pupils. His movements gave off a radiant odor of hatred and suppressed rage, as much as a wild animal radiating a smell that all the others animals know. His teeth were clenched and his lips formed words for which there seemed at first to be no sound. But when he was still, the animal seemed to slink away and he became this silvery delicate presence that wouldn't hurt anyone who didn't deserve it.

"When you came home from the hospital, you were carrying something with you."

"Not that I remember."

"You know Samuel Simopoulos?"

"Yes."

"He helped you get to the hospital when you got hit on the head."

"He met me leaving, that's all I know."

He accepted that.

"Mr. Simopoulos said you were carrying something in a paper bag as you left."

"He's wrong. I wasn't."

He nodded. He expected me to say that. I could feel the man behind me, his eyes boring into my neck. They were communicating, Spollick and that man, maybe without even a glance. I got the impression Spollick wanted to fill the air with meaningless facts, that if there was a forest of fact, then he would find his way, and I would be lost. That was his plan, born with all the anger and ineffectual rage that he had had to swallow in decades of watching murderous hoods go free.

"What do you know about Matthias Follett? He live in your building?"

"Yeah."

"What do you know?"

"Uh ... nothing much. He never complains. Likes women a lot, according to what people say. I never had an intimate conversation with him."

"Know anything about his past?"

"No. I heard he was in jail once."

Spollick eyed me and nodded.

"Didn't show up for his job yesterday. We knocked on his door several times with no answer. Any idea where he might be?"

"No."

I waited and said nothing.

"Guy with a record," Spollick said. "Did you know that?"

"No."

"Yes, you did. You just said you knew he was in jail."

"Well, lots of people have been in jail. Doesn't mean they have a record."

"How about you, Fyrish? Ever been in jail?"

"No."

"Nowhere? Not in some other state?"

"No. I was pretty timid as a teenager."

He waited to see if I would go on. But I said nothing. It was going to be an effort to be silent at the right moments, I could see.

"Back to Mr. Follett. He's not in his apartment. He didn't go to work today, though he was expected. You know how come?"

I shrugged and shook my head.

"I didn't have the impression that Follett was all that punctual,"

I said. "He seems kind of carefree."

"Know what he was in for?"

"No."

"Sex offender. I'm telling you because it's not something we have to be discreet about anymore. According to some people, the more who know the better. We put an order out for his arrest. If you see him, advise him that it's in his best interest to come talk to us. He lived on the same floor with the woman. He might know something."

"Okay."

"Did you know Miranda Dauphine?" I said yes.

"Did you know that was not her real name?"

"No."

"Her real name was Melissa Murphy."

I looked dumb, which was easy. "Well, whadayaknow."

"She was from a little town in Indiana. She left there more than ten years ago. Now, from what I understand, she told you she had just moved to New York when she rented that apartment from you."

"Ah, no … she was there when I moved in."

"Did you know that was not her primary residence?"

"No. I … thought it was."

Valencio belched softly.

"Now you told us yesterday that you went to the dead woman's apartment at …" He consulted his notes. "Around four AM. You still stick to that?"

I hesitated, wondering if I heard right. Did they think I was lying?

"Yeah. It was about then."

"You went into the apartment because she asked you to use your key and not knock 'cause you might wake somebody up. Now, when you found her, did you immediately examine the body?"

"No. I was a little surprised. I looked at her eye, just to be sure. Then … I guess I just stood there for a minute."

"Did you think of knocking on somebody's door, like Mr. Follett's, waking them up to come see?"

"No. I thought the police should be the first to get notified."

"Did you look around her apartment?"

"I looked for a phone but didn't see it, so I just left. I was going to call the police."

Again he avoided the fact that I fainted and hadn't called the police. He didn't throw that up to me. I was sure there was a ploy there somewhere, if I could just see it.

"So it's possible someone was in the apartment when you were there, someone who hid when you came in."

"I ... guess so."

"No guessing, Mr. Fyrish. Is it possible?"

"Yeah.... Well, he would have had to be pretty silent."

Spollick looked at me to see if I would say any more, and when I wouldn't, he went back to his notes. Each time he did this, he modulated like a conductor moving into the pianissimo section of a quartet.

"Let me go over with you where you were at various times in the evening before."

I told him exactly what I had told him and Valencio and he listened as before. He still had the same expression, as if it really didn't matter what I said; he was listening for something else. I went over the business of seeing Bernice come in from work. But since that was after the killing, I didn't see how it mattered, and they said nothing.

"And where was it you went drinking?" Valencio asked.

I told them again about the evening gathering in the cellar, and my trip to the hospital. I could see them talking with Victor and Sam and maybe getting the impression I was an antisocial lush. And wasting more time in the process.

"And did anything unusual happen while you were there?"

"Yeah, I told you. I had a fight and pushed a guy out in the rain...."

"Why did you do that?"

I waited for a full breath before I answered. "Well, I wasn't alone. The guy was making trouble. He was saying a lot of crazy shit and.... Maybe another night I would have just had another drink and forgotten about him."

"Ever seen him before?"

"Yes. He's a homeless person. I shouldn't have gotten carried away the way I did."

"What did he say that upset you?"

"He was insulting a certain woman in the building."

"Which one?"

My heart was beating hard now. But I persisted in telling the truth, wherever that might lead, I had no idea.

"Ms. ... Dauphine. Miranda."

He acted like he knew this already and I was just confirming what he knew.

"You had a close relationship with ... Miranda. Isn't that true?"

"At one time."

"Let's back track a bit, Fyrish. Back to before anything happened to her. How well did you know this woman?"

"Actually, I got to know her a bit when I first moved in. We went out a few times."

He unbent a little. He guessed that. Somebody in the building, like Ms. Peretti, would have told them. I could feel their bodies relax from the weight of what they were going to hit me with.

"How many times?"

"Oh ... three or four times."

"And that was the end of it?"

"She was too busy. If you want to know, I don't think we had much in common. She got bored with it and so did I."

Spollick caught on that.

"Pretty good-looking woman to pass up," he said.

"Yeah, well ... If you just met her. But after a while, other things count too."

"How come you didn't tell us yesterday you had an affair with her? Why keep it back?"

"I didn't keep it back," I countered.

"You didn't just go out a few times. You ran after her. She rejected you and you were really hurt by that. You had a grudge. It ended badly."

"It ended."

"Yeah, how?"

"She just ... stopped ... seeing me. She said she was too busy. She had other things going on. She was making good money as a model and making a lot of new contacts. She just didn't have time for me."

"How did you feel about that? You don't strike me as a guy who would just let that go."

"What was I going to do?"

"So, what did you feel when she told you she couldn't see you anymore?"

"I felt sad, you know. But you got to put an end somewhere. Life goes on."

But Spollick was driving in to make his play.

"Except for you it might not have ended. Some guys are like that. They don't forget. And then the anger builds up in them till they can't stand it anymore and then one night it just breaks out and it gets splattered up the wall. Ever hear of that?"

"Hey, it was over. I've got a girlfriend. What do I need with ..."

"You ever tie her up?"

"No."

"You sure?"

"Yes."

"Sure you have."

I just stared back at him.

"Not into bondage," he said quietly. "Was she? The dead woman? What about her?"

"I don't know," I said.

We stared at each other till I could feel the pounding behind my eyes. He went back to another tack.

"You were close the night of her death. So close you were supposed to show up at her place at midnight and ... have some tea?"

"Yes."

"And when somebody insulted her, you got upset."

"Yeah, I guess I did. I'd had a couple of drinks ..."

"You're kind of a volatile guy sometimes, aren't you, Mr. Fyrish? Your name starts with fire and ends with Irish. You are a very volatile guy."

"If somebody rubs me the wrong way," I said.

"And she did rub you the wrong way."

"I cool off quick enough."

"Maybe you didn't though, this time. You were outraged at her, weren't you? She rejected you, didn't she?"

"Yeah, but that was years ago."

"But she was coming back to you. She was toying with you. You were a plaything for her. You like a woman to treat you like a dildo, like a toy dick?"

I took a minute to think, even though I realized the more I thought the less credible I looked. Finally I sighed. What was there to get upset about?

"She wasn't that bad," I said. "She was a little confused, that's all. We all have our moods."

"But you were angry. It had been building up in you for months. Weren't you angry, weren't you enraged, Mr. Fyrish?"

"No. Sometimes I felt annoyed at her. She changed her mind a lot. I also felt sorry for her."

"Sorry for her? You're kidding. She was way better off than you."

"Well, I mean when she got mugged. I lent her some money to tide her over."

"She pay you back?"

"No. She had no time."

"You go through her apartment looking for the money?"

"No."

"Sure?"

"I'm sure." He was getting off the track now, and that made it easier. He wasn't making me angry. He knew that and stopped himself. He eyed me in that same way, like he was staring down a reptile.

"You went there well within the bounds of the time she died. Did you know that?"

"No."

"She died between one and five in the morning, according to the medical report. Does that surprise you?"

"No. But if it wasn't true that wouldn't surprise me either. I don't know when she died."

"You're a volatile guy who might want to take revenge. You don't take things lying down, do you, Mr. Fyrish? So when you went to the woman's apartment, at four AM you say, you could've killed her yourself."

"No, I couldn't. She was already dead."

"You're sure of that."

"Pretty sure. I could be wrong. I'm not a doctor."

I took a moment and then I pointed at him.

"Let's suppose," I said languorously, "that I did harbor a grudge from our old affair gone wrong. A crime of passion. That's what it would be. A crime where I got out all my angry and aggressive feelings and vented them on a helpless woman that I overpowered and I tied up silently for that purpose. Maybe I even tortured her, because if I'm mean enough to tie her up, I'm probably mean enough to do that too. And then after I got bored with that, I killed her by strangling her. Then I untied her and got rid of the rope. Okay? And then what? Did I call up her best friends and get them to come over and blow her door down? Is that what you figure? 'Cause if it is, I'm asking for an attorney right now."

I didn't say more. After all, everything depended on how much I said, and if I didn't say more, didn't get angry as they hoped, then things might taper off. He had lost the round. I saw it in his face. He had been hoping for a quick kill. Then they would bring in the video camera, let me tell it as it "really" happened, and then they could go home in under an hour. Have drinks on the porch. Watch the sun set. It hadn't worked out that way, and he was disappointed, though I began to see that he believed me. I had too many things to hide that I hadn't hidden.

Spollick got me to tell again everything that had gone on the morning Miranda died. While I talked he looked away most of the time, wincing sometimes, like he was hearing me through a line with static. Like he wasn't listening so much to the words as the way they were said. Only once or twice did he glance at Profumo behind me. I kept wanting to turn around, but they would jump on that. Why had I turned around? Spollick's eyes flicked around the painted-over fretwork at the edge of the ceiling. When I was done he looked around at the folder and picked some lint off the edge.

"Did you go into the apartment the same time they did?"

"Huh? Well, about the same time. I didn't want to get in anybody's way."

"Why?"

"Well, they ... it seemed safe then. They were expecting somebody to be there, but nobody was. Except ..."

"Could've been kind of dangerous, couldn't it?"

"Well, I didn't know that. I still wasn't sure they weren't cops. They just said they were answering a call. I was kind of groggy. They wanted to go in her apartment. I said the buzzer worked but they wanted to check for themselves."

The weakness in all this did not seem to faze him. He was interested in something else, whatever that was.

"Tell me, did they seem surprised by what they found?"

"Surprised ...?" I thought about it. "Yeah. I would say that. They seemed ... damned surprised."

"What about this business of pretending to be cops?"

"They had badges. One was in plain clothes, the others had police caps. They had cards with pictures on them. I didn't look too close. But they were looking for her. And she didn't answer her bell. So ... I didn't see anything wrong with checking to see if she was there. They said they got a call from her and she might be in trouble."

"And you believed that?"

"Sure. What, was I going to chase them away? I could be blamed for that too."

"Yeah, you could," Valencio said. "Did you think they were going to shoot down her door?"

I didn't answer that.

Spollick looked away. He was leaping across mounds of thought. He sighed.

"See, Fyrish, this isn't a mob related thing. It's much too messy. A mob member who made this kind of a disturbance would be severely rebuked. He would be punished, most likely."

Spollick motioned to Valencio, who handed him the mailer.

"I'm going to show you some pictures. You tell me if you saw any of these men yesterday morning."

He pulled out a sheaf of pictures. Some were police composites, and some were just pictures taken on the street. He spread them out on the table.

I pawed through them.

"This guy," I said. "He was the first one in. I wouldn't forget him."

He set that photo aside.

"Anyone else?"

I stared at them.

"No. No one else. Just him. He threatened me."

"How so?"

"He said the more I forgot the better he would like it."

Valencio grimaced.

"You got no problem with this," he said. "Lots of people saw them."

But Spollick was unhappy. Quietly he picked up one of the pictures and held it in front of me. It was a puffy face with clearly articulated lips. The man had a shock of black straight hair. I looked at the picture. Spollick looked at me. Then Spollick held his hand over the man's hair.

"How about now?" he said.

It was Opov with different hair. His hair was shorter now, and what there was was white. And his face had sagged since that picture was taken.

"Yeah. I guess that's the guy that came in last."

"He's going bald now, right?"

"No. His hair is white. Anyway it was straight and lighter than that."

"Opov," said Valencio, nodding.

"Yeah," said Spollick hefting up his belt. He looked at me. "Anyway these four guys, I know where they're coming from. They expected trouble, that's clear. You came very close to getting into trouble yourself. I don't know if you knew that."

"It was ... kind of scary ..."

"You came very close." He held his palms like he was measuring a ten inch fish. "Those men are extremely dangerous. You or someone in your building could have been badly hurt."

"It would have been an accident, of course ..." Valencio added in with his little smile.

I told them I knew the name Opov and I told them about Wyent and the visit to the country.

"Why did you go?"

"Wyent said it might convince Opov that I had nothing to do with killing Miranda."

But even with telling them about Opov, I kept his son out of it.

They listened and Valencio took notes but they avoided talking about Wyent. When I mentioned him they didn't even blink. Spollick grew speculative.

"Well, that's the kind of guys these are," Valencio said. "They almost kill you in the morning and that night they invite you to a party."

"And this guy's the super ... Heeeeyyyy," Spollick said. Even Spollick had a wry smile for me, but right away he was on a different tack.

"Opov didn't do it," he said closely. "You know why?"

"No," I said.

"Y'see, Fyrish," he expanded, "we've thought two whole times we had this thing wrapped up. Two times. First we were sure he did it, that the shotgun blast killed the woman, which was logical enough at the time. That whole thing with those men impersonating cops was very misleading. It's a one-of-a-kind type of thing. It didn't really have to do with the girl's death. The girl was dead before they got there."

"Yes, I told you that."

"Then we listened better to you than we had at first. And we weren't so sure, but we kept an open mind. You see, you'd been hit on the head and you admitted you fainted before you could even dial 911, and so you weren't the most reliable witness to this thing. But then for other reasons it became clear the shotgun blast had nothing to do with it, which we now know, and we thought another guy did it. Young guy who was sleeping with her, knew her from her uptown location. They had a fight a few days ago, and several people heard it, but now we know he couldn't have done it. We've exed him out. We're back to square one. A woman is killed in her apartment, and yet nobody hears anything. All the people in the building. No screams. No fights. It's amazing. You know how many people die in this city every day from domestic fights, from drug related fights? You know? Average five. All the neighbors know. You get twenty French versions of the same story. This lady, the lady in your building, gets herself killed in a vacuum. A vacuum. So we're crawling the walls on this one. And I'm asking myself, what is it we're missing here? Now it looks as if the killer was nobody we even thought of yet. So maybe you can help us."

He looked at me like maybe I had some ideas.

"Hmm," I said. "I've told you about all I know."

"Maybe you have," he said definitively. "You know, Fyrish … you know how we'll solve this one?"

"No."

"The solution to this one will walk in off the street. Mark what I say. Someone'll talk. Someone always does. That's how it'll be solved, not by any of that medical shit. Enough people are upset about this thing that the killer will come running in the door and begging us to take him. Or he'll be delivered."

"Hope you're right," I said.

"So to get back," Spollick said. "She lived in another apartment, uptown on the East Side. Why did she keep both places?"

"I don't know," I said. "But I have an idea. I think maybe she liked to spend a lot of time by herself. I'm just guessing, but she liked to be alone and she didn't socialize, that I saw, with anybody in the building."

"Okay, that's what it looks like. And that isn't so odd. A lot of people who can afford it keep another place. Sometimes in the city, sometimes out of town, a weekend place. That doesn't bother us. But see the way she did it, there could've been another reason. Like maybe she was hiding from somebody."

"Ah, yeah," I said. "I see what you mean. And then finally they, it, whatever it was, caught up with her. Yeah, that could have happened, I guess."

"And it could have been this Russian character. Estonian or whatever."

"Well, you've ruled him out," I said helpfully.

They waited for several seconds. Valencio looked up at Spollick, like he would like to take a break. But Spollick didn't move. I thought about what I was going to say next and took a deep breath. I enjoyed their attention for a second and then I spoke.

"There is one thing, that might open up some possibilities," I said slowly.

"And that is?"

"But I would have to talk to you in private."

All six eyes were on me then. I even felt Profumo staring at the back of my neck. They were hungry for something. Maybe this was it.

"I'm agreeable to that," Spollick said. The other men left with hardly a word.

He waited and watched me as the others left.

I began as simply as I could.

"You have to promise to keep me out of anything about what I plan to tell you. Do I have you're word on that?"

"If I can keep you out, I will."

"No, forget it. That's not good enough."

I sat still and we both shared a moment of silence. Finally he spoke.

"Fyrish, no cop wants a dead informant on his conscience. Our department has a very fine record about keeping informants out of trouble, if that's what you're worried about."

"Oh, you think it's a trivial concern?"

"Look, Fyrish ..."

"If it's not serious for you, it's not serious for me."

We had another long moment of silence. We were each waiting the other out. I began wondering if I hadn't made a fatal mistake.

It was my craziness again. My crazy sense that I had to do something even if I had to pay for it. Maybe I should pay. I couldn't lie to everybody about everything. I had visions of keeping a .45 under my pillow at night and carrying it with me wherever I went. It would alienate Holly, but she should be far from such a crazy character as me. Still I watched Spollick. Finally he started speculating.

"The capo called you out there to tell you something. That you know something he doesn't want us to know. Is that it? Wyent will tell us."

"Yeah, why don't you get it from Wyent?"

"Fyrish, if we get it from Wyent, Wyent will tell them it came from you. They'll believe him before they believe you. And how much time do you think you'll be given to explain these fine points? Five minutes? Thirty seconds? Maybe less. You'll have a better safety record if you talk to us."

I wanted to believe he was right. I had gone too far to back out now. I was competing with Wyent now. If I talked they would ask less of him.

"The biggest reason those guys wanted to see me is that Opov's son was involved with Miranda, and in fact visited her when I was sitting talking with her at around seven o'clock that evening. I didn't talk with him, just a few words, then I left. They didn't want you to find out about that, and I'm trusting you that you won't let that out. Like you say, these are very dangerous people, and they don't want the son to be connected to Miranda in any way. But he was there. In fact he interrupted my conversation with her, and she made me leave shortly afterward. Apparently they had a date. But she was going to be back at midnight to see me, she said. I didn't put a lot of credence in that, but I think now she may have been telling me the truth. Maybe they went out somewhere and she came back alone, I don't know. But there was a recording made of her voice, telling the capo, the father, to come and visit her and giving him the address, which he didn't know. He only knew about her other apartment on the Upper East Side, which he said he gave her. Well, the recording was mind-blowing enough. It was her voice and it sounded like she was nervous. But it was because of that that they went in there that morning, thinking it was a trap of one of Opov's enemies, of which he says he has a few. I can believe that part. I didn't like him much myself.

Anyway, the whole thing was a scam the kid pulled to impress his old man. Since she knew to expect them that morning, she would have to be tied up, or she would split. Well, the kid said he did tie her up, but he denied killing her."

Spollick took this in and sat thinking for a moment.

"So about what time would you say Vincent visited her?"

"Around seven. Maybe eight. The sun was still up."

"Well, Fyrish, if I'm gonna use this lead, and I am, then how do I connect it without involving you?"

He was serious. He really wanted to keep me out of it. I began to believe he would.

"Here's how. He called her up the next day and I answered her phone, because I was fixing the door. You can get the telephone traces and find his number. If you can't, I have it at home. He called between eleven and twelve, I think, after you guys had left."

Spollick went to the door and motioned Valencio to return. He spoke with him briefly out of my hearing. Valencio left. Then Spollick turned to me and we went back into the room with the big mirror.

"Now, Fyrish," he began, "from what you're saying, the killer could have been this Vincent, Opov's son ... "

"I'm just giving you a lead. He admitted tying her up to impress his father. But he denied killing her. It convinced me, for what that's worth. He called twice, and the first time he hung up. When he did talk to me, he seemed to be checking up on her. Like he thought she was still alive. So, I'm convinced he didn't know what had happened to her."

Spollick squinted at the window, thinking out loud.

"Killer commits the crime and then calls the next day pretending he doesn't know what happened. That's clever. Maybe. Or it's guilt. I've heard of stranger things. Killers revisiting the scene of the crime, rituals people go through. It's obsessive with some guys. They go through elaborate retracing of their steps, as if they secretly believed that retracing what they did could undo the crime. Shrinks know all about that stuff. Most of it's useless in what I do. Did you have a long conversation on the phone?"

"No, when I recognized his voice, I made like Miranda was just out that day, partly because I didn't want to go into a long story, and I knew he would read about it soon enough. And partly because once I had recognized his voice, I didn't need any more from him."

"You're a kidder, Fyrish," he said. "Be careful you don't kid the wrong people."

"You just gotta keep it off me."

"Yeah. If it leads to this guy. Which it may not."

"Which it may not."

He made me go over it again, and then he went out and brought Profumo back with him. By that time Valencio showed up too, and we all sat down where we were.

Spollick waited in silence for several seconds, like he was savoring what I had told him. Finally, he turned to me again.

"There's just one other thing I gotta ask you about, Mr. Fyrish. When you discovered the dead woman at four in the morning, she was tied up, right?"

"Yes."

"Did it look like to you she could get loose if she really wanted to?"

"I ... don't think so. She would've gotten loose if someone was trying to kill her, no?"

He placed his hands before me as if he was trying to contain something the size of a bread basket, and he was going to present it to me, and would I take it?

"Precisely how was she tied up, Fyrish?"

"Her hands were tied behind her and her feet were tied to the bed. Her hands were tied to the bed too."

"Uh-huh. About how much rope would you say was used?"

"I don't know. Maybe twenty yards. Maybe more. There was some left over."

"Twenty yards. That's a lot of rope. How much do you think it would take to tie up someone like that if you were to use the minimum amount of rope?"

"I don't know. A lot less. I guess a lot of rope was just extra."

"Did it look any special way?"

"It looked like a lot more rope was used than was needed, that's true. In a way, some of it looked like macramé."

"Macramé!" he said, raising an eyebrow. He nodded, as though expecting each word I said. "So it was elaborate."

"Yeah, I guess so."

"It was a lot more rope than it would take to hold this woman."

"I guess I don't see your point."

He smiled patiently. "How long would it take to tie that woman up like that?"

I thought a minute. "Well, if she let you do it, but she wouldn't ... I don't know."

"No, suppose you had her cooperation. How long would it take then?"

"But she wouldn't ..."

"You're not thinking, Fyrish. There were no screams heard. No scuffle. No struggle was evident in the room, or in her dress. She had to cooperate. Because some people like that, like being tied up. It's not that unusual, actually. So if she was docile, how long would it take to tie her up that way?"

"About half an hour," I blurted. I hadn't the foggiest idea, but he seemed to be leading somewhere.

"So, whoever did this, took a lot of pleasure in it, would you say? It was a challenge to him and he enjoyed it. Hmm?"

"I wasn't there," I said.

"A particular kind of pervert. Guy's gay but he hates gays. And he knows she's bi. A special taste. Special zeal to do this particular thing to this woman. You see? That narrows it down. That narrows it down a lot."

"Well, I guess that's good," I said.

"And then he gagged her. You ever try to gag anyone?"

"No."

"Well, think about it. When you see it on TV, they put a piece of tape over somebody's mouth and that's supposed to keep them quiet. Does that work? Try it. No, it doesn't. The person just opens his mouth and the tape comes off. It's very hard to gag someone so they really won't cry out. Do you know how it's done?"

I just looked at him.

"Like this." With his fingers he pushed the sides of his mouth together. Then he let it go. "You tape the sides of their mouth together, with the jaw wide open. You do that enough, the person can't open her mouth anymore, and can't close it either. Then you put a lot of tape and padding over the mouth. She might've even choked on the gag. That's a very dangerous thing, to gag someone like that. Before long, they can't make a sound that can be heard behind a door. That's the way this woman was gagged. Her lips were still pursed that way even after the killer removed the gag."

Suddenly, he looked at me.

"Do you find this interesting?"

I was glad he asked.

"No. The poor woman …"

"Fyrish, there's a few things I don't think you know. Or you're pretending not to know. Can you guess what I'm talking about?"

"No."

"Ever seen porn on the web. There's a lot. Have you?"

"No."

"Why not?"

"Never got around to it."

"Aren't you curious? Most guys are at least a little curious about what's out there. Aren't you curious? Never turn to a porn station on TV?"

"I don't get cable."

"When you want to see some real action?"

"The little I've seen was pretty boring."

"It might be an eye-opener, if you're as dumb as you say you are."

I let that pass. I just sat there, looking steadily at his eyes, which were beginning to fascinate me.

"See, some people like to tie people up. Bondage it's called. It's very taboo. It's never in movies. Even porno bookstores, most of them didn't carry it. It's a particular sexual game that excites a particular set of people. Specialized. Many guys are excited by it. Especially men like to tie up women, but it goes both ways. Many women know this and they fake an interest, just like they fake orgasm. And conversely, or should I say, conveniently, there are people who really like to be tied up. There are even people who tie themselves up because it's the only way they can get off. When it goes awry, the person, often a woman, can strangle herself. It's called ritual suicide, that's the insurance term for it, because they don't pay, and it kills maybe a dozen people every year. Most people that like to be tied up, and it may be the dead woman was like this, find someone who likes to do it, because, as you can imagine, it bores or disgusts or embarrasses most people. And most people are inept; they aren't dexterous enough to tie themselves up so they really can't get loose. It's safer and easier to get someone who likes it to do it. That's what had to happen with her. She was tied up. Because she wanted to be, because no one heard any sounds of a struggle. And then she was left alone for a time. They like to do that, and in particular this Russian sonofabitch might have been trying to show off to his father as you say, so he left her like that, for his father to find her. So if she was left that way, anybody who could get into that room could have killed her. A child could have done it."

He said all of this very fast, like a kettle of fish tumbling over one another as they slid into a bin. Never mind that I had asked him to keep the "Russian sonofabitch" between us. I had to swallow when he stopped. I pictured Tommy or Gerald doing a something like that. Tommy was pretty cruel—and what do kids know about death? When it's over, it's commercials and you go and get a Coke out of the fridge. And Louis, he was the follower ... any of them might. Kids.

"That's a disgusting idea," I said. "Have you been watching horror flicks?"

Spollick only smirked.

"And then," he went on, "the killer came back. You know why the criminal returns to the crime scene? He wants to get caught of course, secretly, so he can confess. But why does he want to confess? To get it off his chest, maybe. But in a deeper sense he wants to claim responsibility for it. You see, it's his, what he did. He doesn't want it to belong to someone else, because it's a part of him now. Disconnection from it is disconnection from who he is. But you interrupted that. You were the interloper. You came between the death and the return."

Perhaps he was enjoying himself then, and maybe he wanted to egg me into elaborating on his crazy idea. I actually couldn't improve on it. We were silent for a long moment. I had the feeling everyone but Spollick wanted to leave the room, but nobody made a move. He looked like he would nod, but instead he cocked one eye at me and pointed again. He liked to point.

"You know what really killed her?" he asked.

I waited.

"Do you?"

"No."

"She was asphyxiated."

I looked back at him, as blankly as I could.

"It was a pervert killing," he said.

He took a breath and squared away at me.

"The woman was tied up. We don't know for how long. Then, she was asphyxiated. Probably with a pillow. Maybe with a plastic sack. No semen was found. And then the killer untied her. BUT ... he didn't try to make it look like suicide. She died sometime between one and five AM."

He watched me when he said that. He seemed to not care if he was giving out information now; he was on another plane entirely.

"Sounds kinda crazy," I said.

Spollick took a breath and bent towards me.

"There were marks on her wrists and feet." He motioned over his own burly wrists. "But we didn't find any rope. That's another thing. Nowhere. This guy was very neat. He was a neat kind of crazy."

"Well, I'll tell ya," I said, "I doubt if there's anybody in my building that's that crazy. Not that I know."

"You wouldn't. The killer would be somebody that on the outside looks pretty normal. He's cunning. He thinks."

Spollick pointed to his temple and with the wild slant to his eye, I wondered how much he really knew about cunning, crazy, homicidal people—way too much by now. More than I wanted ever to know. And then the way he looked at me made me think maybe he, Spollick, was a little crazy. Wouldn't you get that way from dealing with psychotic criminals every day? And the way he motioned to me, the way he directed all his attention at me, made me think that he thought I was crazy too, that we were buddies that way.

"What did she say about this purse snatcher? He had a key to her apartment."

"Two black guys. That's all she told me."

"They didn't do it," Spollick said.

"Why not?"

"Because street criminals don't think that way. I never saw a purse snatcher who could keep still for two minutes. And nobody saw any young blacks in the building who didn't live there. You gotta remember, he got in the building without anyone knowing he was there. He tied her up without making a sound, killed her and left and wasn't seen. Or left her and somebody else killed her. Either way, it's not a street hood type of thing. Most likely the guy that did this had a lot of patience. A lot of planning. Mind obsessed with planning. Not a street kid. Not an impulsive actor. That's why I wanted to talk to you. I thought maybe you would have some idea, some inkling of what could tie this together for us. I know it's a long shot. But see you were there for a lot of what went on that morning. A lot of it. You might have seen something, anything, no matter how trivial, that could point us to the killer."

Yeah, I thought, though in the mean time I was a target high on his list. Just here to help. Helpful Milo.

"Well, I was there for the fireworks," I said. "But if she was killed as you say, by strangling, then ..."

Spollick shook his finger at me.

"I didn't say by strangling. I said by asphyxiation."

"Okay, asphyxiation. Anyway, the guys with the guns had nothing to do ..."

He stopped me again.

"We know she wasn't strangled because there were no bruises on her throat. There's a bone, right here." He held his chin up and pointed at the top of his throat. "There's a bone there and it often is broken in strangulation. Not always, but often. The hyoid bone. Hers was all right. And there were no marks on her neck."

The way he said "hers was all right" was so personal, as if Miranda had been someone he knew and had maybe lunch with now and then. My tongue felt like it was glued to the back of my hyoid bone.

"Hers was intact," he went on. I pursed my lips and nodded.

"Well ..."

"Well, what?" Valencio said.

"Just well," I said. I wanted time to think. Half a minute would be enough. Twenty seconds. But Spollick took one breath and he was back at me. All of this was intended for me. None of it was wasted. But I couldn't see where he was going.

"See, she was asphyxiated," he went on. "You know how we know that?"

His eye gleamed at me. There was no stopping him.

"It's because of petechial bleeding. You know what that is?"

"No."

"Nobody has petechial bleeding except people who die of asphyxiation. See, there're these capillaries on the inside of your lungs, they're there so you can absorb oxygen when you breathe. The air comes into your lungs, and then the oxygen in the air goes into the capillaries and gets carried off by the blood. Are you following me? 'Cause I can go into more detail if you want."

I nodded that I had caught on.

"So whaddaya think happens when there isn't any oxygen there? I'll tell you. When a person has trouble breathing, the capillaries expand, they get bigger because they want to get every chance to get any oxygen at all. It's like they, every one of them, every cell in her body realizes this is it. This is it, their only chance, now, when the lungs are crying for air, burning for it, for even a single breath. But there is none, and from reaching out and reaching out hoping to get that last bit of oxygen … they expand and expand and eventually they break. You see? And there's blood and that's petechial bleeding. It can only happen in the last moment before death, when the only chance for life is the thin hope that a little oxygen will still somehow seep through. It can even cause bleeding in the eyes, can you believe that? In the eyes. That's how much the body wants to live. You know what the medical examiner told me? She had a quarter cup of blood in her lungs. Yeah. She was fighting that hard. Right down to the last second. This woman wanted to live. There was sweat half an inch deep in the blankets under her."

My tongue was like a log in a sand dune. Sandstone scraped my throat.

"So that was what killed her," he went on. "And that's how we know."

I nodded softly. I breathed in, but the air was like a brick in my lungs. I was holding on to the chair. I was going to be lucky if I ever saw the street again. There would be no space at all soon. All the gaps were filling in. Doors with mottled glass panels tunneled down long green halls where aged spectral figures called and called without sound: "No Air …"

Valencio's eyes were depthless as paper.

Spollick stood up and straightened.

"So that's it for now, Fyrish. Let us know if you hear anything."

18. Lyla

When I got out of there I went home. Just before my door, Ms. Clamper was waiting in the hall.

"Milo, I want to talk to you."

She motioned me into her parlor and I stood as she composed herself. She took a moment without speaking.

"A woman knows things, you know."

"Okay."

"You know that? There are things a woman knows. Just knows."

"Yes."

"I see people come and go and I know. Like I saw you with that poor dead woman the night she died. I know. But you know what the real secret is?"

"I can't guess."

"Your girlfriend."

"Holly?"

"She's the one. Pretty soon everyone will be saying it."

"Saying what?"

"It was a crime of jealousy, Milo. Did you know she was here that night? She knows everything. She has a key to your apartment. And I saw her come and go. I hate to tell you this."

"No, no. I'm glad you did. I want to know all the facts."

"Your girlfriend is the killer."

"Don't you think that's going kind of far?"

"But I won't tell the police, Milo. No. Out of respect for you. I'll keep it between you and me."

"I think that's wise."

"I leave you with the information. It's your decision. You're the one who should turn her in. Or get her a ticket to a foreign place. You can still save her. She's hot-tempered. She's capable of violent acts."

"Well, as long as it's between you and me."

"It is. It is. It's totally what I'm telling you and no one else. You think I'd go blabbing a thing like that?"

"Well, no ..."

"Protect yourself, Milo. What's good for her is to get out of the country."

She stared at me as if to impress upon me the gravity of her conviction.

"I gotta go," I said. "Let's talk later. When I have more time."

I made it to my place, locked the door and got a beer. I lay in my bed by the window and convened with my cat. I didn't want to see anyone for days. I felt like escaping, running away, without even knowing what from, just someplace where nobody would ask me any questions and I didn't have to think too hard. I'd go someplace where people weren't too serious but they still made sense and nobody worried too hard if you spent some days in a kind of fog. Akbar understood. His purr concurred. He would have had a hard time putting up with Spollick's guff too, his look said, and who knows what worse characters Akbar ran into on his nightly prowls? Akbar knew what I meant. I was to be pitied. I sipped my beer and unplugged the phone. No one saw me come in. I could hide for hours.

But then it needled me: what Spollick had said about kids. I liked all the children in the building, and not one of them could I think of as having done anything as mean as what happened to Miranda. Tommy was arrogant and playful, but everything was out front with him, not hidden in some private darkness where no one could see. Gerald had his strained relationship with his mother, of course, but kids lived through that and he seemed calm enough when he was on his own, around the rest of us. Louis was a kind of child of the weather: you got the feeling he was in a dream world as much as he ran around with Tommy. And what about the girls? Letitia was a loudmouth; you could be sure she couldn't do anything without immediately talking about it. A lot of kids couldn't. I went through the list of kids I knew on the street. Who was secretly a monster and you wouldn't know? Children were mean, sometimes, but they weren't as cunning as adults because they usually couldn't keep the same thought in their heads for very long. They'd be betrayed by their own feelings if nothing else. What an awful burden a child would have to suffer if he carried the secret of this crime. How could he ever be himself around other people after a thing like that? He would in all likelihood become schizoid.

It had to be admitted that children, near adults maybe, sometimes did awful crimes as soon as they got their hands on the means. If they thought they could get away with it. Spollick was right about that. He trafficked in that world, and I was happy it was him and not me who had to deal with it. It was another reason why I watched so little TV. But now this whole question was all around me; I couldn't get away from it even by hiding with my cat. And then I remembered something strange: Miranda's hope chest, how she had hoarded things for the future, when she might have children of her own. I saw all the objects and fabrics piling down before me, cornucopia style, tumbling from the over-filled chest as in a sequence in a dream; the chest had contained something that didn't fit somewhere ... what was it? Some idea came to me and then slipped away. What was it that was wrong about all her jumble of stuff? Her dower for an unplanned marriage? Behind all her gaudiness she was just like a lot of other women. She hoped for the things a lot of ordinary girls wanted: to have a family, to make a home, a future full of love and promise. And so she would collect, with all the patience of a dreamer, the bedding, the dishes, the curtains, the toys a child would want.... The impression was too strong and complex to stay in my mind's eye for long and soon, with the beer's help, it wavered in all its varicolored pieces, its soft intimate confusion, and disappeared. I wanted to sip my beer and just stare out at the trees.

Toward evening a woman rang my bell and I answered. She introduced herself as Miranda's sister come from Illinois. She had a deposition from court that gave her the right to handle Miranda's things. Her name was Lyla Murphy and she had cornflower irises that seemed to reflect all the depth of the sad twilight as we stood in the hallway like passing witnesses to a terrible storm we didn't want to talk too much about. She had a flight bag such as flight attendants haul, and she wanted to see Miranda's place.

"I came as soon as I could," she said.

"Your first time in New York?"

"Yes, I don't know a soul."

"Where are you staying? Manhattan?"

She hesitated as though it was a new thought.

"Why, no. I haven't made arrangements yet. I visited the attorney right away, Mr. Ogile, and then I came right here. You must have talked to him."

She showed me a document signed neatly at the bottom:

Osoborne Ogile, Esq.

"No," I said, hoping it wouldn't lead me into meeting another official. Let the Widow handle it, I thought. "I haven't listened to my messages yet."

"He's handling her affairs. Our parents wanted me to come alone."

I got the feeling that she hoped I would let her stay in Miranda's place and it occurred to me that that would be the most convenient thing, if indeed she didn't feel the place was too haunted to stand. We went up to Miranda's. When Lyla walked into the apartment I had the impression she was stepping into a fairyland where there were things she expected to find. She seemed to be walking into it as a strange place she had visited once long before; she stepped slowly, taking in each breath, and a new impression with each breath of air. The light of the evening was just coming through in slanting rays and orange hues that striped the wall. She paused to think about everything she saw. She touched nothing, as if she wanted to leave it all exactly as it was. I said she could stay there while she cleared out Miranda's stuff; I was sure the Widow wouldn't mind. But even to that, she took her time answering, as if it all depended on some confluence of unseen forces that she was going to have to sit down to assess. She sat on the bed for a moment without saying a word.

"I think that would be the best arrangement," she said as she dug out a cigarette and lighted it while she looked at me. "Thank you for the offer, Milo."

"You sound like you're on vacation," I said.

"Well ... sometimes I do temporary nursing. It's the kind of job you can turn on and off."

She blew smoke toward the ceiling and sat silently again. When was the last time I had met a nurse who smoked? I supposed she had a lot of things to think over alone, and I felt like I wanted to leave her to it. I gave her the key I had, since I had another one, and went back down.

"Well, that's done," I told Akbar. "Now the Widow will be happy and maybe the awful pall will clear off this place."

"MMMMMrrrrrrkekkegoooouuue", was all he said.

But then as I sat alone, the feeling of another person in the building felt like a palpable change, a slight disarrangement of all that I had expected and wanted to stay the same when everything all about me was whirling out of control. Spollick had shook me up that much. Wasn't I secretly going to go up to Miranda's place and rifle through the hope chest, and dig out the missing part that had piqued my memory before? Now I couldn't do that. Not with Lyla there. Not that it wouldn't have been sacrilege before, but now I had to wait for her to leave; I could never justify it to Lyla in any way that would make me seem more than a pilfering busybody. And by rights, she could deny me entry now, couldn't she? Get her attorney down on me, something I positively didn't want. And whatever my intimation pointed to would be gone when she left.

I let it go.

Anyway Lyla, it turned out over the next few days, never left the apartment. She ordered in pizza and whatever from someplace that sent a delivery boy that rang every buzzer with the side of his arm and bounded up three steps at a time, like a Marine on attack up the side of a mountain starving for cheese.

One day Holly called me from work.

"They got the guy that did it," she said with precise satisfaction. She had heard it from somebody at the office who got it on the radio. I was heavily involved at work and I did little more than get the name of the guy; it was Vincent. He had confessed, she said.

"To what?"

"To killing her. And tying her up and killing her. The creep."

"I gotta go," I said.

"It's really good they got him."

"Yeah, it's good. I mean it. It is good."

"You don't sound it," she said.

"Well, I just wonder what the repercussions will be ..."

"What could they be? They'll shoot him up his dirty little arm with a fluid to send him on a short trip to Hell, which he profoundly deserves," she said.

I couldn't help thinking of Opov and his pals and if they would blame this on me. Who knew now about what I had told Spollick?

"You want to meet for dinner?" Holly said brightly.

"No, not tonight," I said. "I've got some catching up to do. Maybe Wednesday if we go to that little Greek place up by Columbia."

I wouldn't date her with the possibility that Leo and his friends would be following me tonight, but if we did it right and made a rendezvous that couldn't be predicted, we could take a cab up there and probably not be seen.

"All right. Wednesday," she said and added her lyrical "Bye" that said in one word that all things, given a little love, could be healed by Wednesday. I got a dew-kissed rose petal whiff from her "Bye".

I finished wheeling a tray of glass slugs into the fire room and went to the can and mopped my face. I wanted to think but something told me that thinking was no use, none whatever. In fact it was a deficit, a downer I didn't need and would only make me more tired and less fit for the things I needed to do. The rest of the day went by like a swampy stream.

When I got home, I did my usual: I spread out on the bed and nursed my beer, sharing a dollop now and then with my compassionate cat. The phone rang. I had forgotten to unplug it.

It was Spollick.

"Hey, we caught your boy," he said cheerfully.

"He's not mine. He's yours. And you promised me …"

"And I called to thank you. You were definitely instrumental in the arrest of this pervert."

"I thought we agreed …"

"And guess what we found in his apartment. Go on. Guess."

"Uh … a shotgun?" I was out of ideas with this dialogue between the deaf. Now I just wanted to find out what else he would spill.

"Nah. No shotgun. That's not his type of weapon. Know what was there? Enough pornography to open up a store. All about bondage. Thousands of bondage pictures. And enough rope you could tie down an elephant. Kid's a real lover. He resisted arrest, even though we had him surrounded on the street. Now he's in the slammer and that's where he's staying. No judge in his right mind would grant him bail. There'd be a riot. Because there's outrage about this. Tying a woman up and killing her is worse than ordinary homicide; it's pervert homicide. It's worse than Robert Chambers and that "rough sex" crap. Much worse. Yeah. And he did it. He's the one. He's already confessed. Took two hours to break him because he's too stupid to realize when he's beaten. He's a pansy."

"He confessed to what?"

"To tying her up. He did it that night, after you left for the hospital. And he's bawling to us that he didn't mean it to happen that way. That he did it to impress somebody, he won't say who.

But we know anyway. Little shit."

"Oooo ... kay. Well, I guess that wraps it up as far as you're concerned."

"He's confused, but it's clear enough. With a smart lawyer, and enough delays he could get off without the death sentence—which is what he would get if the trial were held tomorrow. Trying to impress his father, Opov. And he's implicated if we can catch that guy you identified. Impersonating an officer. You can get ten years for that. But Opov might not be implicated enough. A lot of people would like to put him away. He's the big fish."

"Well, I guess you're happy, even if you didn't keep me out of it."

"I did. I didn't tell anyone."

"What about Valencio? Didn't you instruct him to get the phone trace after you talked alone with me?"

"Getting the trace is nothing, Fyrish. It's common procedure. We just hadn't gotten around to it. A lot of people called her in the last few days and by rights we would have to check on each one of them. But whattayouthink? I'm a genius because I picked the right one first try. Doesn't that make me a genius?"

"Yeah, you're a genius," I said.

"Anyway it'll be in the papers tomorrow and you can read it for yourself. Okay, buddy?"

"Fine," I said.

"Oh, and there's one other thing."

"Yeah, what's that?"

"They're under pressure to hold a grand jury hearing right away, and I happen to know you'll be called. I don't know what they'll ask, but you should be in the clear on most of the questions."

"What does that mean?"

"If you have nothing to hide, you should be in the clear."

"But I have something to hide. You promised to keep me out of it. But now you're not helping me. I thought ..."

"We have to tell them what we know," he said piously.

"After all I did for you ..." But I couldn't finish. I was too angry. I hung up without another word.

The papers the next morning were worse. I forced myself to sit in the back of the diner and read every word in three papers. The Times was the only one that had it: "... thanks to an anonymous tip ..." it said. I read the words over and over. Worse, they floated Spollick's idea that Miranda choked on the gag, and how that did not make Vincent less a murderer with premeditation. I could see Spollick dancing on the tombstone. Vincent would not be out in a few years; he might not be out at all. The heinousness of the crime would cry for the death penalty.

I fingered the paper to make sure it was real and to make myself see, if I finally could, that it was only one copy of indestructible thousands that were spread like dust all over the city. I fantasized for a minute that I could burn each one somehow—until I saw I was making myself crazy and I gave up and went to work.

At least that helped. I could dig myself into that and forget for as much as an hour that a gaggle of homicidal maniacs might be waiting till I got home. I just did my job. I worked harder and faster than I ever had. I even got a compliment from Patrice. Sweat poured off me till my jeans were soaked to my calves.

When I got home I ran up to Follett's. No answer there. Across the way, Tartakauer was probably asleep. No sound from Miranda's; I had no idea what Lyla was cooking up. It was she, probably, who had cleaned up the candles and flowers; there were only faint spots of wax and streaks of chalk. No boxes were stacked in the hall. The whole top floor seemed quiet and forgetful; it was just the kind of atmosphere where, ordinarily, I would have loved sitting around talking with people. Now the time for that seemed very far away.

19. Jockey Colloquy

I stopped by Sam's on the chance that he might be in. He answered the door in his tee-shirt and black suspenders. In his muscular free hand he held a red spring bar that he let dangle like a ninja stick he might use on a visitor. He motioned me in. His compact torso fitted straight down into his trousers without an inch of flab. He danced forward on one toe like a boxer and shut the door. I said nothing for a few seconds.

"I need a gun," I said.

"You talked to the cops," he said.

"I ... yeah ..."

He lifted his hands as if offering a lamb to God. Then he sat down in his cushiony chair. He stared into space and shook his head just once and then looked back at me. I had to go on.

"I talked to the cops. They know Miranda was killed hours before those guys came in. And they just caught the guy who killed her. And I fingered him. His father's an Estonian mafia capo or something. He told me not to do it but I did it anyway. It was crazy but I had to do it. I couldn't go on and not say that I knew Vincent was involved somewhere. I didn't know where. I asked the cops to keep me out of it, and they ... tried, I guess. But it says in the paper they got tipped off and ... I'm afraid ... that I'm the logical person."

Sam thought a second. He frowned a deep frown, and nodded even so. He tossed the spring bar on the sofa and suggested I sit down. He forgave me and in a deeper way I forgave myself; I wouldn't take back what I had told Spollick. I was a piece of the puzzle, not the whole game.

"I can get you a gun tonight. Or maybe it'll take a day. Have seven hundred bucks on hand, though I don't think it'll be that much. They won't hit you now anyway, they'll wait for a good time. It won't make any difference whether the kid gets off or not. You know that, don't you? Don't start worrying for two, three weeks. Maybe months. What kind of gun you want?"

"Beretta 9 mm, 14 shot, I guess. Two extra clips. Two boxes of shells."

"Yeah. I may can get you that. You may have a choice of

something else. We'll see."

"You knew Miranda was mixed up with these people, didn't you?"

"I told you I knew. People I talk to, word gets around."

"You know where Follett is?" I asked.

"No." Sam had no curiosity about why I would care.

"He sits around on the stoop sometimes and maybe he saw somebody leave here that night. Also, the police are looking for Follett. Only now he's disappeared."

"Whaddayou, turned cop yourself?" he chortled.

"No. Let's say I don't feel like just standing around. She was a friend and ..."

"Yeah, you sounded like it that night. You and her were way over-involved, but I told you what I thought."

"Doesn't matter. I gotta see Follett."

Sam winced. "If he wants to be seen...."

"And what's this about sex offense?" I said. "Sounds heavy-handed for a guy that likes women. You hear the police tell it, the guy that got to Miranda was a crazy, a pervert."

Sam reached over the flexible bar and held it like a shillelagh.

"It wasn't heavy-handed, the sex offense," he said. "He showed no judgment. I heard how it happened. The girl was underage, that's all. Thirteen. Had nothing to do with hurting anybody. They had a thing going and he said it's off and she didn't like that. She got vindictive, and she went to the police and told her story. And then she told it again and again until finally it got to a grand jury and she stuck to her story. A persistent little bitch. He cut a plea."

Sam glanced at me, like he'd just hit all the tacks.

"It happens sometimes," he said philosophically, picking up another weight. It was as if he kept odds on possessive heart-stricken thirteen-year-olds who would accuse a paramour and then would persist until he went to jail and she ruined his life. "What can you say?"

Follett had relatives in Cincinnati, Sam went on. The cops probably were onto that, even though he wasn't on parole anymore.

"They won't go hunting for him," he said with a sigh. "They'll wait till he comes back. Anyway he wouldn't go there."

"How so?"

Sam stared steadily at the wall while he worked the weight. He didn't care to explain. He just said, "The woman might know. I'm not telling you what to do and it's probably too soon if he's hiding out, because he might be foolish enough to tell her. Either way, after a while, my guess, she'd know. But she probably won't tell you."

"Which woman?"

"Yvette. That's the only one ..."

Sam paused for a few seconds as if trying to remember something.

"... I think matters to him. Although ..."

"Although?"

"Well, Milo, I'm not throwing this up to you, but you belong to a club. There were other guys who found Miranda very attractive. And he lived on her floor. So you might say, he had it over you— by about four flights of stairs."

That he had. I should've expected as much, but I wasn't happy being in the company of a man who seduced, or was seduced by, a thirteen-year-old. What mattered was Yvette. I didn't know where she lived, and she wasn't going to show up at Follett's anymore.

"I gotta find her. You know where she lives?"

"No. And I think she uses an assumed name, anyway. My advice: don't think about it. You won't find him till this thing blows over. Follett's got his own way of doing things. Wouldn't make sense to you or me, but it's his way."

"Yeah, he should turn himself in," I said with my own piety.

Sam went back to his bar and bent it double. His shoulders and neck became a thatch work of wirelike skin.

"It's not the way he thinks," he said. "And he's got some experience to back it up."

"You tell the cops that?"

He smirked.

"No. I let them find their own stuff."

I paused, thinking probably I was still missing something.

"It's weird, the way it's working out. That Vincent would tie up Miranda and then kill her and then make his father and those hoods come running in. Why tie somebody up, if you're going to kill her anyway? Sick."

"Happens all the time. Guys like to be in control. Then they can play with the victim. C'mere."

Sam went over to his computer and punched some keys. What came up was porn where women in very sexy poses were tied up. I stared. Sam tapped more keys.

"Well ... I dunno, Sam. Why are those people tied up?"

Sam looked around at me.

"Are you kidding me? You don't know nothing about porn? What kinda weirdo are you?"

"Sam, I got my hands full with the Widow, you know? And Holly. I never liked television. I guess really, come to think of it, that's at the bottom of it."

Sam pointed at the screen.

"Now look at that. D'you ever see something like that?"

I stared.

"Well, I dunno. Um ... it's just a picture. This is some sick stuff, seems to me."

He showed me more pictures of women in bondage. All kinds of sexy poses.

"See that?" he said pointing. "That's what it's about."

I looked. It was sexy, but it just seemed strange.

"Well, it's sexy enough, but why is she tied up?"

"Ahh, you don't get it, Milo. It's porn, so it's men that like this stuff. But there're plenty of people who like to be tied up. Men and women. This gal, see?"

I stared at the picture, and he flipped to others. All very sexy and very pretty. But it was still disgusting and I turned away.

"I don't think Holly would like that."

Sam clicked again and smirked around at me.

"Don't knock it. Some women do. Y'know, Milo, I don't think you're too smart. See this porn stuff. You think it looks strange. But the emotions here are just like the emotions of any crime, even the emotions of war. Guys want to be in control, and they enjoy watching someone who isn't. It's the same as the delight in inflicting pain. Lemme help you. Think of Mrs. Clamper. I know you don't like her. Now, what if Mrs. Clamper lost her job? Now really, wouldn't you feel a little tremor of delight when you heard?"

"Absolutely not. She suffers enough. She works for the IRS."

"You're too soft, Milo. If everyone was like you, Brooklyn would get wiped out."

"If they were all like me, no one would bother."

I poked his monitor to make the screen go dark.

Sam nodded with a sigh.

"And besides," I said, not only do those Estonian sonsabitches hate me, the Widow wants to throw me out."

"I figured she'd be on your ass."

"She blames me for Miranda getting killed. And she talks to Patrice. Just called him up out of the blue. I hate clairvoyant people."

"Yeah, well," he said thoughtfully. "Better she blames you than you blame yourself."

I was silent when he said that. I said adios and went to the door. "Hey ..."

I turned and Sam extended his finely articulated arm. In his hand was a little piece of wood, a pawn from a chess set.

"You slipped on this when you hit your head. You ought to keep it as a souvenir."

I took it and stuffed it in my pocket. I left Sam.

20. The Little Sister

Around midnight Sam called me up. He had my gun. Two clips. Only one box of shells. Five-fifty. I paid and went back and lay in bed, lovingly fondling this shiny machine of miraculous power. I loaded it, put one in the chamber and uncocked it. I stuck it under my pillow. Did I feel safer and stronger? No. I felt like maybe I was a fool and liable to make mistakes, now I had more power to make them.

A couple of days went by like the slow hot summer. I went to work religiously, so intent on my job that the notoriety people wished to confer slipped off me like a dry coat. I stopped spending any time at all in my apartment. I preferred working in the shop down in the cellar, and I got some more shelves put together that I was rather proud of. In the process I found a bunch of old folded boxes that somebody had left when they moved in. I knew people would ask me for that kind of thing, and so I had saved them. They weren't damaged. I thought I'd take them up to Lyla and help her out a little. To use them, all you needed was wrapping tape, and I even had some of that I could give her. So after work one day, I carried them up, figuring if she was out, I'd just leave them in front of the door.

But when I knocked, I heard her voice simply say, "Come in."

It was as if she expected me and hadn't moved an inch because of my knock. She was in a pose Miranda might have taken: lying on the misplaced bed, in a corner with pillows piled behind her and the light on a newspaper she was reading. She was wearing cut-off jeans and a shirt with no sleeves. She had a drink and beside her on the bed was a wadded-up towel and an ashtray.

She only moved her eyes to look at me, and her stare seemed to be impinged upon by my very presence. She glanced down at the boxes and then at me again.

"Well?"

"I found these downstairs and I thought you might need them," I said, looking around. What had she been doing? Nothing had been moved, nothing had changed. The empty room, the kitchen, certainly not the bed, she was using the same sheets. I dropped the boxes on the floor of the empty room. The far room, that contained Miranda's writing table, seemed untouched.

I straightened up. She was watching me like a cat all the time, her free hand poised on the wadded-up towel.

"Milo, tell me something. Do you want me to leave?"

"No ... I hadn't given it much thought. The owner hasn't put a deadline on it. If you don't need these boxes, I can ..."

"Leave them where they are."

I paused by the door. She wasn't speaking to me like I was a servant, as Ms. Kissich did, but she wasn't exactly kind in her tone. It was entirely different from how she had seemed when I first let her see the place. I had a palpable feeling even without her saying another word, that she was deeply, intensely angry, and she didn't care to explain it or give a rat's ass who knew it. There were newspaper clippings on the bed in a little pile. All about Miranda and the arrest of Vincent. At one time I would have felt pique at her attitude and her lack of gratitude for my little gift, but now I only felt a little sad: why wouldn't she be angry, reading about what had happened to her sister? She even had a right to be angry at me, didn't she? If not for the missed tryst, which wasn't in the papers, then for the simple fact that I was alive in this world, where her sister was not.

"You can stay as long as you like," I said. "The owner won't complain. Not right away anyhow. I know her. She has other things on her mind."

Lyla just looked at me, her eyes not filled with rage so much as incisive cunning and inner solitude like I had never seen before. She relaxed with solidity and determination that seemed effortless and unquestioned. Her hand still lay over the towel: I felt sure there was a gun under it.

Now I had my own, I carried it in a little box in a shopping bag with a rag thrown over it. And I took it most places I went, so now I saw guns everywhere. I hated guns. I hated them before I had one. I didn't want to carry one, or see one, or even suspect that there was a gun in the room. I didn't want them banned, so much as I wanted them disowned, repudiated, disregarded so I could disregard them. They had an ineluctable aura that changed the atmosphere of any room, even a room where you made love. They changed the temper between people, even people you met casually on the street. They didn't make me safer. They could never do that; they only made me more cautious.

But nothing in Lyla's gaze told me what was under her hand. I was no threat, unless she was afraid I would try to rape her, in this apartment house filled with curious retirees who would like nothing better than to have a reason to call 911. Perhaps Miranda had told Lyla stories, maybe even a story about Follett. Or just stories about the big city which a Midwest girl wasn't supposed to know. Then, I reflected, on the other hand there was her incautious "Come in" as if she expected me in particular and left the door always unlocked because that was what neighbors did. As if this was her dream space and my walking through it made no more difference than a sleeping moth that had become part of the wall. She hardly moved when she spoke.

"You know what I think, Milo? I think you didn't come up to deliver boxes, but you came up here to spy on me and see how much progress I'd made. Well, I haven't made much? I don't know what I'll take out of here, besides the smell of death. I believe in ghosts, Milo, and you will too if you stay here at night. My sister went through an anguished, bitter cheating of the only life she had right here. And I can see who did it. Even without reading the papers. But I read them. I read them anyway. You know how it feels to commit a crime and get away with it? Well, let me tell you. It feels fine. Just fine. You ever had something stolen from you and wanted the thief to roast in Hell? But you can't make him and you know what the thief feels? He feels glad. He got away with it and it doesn't matter what you think, or feel or lost. It's that way with a killer; if they get away with it they feel good, that's what they feel. They feel sweet and grateful and good. Real ... good. And blessed. And there's something else."

"Yes?"

"You didn't know her that well, did you, Milo?"

"Well, I wanted to know her better. If I could."

"If you could." She smirked and took a sip of the drink.

I felt on guard with her now. I got from the sound of her voice that she was going to blindside me with some meme or code word that only gay people would know. That I was the outsider as she meant to show Miranda, despite her worldly intrigues, was an outsider beyond anything I knew.

"Too bad you showed up late."

"I've thought so many times."

She didn't want to pursue that relentless tack. I got the feeling it was too simple for what she had in mind. She waited through an embarrassing silence.

"I don't care who killed her, Milo. I really don't. You believe that?"

"No."

"I don't. I just know why she was killed. She was killed for being different, Milo," the little sister said.

"I should know. I'm a little different myself. She went for being the other. The one who gets excluded because you're a little strange. And so she decided not to be strange. Not to look it. She had the looks to get away with it. But somebody knew. And decided it was too much. You don't have the right to be so strange, they said. And then came along with the plastic sack."

"Lyla, I don't find this is something I can take too much of. I cared about her."

"You know how close sisters are? We were very close. Too much. That's why she moved away. Came here. Get away from it. The it that haunts you for being what you are. For loving something that other people think shouldn't be there. Thanks for the boxes, Milo."

She inhaled from her cigarette and impatiently blew away a cone of smoke. Then she returned to reading her newspaper. I wasn't in the room anymore; as I walked out, I felt as if I'd left thirty seconds before.

I didn't call up Holly that night. I sat by the window, watching the evening darken, and I reflected on things that had nothing to do with Lyla or Opov and his crazy gang. I just felt remorseful, and like I had been thinking wrong before. Even a simple glance at the sky and the gentle ruffle of the leaves seemed to have a meaning I had missed before. I had been blaming myself, when what really mattered was not what I felt or what happened to me. I had been unkind to Holly, or thoughtless anyway, which now seemed like the same thing. I wanted to make it up to her, but just calling her and asking her to go have dinner someplace didn't seem like it was enough. And behind all that I had a strange feeling that I saw my own life as if I were outside something else looking in, as if I was beside myself, about ten feet off my right shoulder, and I was watching how I said things, how I spoke, how I looked at people, and the body I moved I manipulated by remote control. The things that gave me comfort before, like even this beer, seemed like instruments of my own capacity to make mistakes.

And I must have fallen asleep with these thoughts because it was completely dark and silent when I looked up next. And the door was ajar, I could see it from my bed. Light from the hall slanted in and nothing moved. I wanted to get up and shut the door but I didn't feel like I could move, or that I should move, even a muscle. I shouldn't lift a finger, I should just watch, because this was different now, and I had to rest back and that would be good too; that would be enough. I was free from having to lift a finger, free of all responsibility that wedded me to the world of doors and walls. Free to drift ...

As the door glided silently open, there was another light, not the one from the hall. The hall light was yellow; this light was white and it glimmered as the figure advanced, walking on bare feet under a robe so light it seemed to float in the air around her arms. It was Miranda, only she was smiling, as if she had come to make me a gift, and she would not be stopped by anything. She advanced slowly and gently, as if not to disturb a single petal of the flowers beneath her. And streaming off her hands and arms where strands of rope cut roughly at the ends. From the side of her neck hung a long piece of tape like a dangled earring. The ropes, though, were a hundred tassels draped down like the threads of some shredded gown. From her extended hands, her long white fingers reaching in the air and with the lightest movement they could rise and make her rise effortlessly in the air. Her face was streaming with sweat so much that strands of her hair stuck there, and she brought back each strand like she was spreading a veil, letting her face be seen in simple clarity. Her skin was glowing and white and on her negligee was a fine design like the window of a church, a window of leaded glass where you only saw the red circles and fine multicolored arcs at the apex and then a long thin line down the center with vacant pastel panels on each side. And below that in the window were long thin leaves and a blue lake and a single cabochon in the center with the date: 1968.

Behind her, leaning against the doorway, was Lyla, only now she was dressed in dungarees and leather boots and light flannel shirt. Cocked in her right hand was a toy pistol she leaned against her hip. The look in her eyes said she was interested in this visitation, but indifferently so, as if she was mildly curious about what was going on, but unimpressed and uncaring, as though it would change nothing, that what was happening was not just one thing but a whole progression of threads that would come together only in what she intended, and her intention was a glow all around them both.

Miranda was closer to me now, her hips level with my eyes and I looked up at her as if she were an opaque glass statue that moved and breathed and entered into communion with me because we breathed, for that moment, the same air. Her skin seemed luminous even more now, bright before the darkness of the door and the silhouette that Lyla made in the light of the hall. The two women seemed parts of different dreams, yet the ropes that streamed off Miranda and trailed into the air reached all the way back to the hall and brushed the top of Lyla's boot. Miranda's hair was gracefully disheveled in a way that would have seemed sexy at another time, but seemed only now to be the radiance of love in the person I loved. Miranda bent closer to me, as if she wanted only me to hear, but her voice was very clear and open:

"Don't anymore. You understand? You are half way there. Love a little for now but then, when it's all clear, you can't love me ever again."

21. The Surgeon

When I woke up I felt a strange sense of clarity and sadness all at once, deep sadness, so deep I was glad to wake up, to see a world where not everything was that sad. I remembered every detail as if I had painted the vision myself—and I remembered every word. I even wrote it down, because it seemed like something I should keep. Half way there, she said. When I was all the way there, I would burn the paper it was written on. Yes. It wasn't for the rest of my life; it was only for now. I just sat in the dark before dawn and thought of it for an hour. Then I went to work like any other day.

The grand jury hearing was like a locust conference in a hothouse. People were led into unventilated rooms and made to wait for nothing, it seemed, then they were led someplace else, and asked to wait there. Most of them seemed not to know where they were going. I had to wait for only an hour to be called, and when I was called, I was asked a few pointed questions.

Profumo was at one desk with a chubby senior partner. Profumo asked the questions.

I was asked to identify myself and tell how I was involved with what had happened. I had to tell them I had met Vincent on the night of the crime, but then they let me tell how I had caught his call the next day.

"What did he say when he called?"

"He asked for Miranda."

"And you said?"

"She's not here, would you like to leave a message?"

Someone on the panel snorted. Profumo's friend smiled and his eyes twinkled at the jury panel.

"Now, if you'll pardon my grammar, that was something of a smartass thing to say, wasn't it, Mr. Fyrish?"

"Yes sir, it was, but I wanted to keep him on the phone long enough to make sure I recognized his voice."

"And did you recognize his voice?"

"Yes, it was Vincent Opov."

"And you deceived him into believing that the deceased woman was not deceased."

"Well, I'd say, I didn't inform him. He seemed not to know."

"No further questions."

Profumo's friend got up. He was a little paunchy and slower paced, but he spoke easily from thirty feet away.

"You're a smart guy, Mr. Fyrish. If what you say is true, the defendant didn't know the woman was dead and so could not have killed her. Isn't that so?"

"All I know is he didn't seem to know she was dead. He called twice. At least I think it was him the first time, because the first time he hung up when I answered and then a couple minutes later he called and asked if she was there. He seemed worried about her. I was sure it was him, and it convinced me at least that he didn't do the killing."

"And you asked him if he wanted to leave a message."

"Yes, sir."

"Now, tell me, Mr. Fyrish, is it true that you discovered the dead woman at around four AM that morning but failed to call the police?"

I expected someone to object, but no one did.

"Yes sir. I fainted."

"You fainted before you could call 911?"

"Yes, sir, I had been hit on the head the night before and I had to go to the hospital and get fourteen stitches in my scalp and I had just discovered a dead person and I was feeling nauseous. I also hadn't slept much because I had to go to the hospital and that kept me up."

There was a pause.

"That's enough," Profumo's friend said raising his hand. Profumo nodded and said I could go.

I felt good about the whole thing. I had gotten out what little I could do to help Vincent and that was bound to get back to Opov some way. And then, as if from a plume of mischievous thought, from some door in the hall, out popped Wyent. Apparently he had heard the whole thing from behind a partition and he vigorously shook my hand.

"You did great," he said. "You were very convincing. The prosecution will hit a snag over that one phone call and plant doubt in the jury's mind. Trust me. We may not even have to plea bargain."

I doubted that, but I didn't say so. I left Wyent and took the subway back home.

I watched the papers for only a day, and then Vincent's story came out. He was indicted for involuntary manslaughter, which was better than anyone expected. And there was a bail hearing the next day. He was let out on bail of a paltry 50K. I sat back after work reading the paper. I felt desire again for hammer blow vengeance that most people had for the person who had committed this crime. And I couldn't help wondering if Vincent had been better off in the slammer.

But then I went over the papers again. I had been collecting them since Klondyke had got me to read the first. From wanting to hide my head in the sand, I had gone entirely the other way: reading three papers a day and cutting out the articles and marking them with the dates of each. And I began to have some doubts all over again. The articles today were not nearly so descriptive as before. Really, they weren't as angry. Some of the articles focused on the drugs found in Miranda's Manhattan apartment and the rumored connection she had to organized crime. No one said it, but the implication was there nonetheless: she wasn't an innocent victim, she was cheating the system, playing by her own rules, and maybe, if you read between the lines, just maybe, she got what she deserved from hanging out with the wrong kind of people. Vilifying the victim was actually a defense attorneys used. Who was there to stand up for her? She had money, she was beautiful and smart in her own way, so there was no outcry at the light indictment. There was no demand for a second grand jury hearing. It wasn't front page news anymore. I read the story over and I saw how they could have said much worse things about Vincent. They referred to what he did as "bondage play" and as a "consensual sexual game"—and I realized how that kind of language could soften the fiber of a vengeful crowd. Which we all were—why exclude myself?

Anyway, if he got off or got off light, it would be better for me and I could forget the whole thing about Opov and his vicious friends.

Everything seemed in place, in a way. I sat alone in my apartment a lot the next few days. We eased into the doldrum days of August like a dancer pirouetting and coming back to the same pose. Not that I wanted time to think; I couldn't think. Everything in my mind was a mass of confused rubble from the whole affair. And yet in external ways, it had all been resolved, no? And so how could it matter what happened next? There would be a trial, I would be called for that, injustice would be done (just as it was to Robert Chambers, who got a light sentence for strangling a girl in "rough sex" and laughed about it afterwards—the victim, so ran the defense's song, was really a slut.), but the whole thing had been explained away into vaporous remorse that somehow was going to dissipate like smoke in air. We couldn't mourn forever, and so we couldn't seek revenge forever. As a city, that's the way we behaved.

A few nights later, though, around midnight, the phone rang. It was Spollick.

"I'm glad I reached you, Fyrish," he said as if he was biting into a hard bagel. "Something has happened that I think you ought to know about."

"Oh, yeah? Let me guess ..."

"Don't guess. Vincent Opov got hit."

I went cold hearing this. Spollick waited silently, then he went on. I could feel he really didn't like telling me this, because he was, quite simply, warning me of impending danger. I wondered if maybe he had a delicate side to him that offset his vise-like temper. He went on.

"But he'll live. That's sort of good news. See, some woman, he said, put a gun in his back in the parking lot below his building. She made him stand up against a wall and she plugged him twice in the lower spine. Nobody heard nothing. And it must have been a silencer, but the trouble is, he was shot twice in the spine and then there was an incision, which the medical guy told me about. He'll never walk again, of course, but there's more. He'll have to use a colostomy bag for the rest of his life. The medical guy said if you make a certain kind of cut ..."

"I don't want to hear it," I said. "The bottom line is he got maimed and not killed."

"Yeah, isn't that beautiful?"

"Not the way you tell it."

"I mean, think about it. What a kick, huh? She could've killed him, but ..."

"You're enjoying this."

"Hey," said Spollick, "I can't weep for that guy. Pressure to indict will dry up now...."

What he said after that I didn't hear. I just blanked out. I kept seeing my last image of Vincent, with his arm raised to his father, in complaint maybe, but also pleading: as if he could make his father love him. And now, if it was Lyla, well, this was her revenge. Vincent wasn't dead; he was just going to wish for death a million times before he eventually drugged out or dragged himself to a lingering death. Spinal injury. No way to stop the pain sometimes.

"... and it was a small woman did it; a blond he said."

Lyla wasn't blond, but what did that matter? A wig would be good enough and could be changed as fast as a hat.

All I could think of was where my gun was and where I was in relation to the street, the cars, the overwhelming complexity of the city where a hundred people went crazy every day and suddenly felt they had the right to blow away somebody. I had to speak. Say something rather than be left alone after this call.

"Well, you must have some clues to go on," I said as if we'd met at a cocktail party.

"Oh, no way, Fyrish. Oh, we got clues. We got the slugs, hollow point, if you want to know." Spollick chortled. A big barbecue fire laugh like he had had enough beers to make him really at ease. "But no way in Hell. See, that's the subtlety of it. Not our kettle of fish, I just heard it from a friend and I wanted to pass it along to you, 'cause I know you were worried. See, it's not homicide, so it's out of our department. He got mugged, far as we're concerned. Assault with a dangerous weapon. So? Someone took his wallet. He could sue, if the assailant were ever found, but it's not like there's a city-wide manhunt going on. It's not in the same class with murder, from a legal point of view. And you know a lot of people will be saying he got what he deserved. The guy will never walk and he'll sleep in a puddle of shit every night. You think we're going to put ten guys to work on this? Ha. Ha. Well, if you want to know what I think and what the doctor thinks? It was a surgeon did it. How many people would know how to shoot someone like that?"

A nurse, I thought. Spollick went on.

"Had to be a genius, 'cause it's a lighter crime, but, in a way he's worse off. So it's not in our ball park. If he had died, then it's a different story. But now it's not a priority for anybody. They'll wait six months, when something else is on people's minds, then they'll quietly drop it. He should never have gone out in public. I know he hung around with his father for a few days and then got antsy and came back to town. He went to his own place. He should never have done that. Someone knew his car and waited for him."

"He should never have gotten out on bail."

"Yeah, that was stupid. But his attorney did that by request. The kid asked for it. They can't blame you for that."

But I helped. Helpful Milo.

"You gotta get me a permit to carry," I said.

"Aww, I don' know about that, Fyrish. I just called you up to ..."

"Listen, you owe me something. I helped you, made you look like a genius. You said so yourself."

"I don't think you're in that much danger, Fyrish. Honestly I don't. Besides, you told me Opov hates his kid."

"Parents often do. Then they murder someone who spits on the kid's shoe. I don't think you're familiar with the craziness of these people."

Spollick breathed heavy.

"Don't insult me, Fyrish. I deal with more craziness in a day than you do in a decade. You're not in danger. They could've killed you when you were out there. They let you go."

"Why'd you call?"

"I just thought you ought to know. If you carry and you get caught, I'll do something for you. But getting a permit ... not that easy anymore."

We argued about it a while without any change, so I gave up. He didn't think I was in imminent danger, so I wound up hoping he was right.

I fell back in bed in a steaming funk. Nothing could have worked out worse than this; it was revenge, all right, but a particular type of revenge, where the woman had thought about it, thought deeply. I knew it was Lyla. I had even had a dream ...

I got dressed and went up to her room. She didn't answer and the door was unlocked. She wasn't there. The keys on the bed. Her luggage gone. All that was left were the mound of clippings she had collected just as I had. Nothing was marked. A pile of newspapers. Pizza boxes stacked on the sink. In her way, she was neat. She came with a mission and she got it done. Smart Lyla, I thought.

I knocked on Tartakauer's door.

"Lyla moved out?" I asked.

"Did she?"

"Not there. Left the keys."

Then he was silent. No reaction. Yet from his voice I could tell he knew who I was talking about. It was the one moment when he seemed to have nothing at all to say.

I locked the place up and went back downstairs. I queried for information to find the phone number of Osoborne Ogile, the attorney. After a while I decided he didn't exist, attorney or anything. He wasn't in my three-year-old phone book. He wasn't anywhere.

I went back up to Miranda's and quietly shut the door behind me. I went to the hope chest and opened it up. Lyla might have taken something out, of course, but it didn't look like it. Surely she would want the Bible, to keep that in the family. But the Bible was still there. The police had probably been through it, but since I wasn't looking for a smoking gun, that might not matter.

Beneath the layers of bedding almost at the bottom, were the children's toys Miranda had collected for some, you could guess, imaginary child. I found the alphabet blocks and a toy pistol and a colored toy with a hammer and the painted rock. And then it dawned on me what I had missed before: the painted rock hadn't been bought; it had been painted by a child she already knew. It wasn't a planned toy for the future, it was a relic from some childhood passed. Her own? That didn't seem right; there was the pistol and there were no dolls or paper houses. Nothing for a girl. It was not some child in the future which she dreamed about, not some unborn creature whose sex had yet to be decided. Could it be that she had already had a child and lied to me? Possibly. Who was the child in the picture with Simone? Then I started removing things and looking deeper and it was there at the bottom I found the paintings and crayon drawings. I stared at them. Here was the naked blossom of a new eye looking, perhaps for the first time, in its own way, unique and strange, at the ever-rich world of a child. There were suns and trees and houses with stick figures; serpents and dragons. These were not things of the future, but of the past. And she had insistently closed the lid so I couldn't look further. She hadn't wanted me to know. Why not?

I put everything back and closed the lid. Then I went back down.

The next day I called a friend to get him to check on the Internet: Osoborne Ogile existed but wasn't an attorney; he fixed watches in Phoenix, Arizona.

One nice thing that happened was Follett showed up. I met him on the stoop one night, crouched like a guardian monkey outside some temple that was sacred and revered for its age and the strange rites enacted in its depths.

"Yeah, I went to Mexico," he said.

"Hot, huh?"

"Like a sonofabitch, but not in Mazatlán. And the women, man ... American secretaries are so lonely, they disassemble all boundaries. Know what I mean?"

"You went alone?"

"Yeah, I had to. Yvette wouldn't go with me. Well ... I wouldn't pay her way."

I hauled out the picture I had gotten from Yvette, since I'd gotten it when I saw he was on the stoop.

"Here's your picture," I said.

He smiled and shrugged and looked away.

"Yeah. Th ... that was a long time ago."

He still looked at the picture with fondness and stuffed it in his shirt.

"Who's the kid?" I asked.

"I don't know," he said, sucking a tooth and looking into the distance. That was all I was going to get from him. He got up to leave.

"The police were looking for you."

"Yeah, I know. I read my mail. They tell you to let them know when I showed up?"

"No. They don't even care now. You could do it just to show them a courtesy."

Yeah ..."

He blinked at the streetlights with the tick in his left eye. He was always antsy like he was thinking a hundred things all piled on top of each other.

"I gotta go," he said, but I stopped him because I had a clipping I wanted to show him. I fished it out and showed it to him. It was the best picture I had of Vincent.

"You see this guy that night?"

Follett looked at the photo closely, but you could tell he didn't want to be involved.

"I can't really say," he said. "I wouldn't want to tell the police anyway. I ain't fingering nobody. It can come back to you."

"Yeah, guess you're right. But was he going in or going out of the building?"

"I didn't see."

"When do you think it might have been?"

"Well, if it happened at all, about eleven in the evening. I remember because I remembered almost everything I saw that night after what happened to you. I had to get some sleep and that's when I turn in. Yvette was already asleep. But ... I wouldn't tell anybody but you.... Cops ask me, I tell 'em I don't know. It mighta been him. Might not. I ain't fingering nobody."

"Okay," I said and funneled the picture back in my manila envelope of clippings.

"I'd like to help you, Milo. Have you got a new job, private investigator or something? I know it ain't cop. Takes six months to become a cop."

I diffidently said it was just that I was a friend of Miranda's and wanted to find out what I could. He nodded like I had just introduced him to a vegetable he had never seen before, from some tropical island he never heard of. He was unimpressed by the taste.

"I'll see you later, Milo." He winked with his tick and shoved off the stoop and down the street.

22. Luggage

The day after that was a Saturday and I knew the Widow read the papers and would be asking soon enough when she could rent Miranda's place. I decided to bite the bullet and not wait anymore. I'd move Miranda's old stuff into Salty's room, where it could be made to fit. Maybe someone would come to claim it someday since Lyla didn't want it.

Salty's room was a mass of paint cans, odd tools, doors and sinks, curtain rods, discarded bedding, rugs left by owners in a hurry to move out. There were times when I just left a stuff from a previous tenant, but I wasn't going to leave Miranda's hope chest, her chairs and writing table. And I wouldn't leave her bed, if I could take it apart. I didn't want to move any more than I had to, but I knew that her stuff might stay there for a long time and I might need to get to other stuff sooner. The paint and roofing compound in particular, and assorted junk. Anyway, half way through this nonsense, I realized I needed tools to take Miranda's bed apart with. I'd have to walk back down when there was probably some here.

After looking around the front room, where I kept most of the stuff, I went back to Salty's kitchen, where the sink I had put in was caked with dust because I never go there, and I started looking in the doors under the sink.

And pretty soon, I noticed something that made me go cold all over: there behind an end panel, where you would never look, was a valise like Vincent had carried the night Miranda got killed. I opened it up. Inside were masses of tangled and knotted rope, frayed and cut and wadded up and left with the complex knots I had seen that night. There was the mass of tape still sticky with threads of hair. In a way it was as gruesome as finding Miranda herself. Had that been there the day I fixed Miranda's door? Of course; I hadn't looked in the Salty's kitchen in ages. And I nailed the window to the fire escape shut: no one had broken through that.

But the night of her death, the reverse-thief had come and gone that way. A child could have done it. Only a child could get in that window. Now it was obvious: a child had done her in.

I took the valise and locked up Salty's place and went down to mine. I dropped the valise in the middle of the floor and sat there thinking. Akbar came over and gave it a curious sniff, so I opened it up and emptied its contents on the rug. One sniff of the tape and he leaped back like a snake had bit him. He hissed, then licked his lips and composed himself. Soon he grew curious again and sniffed over all the things. He pawed at some of it, but he didn't want to play. Then he looked at me and meowed. He walked in a circle around the pile and sniffed some more. Then he got up on the sofa with me and calmed down. After a while of staring at the rope and not knowing what to think, I gave up my ruminations and packed the stuff back in the valise and put it behind the sofa. Akbar seemed to like that. He stretched and went to the back bedroom, circled himself and plopped down for a snooze.

I hadn't the foggiest idea what I was going to do next. For some reason, I felt vaguely sure I wasn't going to call Spollick. I was alone; I didn't have to tell a soul. Maybe I wouldn't tell anybody. Leave the dead past to the dead, whatever that meant. They can sort it out better than we can. Akbar knew what to do; he was in a doze. That was good enough for me.

But I wasn't like Akbar: I couldn't sleep with the thing in the room, no matter where I put it.

I ambled down to the shop in the cellar and began poking around. Pretty soon I found a heavy suitcase someone had left some time before I came. It was filled with old clothes, nothing of value. I aimlessly added a block of wood and solidified brushes I didn't want. Then I closed it up. There was a coil of clothesline Follett had been playing with that stormy night, and I took that and wrapped it around the suitcase through the handle several times. Each time I wrapped it I tied a massive knot to lock it in place. Then I wrapped it the other way and tightened it all the more and again put down a massive knot. At the end the thing looked like a lost suitcase which some mysterious departed tenant had fixed with the Gordian Knot of Brooklyn to hold it closed. Anyone who looked at it couldn't help but wonder if there was something important inside. You'd have to be mighty uncurious not to think so. To top it off, I grabbed a handful of dust and sawdust and sprinkled that over it. Then I went out on the stoop and sat with it across my knees.

It was hot but there were people about. Tommy and Gerald were arguing over how to construct a kite, but soon Tommy became disinterested and looked up at me.

"Whatcha got, Milo?"

"Old suitcase I found stuck away in the cellar. Left by some poor guy who said he'd pick it up someday, I guess."

I leaned back and surveyed the sun-splattered line of houses up to the playground. I emptied my mind and thought as little as possible. Tommy stepped closer, looking at the suitcase.

"You watch it for me, okay?"

"Sure," he said and I went in and got a beer. I took a little extra time. I stroked Akbar a few times, waking him from his nap. I looked out the front window from behind the shade to see if anyone was making off with the item in question. No one was. After a time I went out and sat on the stoop again and drank my beer and yawned.

"Aren't you gonna open it up and see what's in it?" Tommy wanted to know.

"Yeah, well, these knots are pretty tight. I really need a marlinspike to open them up."

"What's a marlinspike?"

Gerald got curious and came up to the stoop to look. I picked at one of the knots but made very slow progress.

"Why don't you just cut the rope?" Tommy said. "It's no good anyway."

"Well, I don't have a knife," I said, still picking away and never looking up.

"Get a kitchen knife. My mother's got lots of knives."

"All I have is butter knives."

"Gerald has a knife."

"Oh yeah?" I said without looking up.

"Yeah, go on and show him," Tommy said.

The more I got into the intricacy of what I was trying to do, the more I felt the shadow of Gerald coming closer.

"Cut it for him, Ger."

"Yeah, if I had a good knife ..." I said continuing with the picking and pulling.

"Here," Gerald said and he pulled out a folding knife that locked back. "You want me to cut it?"

"Sure, if you would," I said, shoving the suitcase forward.

Gerald's knife went through the ropes with easy snaps on each one. The blade you could see was razor sharp and had a serrated portion at the base just for cutting lines. When he had finished, Gerald pinched the key and folded the knife back. It disappeared in his pocket. There were no cuts or scars anywhere on his hands.

"How much a knife like that cost?"

Gerald smiled while looking down. He didn't want to look at me. "Fifteen dollars. Maybe twenty."

"Your mother gives you money like that?"

Gerald didn't answer right away.

"Sort of," he finally said.

"That's a pretty big knife for a kid your age. How old are you?"

"Six."

"He's not six," said Tommy.

"Does your mother know you have that knife?"

"No. She doesn't care."

"What's in the suitcase?" Tommy piped up.

"Who else has a knife like that?" I asked. I wished Louis was there but I didn't see him.

"Nobody."

"Open it up," Tommy said. I handed it to him. He dumped the contents out on the sidewalk and then kicked them into the gutter in disgust. At that moment the homeless man with the strange tan and the torn yellow shirt came up the street and then walked back. Then he came again and made it as far as my stoop. He reached out.

"Change?"

I fished out a dollar and gave it to him. He nodded his thanks from the waist down.

"Spare change?"

"Take some clothes," I said. "Cold weather's coming."

He understood me enough to look through the contents of the suitcase that had just explained the world to me. I wondered if Sam still thought I was like this man. He held his hand out to Tommy, who returned an obstinate "No!"

Gerald turned to go, but then stopped and looked at me as if for the first time.

"You won't tell my mother?" he asked.

"Of course not," I said. "A man has a right to have his own things without having to wonder about the jealous thoughts of other people. Especially his mother."

Gerald smiled a kind of private little smile like I had never seen before. It seemed to carry a glow of inner joy welled up from his child's heart. He nearly stumbled down the stoop, then ran on as if suddenly released. By so few words.

Small things make a difference, I reflected. I watched the man in the torn shirt back away with some shirts, and then go forward, and then back away again.

23. Five Keys

I ran down to Leonard's and found he was just closing up.

"Hey, Leonard, I got a question for you."

"Yeah, Milo. Anything. How's your head? You really got whacked looked like. Not much blood though. That's why I thought maybe you were dead 'cause dead people don't bleed. I'm glad to see you're alive. But what is it, your question?"

"Did any of the kids in my building ever have keys made?"

"Your building? Sure. That kid that was playing chess the night you got clocked. I remember him because he asked for five copies of the same key one day a few months ago. I asked him why so many? He said because he's afraid he might lose one, since he's always losing things. So. It's not illegal to sell keys to minors? I don't think so."

"Any of the other kids?"

Leonard had to think a bit.

"Kids don't buy keys usually. It's rare. I think I'd remember it. No. No kids in this block. I'm pretty sure."

"Thanks, Leonard."

"What's the problem? Somebody stealing stuff?"

"Uh ... yeah, little stuff from one of the vacant apartments. It started with soap and toilet paper but now it's advanced to water fixtures and paintings right off the wall. You wouldn't believe. I'll just change the locks. All you can do."

"Hey, when we gonna get together again down in your cellar and have a few beers? Maybe watch some TV or play some poker. Whaddayou say?"

"Well, next time it rains, for sure. Maybe sooner."

"Or if my old lady says one more word about my key business, I'll rent that apartment and move out tonight. I'll call you."

"Gotta run right now. Thanks."

"Okay. Any time."

Kids. Five copies of one key. What would he need that for? But in a way it fitted, if a kid valued something a lot, whatever it was, and he felt unsure about what he might lose, then maybe it made sense. He would tuck one away someplace and then another in a secret place no one would look. And so on. Anyway it certainly seemed like Gerald had more money than other kids.

As I came into the vestibule, another kid was just going in. Louis, whom I hadn't seen anywhere on the street.

"Hey, Louis, you got a minute?"

"What? Sure, Milo."

Louis was older than Tommy and Gerald, by maybe a year. But somehow he seemed less secure and so he hung around with Tommy and Gerald, maybe because he couldn't find anyone older that was congenial.

"You have to be someplace?"

"I want to be home in time to watch *The Simpsons*."

"Just take a minute. I want to show you something."

We went up to Miranda's apartment and Louis looked around, especially at the big empty space. He spun around, swinging his arms.

"Woooooo!"

"This won't take a minute," I said, and I spread out the paintings on the floor. "You ever seen anything like that?"

He looked at them and then turned away as if in thought. He turned again and shook his head. He did recognize them, I could tell, but he didn't want to say so. I had left the door open. He could run out any minute if I said something too insensitive. But what did he see? I sat on the floor and relaxed back against the wall. I rolled the painted rock across the floor. He picked it up. He paused a long time; I could feel that every second was in my favor because nothing was going to bring him closer to telling the truth than the simple freedom to wait.

"It's probably Gerald's. See, it's a secret," he said finally. "Nobody is supposed to know. But now ..." He paused.

"I won't tell a soul," I said. And I meant it. Maybe, because I wasn't about to lie to this child, he came around to trusting me. He held the rock in his hand and came over and handed it to me.

"It's a secret."

"Okay. What secret?"

And then I sensed that he actually would tell me, that he probably had always wanted to tell somebody.

"The secret is ... that Gerald says ... that Miranda is his mother. That's the secret. See?"

"Well, okay, um ... then who is Bernice?"

"Oh, she's his mother mother. But Miranda was his 'best

mother'. See? His 'best mother', he says. Because when he was really small, she taught him to paint and she took him on trips and things and he would tell us about where he'd been. And he painted these paintings right here on this floor. I watched one time, but after that she kept the door closed."

"How old was he then?"

"I don't know," he said giggling at the stupid question it was.

"Where did he go with her?"

"Places. Parks I guess. They go and eat. Uh … to the beach. She was his babysitter. She's still his babysitter, see. I mean she was. He said we shouldn't tell about Miranda because his other mother wasn't supposed to know. But she did know. She got Miranda to babysit in the first place. See?"

I paused. I was beginning to see.

"Yeah," I said. "And I'll keep it a secret. It's our secret."

"It's just I promised not to tell. But now Miranda's gone to Heaven, what's the difference?"

"I won't tell anyway."

"Can I go now?"

"Sure."

He walked out and I didn't thank him because I didn't want to put any more weight on what he said than there was already.

The whole thing was taking a stranger turn now and I wondered if anyone had ever seen Miranda taking Gerald for an excursion. But then I thought of the pictures with Simone and the infant, and the shadow of whoever took the picture. The child in those photos had to be Gerald. He had known her since before he could remember. And the two of them kept it secret. Why?

I had to talk to someone, and so I got the valise and went up to Sam's and knocked on the door. He wasn't there. For some reason, it felt urgent and I didn't want to wait around. Who else did I trust? Not Follett. Not Ms. Peretti. Tell her and the whole street would know. Not Holly, because I wanted to keep her mind as pure as I could and I didn't want her involved in the dark stuff I was caught in. Who, then?

24. The Alchemist

Tartakauer. He had seen everything. He might keep a secret. I went up to his place and knocked. The second time I knocked hard. He came to the door and beckoned me in. His face was frosty with a three-day beard. I closed the door behind me.

"You read the papers about Miranda?" I asked.

"Yes." He cleared his throat. "Terrible thing. It's best forgotten, I suppose, but it's a hard thing to get out of my mind. I keep imagining the horrible helplessness of that woman."

"I met the father of the guy who did it."

"Hmm? And did you find that pleasant encounter?"

"No. But the guy didn't come back and untie her. It had to be somebody else."

Tartakauer nodded thoughtfully. He was willing to listen if I had a story to tell, but his skepticism was implicit, always there, no matter what I said. I held up the valise.

"I found this in Salty's apartment. Hidden under the sink."

"And so?"

I opened it and showed him the jumble of rope and tape. He reached in and thoughtfully fingered it. It seemed to mean a lot to him, the factor of touch, as though the touch of something told about its history as well as what was inside it. He was a doctor after all. He muttered softly as he looked it over.

"Hmm. So the killer was able to hide it there. And saw some reason for doing so. But if they got the guy, it doesn't matter now. Unless you want to make more trouble. Milo, is that your intention? Make more trouble?"

"I'm not so sure. The guy that got blamed for it didn't do it, I'm pretty sure of that. I even testified and said as much. That's why they let him out. Not in his best interest, turns out."

"Why'd he get blamed?"

"He tied her up."

"But didn't kill her?"

"No."

Tartakauer pointed down at the jumble of rope.

"Then this is the killer. Whoever did this."

"I think a kid did it."

Tartakauer eyed me with a clinician's caution. If I'd suggested radical surgery, he'd have had such a look.

"It's only kids can get into Salty's room."

"Mm, maybe so," he said. "But that only means a kid hid this. Doesn't mean a child killed her. I don't believe Gerald would do that."

"Nobody believes it before it happens. Every killer was normal as grass before the crime. You read about it all the time. Thing to figure is, why untie her after she's dead?"

"Interesting question," Tartakauer said. He walked to the window and stared out past his curtains. "I can see why you didn't go to the cops yet. You want to solve this yourself."

"Yeah, I do. But frankly, getting this in the papers and the social worker bureaucracy, I'm not sure that would be good for the kid. For one thing, it could have been an accident. Whatever she went through, whoever put her in that position, she wasn't expected to die. Perhaps nobody wanted it."

"Yes," he said, pointing at me. "And whatever it was, the kid might be scared enough already. You're right there. But why untie her, you ask? Actually, I can tell you."

"Can you now?"

He strode to his bookcase.

"Where is it, now?" he mused, looking over the shelves. He pulled out a book and paced over the rug, thumbing pages.

"Hm. Yes. Here it is. It should be read by a real poet, but I can read it well enough.

> Before me floats and image, man or shade,
> Shade more than man, more image than a shade,
> For Hades' bobbin bound in mummy-cloth
> May unwind the winding path;
> A mouth that has no moisture and no breath
> Breathless mouths may summon;
> I hail the superhuman;
> I call it death-in-life and life-in-death."

Tartakauer paused and looked up at me with a delighted smile. "Isn't that marvelous? You can find everything in Yeats."

"Yeats. I don't think Gerald read that."

"No, no, Milo, you don't understand. People follow things they do not know. The part about the bobbin, don't you see? Here, let me show you."

He set down the book and rummaged in a chest on his desk. Eventually he pulled out a little doll, as if he kept an inventory of magical charms, which I guess he did. What he presented to me was a small white doll. He held it up to me, smiling. I saw it actually was a little mummy, all wrapped in white gauze.

"Look at this."

He twirled the thing in his finger and the doll spun down, unraveling the strip of gauze till it fell at last on the floor.

"Yeah, so?"

"Why did the Egyptians wrap the dead like that?"

"I don't know."

"Yeats knew. Because at the last day, they'd be unwound and brought back to life again."

I shrugged at this and looked around his kitchen alcove.

"You have a beer?"

"Don't get distracted, Milo."

"Look, Doc. None of this has to do with Miranda getting tied up and killed and then untied. Gerald, if he did it, knows ferbonk about Egyptians."

Tartakauer held up a finger.

"He has a child's mind, Milo. So had the Egyptians. What do we see in these relics but some pathetic grasping to refute death? But it wasn't pathetic to them. It made perfect sense. Death went with wrapping. For if death could be wrapped up, then the wrapping caused death, and life was intentionally impeded. Then, death didn't just happen. I had been willed—and so the flow of life could be released and time reversed and death undone. If you undid what you did, you'd bring the dead back to life. It's not the way you and I think. It's the way a child thinks. You're right. A child probably did it, then felt remorse, and then went back and tried to reverse the crime. You have to think like a child, which is difficult for us smart people. And many adults also want to reverse the past. Why do we want revenge, but to deny the past? Well, of course. Why would people always be saying that you can't change the past? Because in some way we need to be told. Many people, if they knew it, have an unresolved prior question they keep circling back to, but never quite meet. You might too."

I turned away from Tartakauer.

"Maybe."

"And besides," he went on, "why do we solve mysteries, but for the hidden fantasy it will bring the dead back to life?"

How I admired Tartakauer then, for in his aged way he was filled with childlike thoughts. I sat back on his sofa and stared at the valise. Now I no longer liked my own idea. But at least I wasn't alone.

"What, Milo? Are you depressed?"

"I dunno. I'm not sure I want to do anything right now."

"Well, you have to do something. You have to call the police."

"Maybe."

Tartakauer repackaged the little doll and stuffed it away.

"You know," he said philosophically, "there could have been another reason for preserving the rope this way."

"What's that?"

"This stuff may have had an emotional meaning to the person. Child, as you say. He may have wanted to preserve it. A valued remembrance, or a frightening one. Whatever, it could have been important not to lose it forever. I think that was so. I think the killer had a peculiar mentality that would make him susceptible to feelings ordinary people might not have."

Tartakauer made a long low sound from deep in his chest. I looked up at him. I was glad he'd put away the poetry book.

"He's crazy, you mean? Well ... I can't think of anything more reasonable than that. Did you know that Gerald knew Miranda almost from infancy?"

"Yes, I did. She babysat for the kid's mother, who works. I would sometimes see them going out. You could tell, from the way they talked, that she was almost a second mother for Gerald. She loved that child. But she spoke to me and let me know she wanted it kept quiet. So ... I didn't tell anyone. And when they went out they would go separately, so people on the other floors would never see them together. So I said nothing, even to the police when they came the other day. Why involve a child?"

He looked at me and shrugged. It was a closed book to him.

"Well," I said, "Gerald had a key to Miranda's apartment."

I expected Tartakauer to be doubtful or puzzled by that, but he surprised me.

"Oh, he did," he said. "I saw him use it. That child sometimes used her apartment to get away by himself. It was his when she was away, it seemed to me. But I don't think either of them wanted his mother to know, so naturally, I kept my mouth shut about it."

What a strange man, I thought. He did the exact opposite of so many other people, who couldn't wait to tell some juicy story to whoever would listen. There were such people, I reflected, non-gossipers. They just didn't bore you with stories and so you never knew.

"You really didn't tell the police?"

"I heard nothing, Milo. What was I to tell them? That she had a friendship with a child who lived in the building? I am not going to fill the air with nonsense, Milo. And you shouldn't either."

"The child carries a knife that could cut through steel."

"Ah. So now you know he did this," he said pointing to the valise. He fingered it with that delicate European way of giving soft attention to hard detail. He couldn't help fingering again the frayed ends of rope. They meant something to him because of their secret.

"You may be right," he added thoughtfully. His eyes dwelt downward as if to some incredible depth. "His mother may have poisoned his mind against Miranda and the child turned against her when she was tied up. Children are capable of great cruelty, we all know that."

He sat back and stared at the valise. He breathed heavily, as if his mood had sunken into reflective gloom.

"I hate to turn in a child, Milo. But there are psychoanalysts who could make a difference for such a child. In any case, I suppose you haven't told the police, or they would have confiscated this thing for evidence. That's the next step. It's no good just showing it to me."

I felt a bolt behind my eyes go icy hard when he said that.

"I told you because I think I can trust you," I said, enunciating each word. "I'm not going to the police. I'm not turning in a child."

He patiently shrugged, as if there were no argument to what I said. There was no dispute, in his mind.

"You have to. The child will be burdened by the guilt all his life. The only way he can exorcise it from himself is to let it be known. Besides, you don't want to be accused of concealing evidence, do you?"

"I can put it back where I found it. Nobody knows except you and my cat. My cat doesn't like police."

He shrugged again, but his face was reddening now.

"You have to … you can't …"

"I'm not turning in a child," I said again.

Tartakauer looked at me as if he didn't believe what he was hearing. His whole manner changed; from stating obvious facts, he now had to turn to a harder task, convincing me that I was a fool.

"You're serious?"

"I am," I said. "And if you call the police, I'll get rid of this thing and deny the whole business."

"Oh, Milo. Think of what you're saying."

I was. I could win a standoff with Spollick and Tartakauer both homing in on me with their missiles of hard-to-deny facts. Spollick would be half on my side; he had the killer already. What did he need this for?

"Look," I said, "I came to you to share this, not to blow it up in my face. What kind of friend are you?"

"Milo, I am your friend, but I'm also a human being and a crime of this magnitude … that a child could do that … You have to bring it to light."

"And what about this," I said, since this was the last arrow in my quiver, "What if somebody else killed Miranda and then the child untied her afterwards and hid the evidence?"

"Why would he do that?"

"You just explained it. Like you say, psychotics and people with infantile minds sometimes think they can reverse a crime by retracing it and unwinding the sequence of events back to where they started. Spollick thought that. It's why people return to their crimes. Well, you're saying a child might think that way."

"Yes, of course."

"What if there's even a chance of that, that he didn't kill her but only tried to undo the crime? You say that's how kids think. Then are you right to let the whole thing into the open? Remember, he's just a kid and how smart is a kid going to be in defending himself?"

Tartakauer's eyes got really big.

"If that's even possible, then the police should be brought in right away. The real killer would be at large. He could kill again."

"A serial killer?"

He shrugged.

"Someone is guilty," he said simply. It was a mathematical theorem to him. "That's even worse, Milo, because an adult cannot be healed. The adult will do it again."

"I don't like involving the kid," I said.

Tartakauer wiped his forehead with a towel. He kept the air conditioner off even in this heat.

"Milo, you're playing cop, and that's not your job. You let the police know or I will go to the police. By telling me, showing me this thing you found, you have made me an accessory after the fact, and I respect the law of this country. No, not this country, of my country ..."

He said it with deep, even reverent, conviction I had never seen before. His eyes trailed away like he might be lost and wondering how much to say. He was glancing every which way for some way out of this. I had no idea what I could expect from him. We sat for a long time in complete silence. I felt that anything more I said would only make matters worse. I had probably made a mistake coming to him like this, but in fact he had surprised me. I don't know what I expected, but I hadn't expected things to go this way. He slowly lay back on his couch and breathed deeply as if he might go to sleep. But his voice came out from deep in his chest, so deep it seemed at first like he was humming a song to himself.

"You know, Milo, I never told you, because I never tell other people about it, but do you know how I came here, to America, to my country?"

He paused, gathering his voice, because obviously I didn't know.

"When Hitler had control of Germany, in 1938, I realized he would start a war. I wasn't the only one who thought this, but I was the only one of my friends who knew he would lose. I argued with them. They wouldn't listen. I said Hitler would unify his enemies, something no leader ought to do, and that in the end he would lose. They did it in 1918, and they would do it again. Hitler was not a careful diplomat; he was very daring, an undeniable genius, but only an inspired genius, not a diplomatic one. None of them believed me. I am not Jewish; I would not go to the camps if I kept my mouth shut. But I was in love with a young woman, and she was Jewish. And I said we ought to leave for America and get married. She agreed to marry me, but her whole family was in Bremen, and she would not leave if they would not leave.

And we had horrible fights about it, so bad we were screaming at each other, and I would break down in the end and fall on the floor and hug her knees because I loved her so much. We talked and talked, and finally she gave in, if I would go first to America and make a home for us. Because of her parents' suggestion, it was best we got married then. I said I would. Her family tried to hold her back but she said she would disobey them, this once. I remember the last time I saw her; I was getting on the boat with my luggage, which was very little, and I stumbled on the pier and went sprawling like the ignorant fool I was. And she knelt down beside me and held my head in her hands to make sure I wasn't hurt, which I wasn't. But I remember how she looked down at me, the love in her eyes, so open and free and yet with no fear. Absolutely no fear, only love. I will take that look in her eyes to the grave.

"I went to America and we exchanged letters for twelve months. I got a job right away, and I got an apartment. But she kept telling me there were new reasons she could not come, or come later, and I believed them all. Then, one week, I got no letter. I didn't wait. I wrote to a friend and asked him to go to her house and ask her family if she was on her way here.

"My friend wrote back that the house where she lived was occupied by a German family that had just moved in. They would tell him nothing. They laughed at him for wanting to know. But the neighbors knew, and they told him. A van had arrived one day and everybody in the house had been made to leave. The police, not the Gestapo. And she and her family took only the little luggage they could carry. That was all. And then, in the remainder of the letter, a long harangue, my friend upbraided me for deserting the Reich, and for forsaking the heritage that was my due as a true German. I knew he was wrong but in some deeper way, I felt very sad. Because in some way he was right. I felt it terribly all through the war.

"I prayed night and day for a letter from her, but it never came. After the war, I found out what had happened: she had been sent to at Bergen-Belsen after her last letter to me. From there she was later sent to Auschwitz. I made the best of my life. But I never was happily married. So you see I was very prescient. Very smart. And you see how I traded a quick death, or great guilt and hardship, for a long comfortable life. So you see what I gave to come to my country, my new country. I won't disrespect her laws."

I sat in silence as the clouds built up over the house tops. They were pink and orange now and the light shed a strange glow over his snowy face. He could say no more. His mouth hung open like a cored plum. I could say nothing either.

"I give you a day," he said. He waved his hand the way tired old men do. We both understood.

I buttoned up the valise and walked out, shutting the door softly behind me.

25. Denouement

Back down in my apartment, I hid the valise, just to get it out of sight, but I couldn't sit still with my thoughts. I called Holly and begged her to come over, that I would get food, we just had to stay in that night, that I needed her just to be there with me. Miraculously, it seemed at the time, she said yes. But she wanted to get the food, using, in there somewhere the phrase, "... because you don't know how to shop ..."

Whatever, I thought.

I went out on the stoop and found Gerald mending his kite from his latest excursion to the playground. I sat silently for a while and then ever so gently, asked Gerald if he wanted to play chess. I showed him the pawn Sam had given me. His face brightened at the sight of it.

"Perfect," he said, and he went to chase down his board and pieces. We played for an hour before Holly showed up. Gerald beat me three out of three, but was willing to keep playing as long as I would.

"Keeps the men out of the kitchen," Holly said as if to herself. She had a bag of stuff and pretty soon we had a delicious dinner all laid out for us. I resigned the game, which I was losing anyway, and then Holly rushed over to Gerald and enfolded him in her embrace. She kissed all over his face and hugged him for a long moment which I would have thought he would reject, as too "mushy". But he did nothing of the kind. He seemed ebullient as if he had just experienced that warmth and closeness for the first time.

We had a table-size bottle of wine, hamburgers and crepes, cheese and desert, the whole bit. She even brought tooth picks that don't bend. It was a great meal, and best of all, she didn't make a flurry to clean it up right away. I asked Gerald where his mother was.

"Work," he said.

"When's she coming home?"

"I don't know."

Then I knew he was lying. A kid like that would know to the minute when his mother was due home.

"Well, I was going to do some fix-up in Salty's place," I said. "But I wasted the whole afternoon looking for the key. I don't know where I put it. Say, Gerald, you ever hear of some kids playing around in Salty's place without me knowing?"

"I don't know."

But the way he said it, quick and like a singsong answer he gave to any question that was too close for comfort, let me know he was lying about that too.

He did know. But I was at a dead end if he didn't want to tell me.

"Let me show you something," I said, and I went and hauled out the valise. I sat down on the couch and emptied the contents on the floor. Holly looked at it curiously from behind her wine glass. Gerald's face grew very red.

"You know about this?" I asked.

"No."

"Found it in Salty's place. Somebody put it there and just left it. Had to be somebody who … I don't know … I thought maybe you'd know."

I was looking at the rope and pawing at it with my hand, trying to convince him that I wasn't going to look him in the eye, but when I did, Gerald's face was deep red and tears were coming down his cheeks.

"I don't know. I don't know," he shrieked. Holly immediately moved to comfort him, exactly as if she knew what was going on. When he saw her coming he almost leaped into her arms, and his face opened with tears and a high moaning squeal.

"I don't know. I don't know," he went on when he could catch his breath. Holly looked at me, beseeching me with her eyes to put away this pile of trash that was causing such an uproar. I started packing the rope and tape back into the valise and had just snapped it shut when a knock came at the door.

I went and opened up. Bernice, with a look of pinched anger, strode past me as if the place wasn't even mine.

"I thought I heard you. So here's where you've been hiding," she said to Gerald, not even glancing at the rest of us. "I've been worried sick about you."

But oddly, Gerald just crept deeper into Holly's warmth. He hid his face, not wanting even to see what was coming next.

"Come on," Bernice said, reaching out to take his hand. "Let's go home."

But the kid wouldn't go and Bernice just repeated herself like a mechanical clock, her voice dead and insistent, as if nothing around her was of any concern whatever, I and Holly didn't exist, just Gerald. She bent next to his ear and said in a loud whisper:

"You come with me and you come now."

She whispered it as if that would leave Holly and me in the dark about what was going on. But her whispering didn't work now as it had before. She plucked his arm off Holly's chest, but Gerald was too strong for her and he snapped his arm away and tightly held it to his chest so she couldn't get her fingers around it. Holly looked at Bernice like she had never before seen such behavior. This was the crazy farm. Even as she tried to coax Gerald to go with his mother, Gerald wouldn't let go, and it wasn't clear he could be pried away.

Bernice tried again, her fingers grasped more sharply now, but again Gerald held on. He had his nether hand gripped on some part of Holly's clothing I couldn't see, and that was next to the table where Bernice couldn't easily reach. But when her hand flipped back from his wrist, I saw the scratches immediately bleed. Maybe that was what triggered me. I did the unthinkable, I stepped between the child and his mom.

"Bernice, I think there's something different going on here. I think you ought to pay attention."

She turned and yelled full voice at me, all her pent-up anger, so long dammed up behind the pretense she had molded into a wall around herself and her son, burst out into my face: "Pay attention to what? Are you going to take my child away from me? Who are you? WHO ARE YOU?"

I think she would have scratched my eyes out, but I insolently put the valise between us and snapped it open. She saw and her eyes got big as shiny eggs.

"I think this changes things, just for now," I said. I watched her for a moment since she was speechless. I motioned at Gerald.

"Let him sleep and then I'll bring him up to you. I promise. I just think we ought to have a talk, or else I'm calling the police. Now you let Gerald lie there and sleep and we'll go up to your place and we can have a quiet talk about what we're going to do. The police don't know yet, or even care. But it might matter. They don't have to know, if we talk this over. And then I'll bring Gerald up to you. I promise. Is that a deal?"

Her face broke to a shimmer of anger and a mask of pain and hate. Her mouth was open but she couldn't speak. She nodded and turned away to the stairway. She made like she was leading me as she went up several steps. Ms. Clamper poked her head out the door and asked in a plaintive whine if anything was wrong. I closed the valise and took it. Holly shut the door behind us. Bernice was stolid till we reached her place. Once inside she seemed distracted. One after another she picked up objects on her dresser and then set them down. She aimlessly looked around, as if she might take up a mop or start dusting.

"What have I done?" she muttered. "What have I done?" Over and over she repeated it as if she knew there was no possible answer. "My own child. Hates me. My own son. What have I done? I didn't mean to …" Then her mouth was open as if it was never meant to be used for words.

We walked through a short corridor to the bedroom. On the bed I plopped the valise, and Bernice said: "I have to get tissues. I'll be just a minute."

I was up and beside her like a terrier.

"What are you doing, Milo?" she asked wiping her face. "I'm not going to hurt you."

"That's right, you're not," I said.

But her hand was reaching for the drawer to the dresser. I opened the drawer, and there was a box of Kleenex. I fumbled in behind that and came up with an empty clip for an automatic. I stuck it in my pocket.

"Where's the gun?"

"Threw it away," she said wearily. "Of course, when Gerald … I'd have thrown that away if I knew it was there."

I looked in the other drawers, even in the back, and found nothing.

"There's no gun," she said with a forced laugh. "You're just suspicious because you think I'm unpredictable, is that it? Well, I'm not so unpredictable." She was crying.

She took the box of Kleenex. I straightened up and tried to relax.

"What have you got to drink?"

She had some wine and I poured two glasses. There was no couch so we sat on the bed, like two lovers who'd just had a spat.

I kicked off my shoes and with one foot pushed the valise to the far edge of the bed. We were silent for several minutes while she went ahead crying: inconsolable, total, uncomprehending, lost in her forest that I had just invaded.

"I've had no let up," she said. "I'm always tired. I hate my job, people are so mean. A woman alone over forty is dog meat. Not just here. Everywhere. I'm not pretty. I have this scar. No one wants a woman with a kid. I have no time. He's growing so fast. I can't catch up. I try to speak to him, he just looks at me with his eyes … his eyes are full of hate. But it's not like ordinary hate; it's that his hate never dies away. He doesn't trust me; he lies without a thought of how it hurts me; if something happens to him, I'm the last to know. I'm an unfit mother, you're probably thinking."

She stopped herself. Maybe she was saying way too much to a man she hardly knew, not a shrink. For all she knew I might blab anything to anyone.

"I won't tell a soul," I said.

"You won't tell them about that?" she cried and her hand flashed out at the valise, as if to drop napalm on it.

"Not even that," I said. And I almost added: "If you tell me the truth." But I didn't say that. I caught myself. What did I deserve of her truth? And was the truth something you get closer to if you bargain for it? I could still destroy the valise and defy Tartakauer and let him stew in his own lifelong juice, if he wanted to go to the police. Knowing Spollick, I doubted that tough nut cop would listen for very long.

"I'll destroy it," I said. She was only silent. Her face was darkened and crumpled with pain.

"Where you from, Bernice?"

She gulped her wine. She was trying to get out whatever ghastliness she must have been living with, but she also must have felt some need to talk.

"Oklahoma. Small town. My father was a preacher who drank too much, lost his wife and congregation and married a woman who had property. She hated me. When I was fourteen a girlfriend told me I wasn't even his child, I was adopted. I cried all the way home. It was true, they said. She even knew where the adoption papers were and she showed them to me. My real parents just disappeared and someone said they died in a fire, but I don't think it was true. I hated fire after that. My first husband died. He had cancer all through his body. Then I met another man and we came to New York and he was Gerald's father. That's when we moved into this place. The night I went into labor, he laid down in Central Park on a bench and overdosed. The nurses wouldn't tell me for three days. Afraid I would freak out. All I wanted was to be happy with my child. For us to be happy together.

"I met Miranda on the train. It was like nothing I ever knew. We fell into each other's arms. I got her into this place. We spent nights together. We loved our bodies. It was a time of peace I'd never known. We loved … Gerald was just a toddler. She was good to him. We were perfect together. She kept him on days I worked. We needed no man. We were perfect.…"

At the word "perfect" her face broke like a paper vase and she couldn't speak. She was silent for a long time and I waited. Then without warning her body bent in sobs. She wiped the tears sometimes and sometimes she let them go. Finally she straightened up and looked around at me and then quickly away.

"And we used to talk, and she told me she liked to be tied up. I did it a couple of times, but I really just wanted to be with her. I didn't care about the rest. She felt it was a big release, as if she was free for the first time, released in time and not lost, not aware, nothing, a kind of bliss she said. She felt the extreme of being exposed and safe at the same time. It was like an embrace, she said, a special embrace. And all her anger and fear, she could let go of it then. She wanted to be held back, to have no freedom at all. It was like throwing herself off a cliff and not knowing how she would land, but at the same time trusting that she would survive. Even with me it was a way to get off. I said it sounded like suicide and she said yes. She said it was like a little suicide so you didn't have to do the big one. And she always felt better afterwards. Somehow she knew Vinnie. That was that."

"And Miranda was beautiful, always had money, and she had time for Gerald. She could take him places I couldn't. And she had men friends who could act like a father. I thought that was good and I was grateful. But then, one day, I started to feel, I don't know why, I had this crazy fear that I was losing my son. I had lost him. I started to realize they were really becoming attached to each other. That he really loved her more than me, his own mother. And she let him play in her apartment all day. She even had a special mat where he could sleep. And I'm sure when he got past four she gave him money, but he wouldn't tell me. And as he grew ... so fast I couldn't keep up ... she knew what he liked when I had no clue. I would try to pry it out of him, but he would just clam up with me. I'd come home tired and depressed, but I always tried to manage a smile for him. I tried everything. I tried and tried. Everything I could think of. It made no difference. We'd fight about the way he dressed, junk food he eats, and that's all we do: fight or else silence. His silence is awful. It's more cutting than words. I don't understand it. I live my whole life for him. I tell him I love him a hundred times a day. I tell him he means everything to me. Do you think he hears?"

I had the feeling that I was listening to someone else talk, to a stranger who had just walked into the room and by silent insistence made the real woman keep silent while this intruder spoke for her in her bony bare legged skin. In this pleading I detected the voice of another child, a little girl, abandoned and alone, desolated by loss she could never agree to and which she could never tell. But now Bernice seemed to grow wistful. It was that other person speaking.

"And now we're no longer lovers. He hates me. I try to talk to him, he's silent. If I give him a gift, something I think he'll like—anything, he goes and sells it. I don't know where I stand. Why, I just found out the other night, he even has a key to her apartment!"

She said that and then bent double holding her sides. Finally she looked at me as if she wasn't sure I had heard and maybe if she didn't say it again, it would get unsaid and go away. She straightened and let out a deep sigh.

"And that's it," she said with a gasp as if that settled something. She drank her wine, her hand trembled so most fell on her shirt. The time between us was an iceberg over endless seas.

"Yes, he had a key," I said.

"You're saying I didn't get the last one, is that it?"

"Yeah. I'm saying that. I'm saying that after you went up to Miranda's, you left and locked the door. You must have gone for a walk, 'cause you needed time to think, I imagine. Because I saw you coming in about the time I did, around four AM. You didn't go to work, although you said you did. And then when you were out, Gerald went up to visit her. Which he wanted to do, now you were gone."

"He was asleep when I came back," she said. Then she started to mumble: "Oh, oh, Milo. He'll listen to me tomorrow, after he's slept ... we can make up ... can't you? ... sometimes I just wish he was one again ... that's all I hope for ... everything's alright if you can just smile ... I love him. He didn't kill her. Gerald wouldn't. He didn't. He ..."

"No, he didn't," I said. "You're right there. He had no desire to kill her. Someone else did that."

As I said that I was ready if she tried to stare me down. She did look back, just for an instant, but what I saw there was no defiant killer, only a frightened woman, a frightened little girl who was afraid I would hit her, so afraid she cringed as if I would. She put her hand in front of her face. She was washed in tears and mumbling.

"I went there looking for him. And there she was on the floor like that. And I thought: do it now. It's so simple. Do it and it's over. Just gently, while she's lying there. That will solve so much. Oh. Don't hit me. Don't hit me! I'm not ... I loved ... her ..."

Her face made itself over, as if she had just put makeup on. She even smiled.

"Oh, Milo. Don't think bad of me. Don't disappoint me. You're not going to talk to anybody, are you?"

I held back. Some tiny bolt of certainty.

"No, I don't think I will. No. There's no point. Gerald would be without a mother."

I was naive enough to think she'd be grateful when I said that, but when I looked around, her face was shapeless as if I'd hit her with a club. Her lips were going up and down with no words.

"You like me, don't you, Milo? Could I just lean over on your shoulder?"

I had to look away to keep from letting her see how unready I was.

"Yes."

It was enough. She did lean over. I slid down and cupped her head in the hollow of my arm. She nuzzled in like a little child.

"So sweet. So sweet to be like this. I like your shirt. You have no idea, how long it's been ..."

She was right there. I had no idea. But I decided: if people are hurt badly enough, they can never tell you about it. Even

Tartakauer, what he had been through, at least he could say it. Bernice would never find words. If too much is destroyed, then there is no story and no mystery, there's nothing to know or find out. The shell remains and tells you nothing. She turned in my arms.

"He loves me. He loves his mother, doesn't he, Milo?"

"Of course," I said without thinking. She sighed and curled in my arms. I stroked her hair. In minutes she was asleep. I knew no way out of this. I couldn't figure out what to do next and so out of ignorance I did nothing. I simply lay there stroking her hair and held her until she caved into deeper sleep. I made myself motionless for an hour. Then more. Then I slipped away and propped a pillow beneath her head. I put a blanket over her. I turned to go but something caught my eye: the cross over her bed. I had no truck with the victim god who had deserted this huddled piece of flesh whose only gift was sleep.

She would be all right, though. We could talk the next day, if she wanted to. I had lost all zeal for caring what was right. Did I mean it that I wouldn't call the cops? Emphatically I did. So what would I do if Doc called them? I didn't know. The sky might fall. I decided one thing: I wouldn't lift a finger to help any sky fall. I took the valise back down to my place and hid it. Gerald was asleep on the couch with a sheet thrown over him. I wasn't going to hold up my part of the bargain; I wasn't going to carry him back up there. Akbar was curled at his feet, but came over when I entered. With gentle strokes I consoled my cat.

Holly was asleep in my bed, but she turned over when I came in.

"You had a long talk."

"Yeah. I got her to go to sleep."

"That's good. She'll be all right tomorrow. He stopped crying when she left, but he seemed depressed. Then I gave him some ice cream and apple pie. And that seemed to get his mind off it. He's okay. Are you coming to bed?"

I undressed and slipped in beside her. I felt her loving form, and that was enough. When my head hit the pillow I slipped down a long funnel of thoughtless rails to oblivion.

26. A Trip to the Altar

About dawn the next morning the phone got me up. I picked up and went into the kitchen. It was Spollick.

"Is this bad news?" I said.

"Yeah, it is. Well, depends. You ready for this? A woman in your building died last night. Bernice Durand. You know her?"

I paused, not wanting to say anything quickly.

"Um ... a little. We ... um ... I fixed something in her apartment ... or was it ... no, I don't really ..."

I mumbled something else incoherent. I was getting this from a dead sleep and I felt like Spollick, the jolly cop, was hitting me with broken glass in the face. I went in the back room and closed the door.

"Don't you ever sleep?"

He didn't answer at first, then he got his avuncular tone.

"It's thought that it might be connected with that other event in your building, which is my responsibility. You think it's connected?"

"Um ... I don't know. Why? What ... the woman's dead?"

"Just coincidence you think? Well, that's one vote." He wanted it to go that way.

"How would I know?"

Spollick seemed not to hear me, or care.

"I don't know if anyone's going to believe that," he said in a speculative way. "Might matter, might not. Well, did she know the Dauphine woman?"

"Who?"

"Durand. The woman that I just told you. Dead. Did she know the actress? The deceased I mean."

"Ah ... I don't know. I don't think so. Most people don't know their neighbors. I can ask around."

Spollick sighed. I imagined him sitting at his computer with a dozen other incidents trotting through his head.

"Would you?"

"Sure."

"I'd appreciate it. And get back to me."

"Sure."

"Yeah. Well, all right, Fyrish. I'm not sure what's going on around here. Everybody says something different. But if they didn't know each other, then it's probably not connected. I can go back to sleep for a few hours."

"What killed this woman?"

"Huh?"

"How did she die? The woman you just called me about. I guess you're looking for the killer."

He gave a high thin joyless laugh.

"No killer. No killer, Fyrish. Did I say killer? No. The Durand woman, no, she broke into a church and shot herself in front of the altar. Happened just before dawn. Priest freaked out. Nine shots in the head."

There was a pause when he was waiting for me to say something.

"Nine shots."

"Yeah," he said finally. "How can you shoot yourself nine times in the head? An automatic .22 with no clip. So how did she do it? I'll tell ya. She had to insert one round into the chamber every time. And then she missed, or sort of missed, each time. She had more bullets, more than the nine, I'm just saying, but she just stopped being able to load them. Loss of blood, what they said. That's how she went."

A lonely death was all I could think. But Spollick was conversational.

"Now think about it, Fyrish. Why? Why she didn't put the gun in her mouth, I don't know. Everybody knows if you want to go, the way to do it...."

"I don't think she watched much TV," I said.

"C'mon. It's so obvious ..."

"I don't think she saw many movies."

"Who knows? I just got the call. I'll be over in the afternoon. Could be she left a note."

I didn't say no, though I doubted it. Bernice felt too alone and deserted to speak to any of us, even her son. I got off the phone and stared out at the new day. Then I figured to go up to Tartakauer and head him off. I wanted the valise full of rope to just disappear. But when I went out, there was a plastic bag hung on my doorknob, full of newspaper. I took it back and emptied it on the other bed. In the newspaper was money. Stacks of hundreds and twenties. All tied with thin ribbons like you see at Christmas. And there was a strip of torn paper with the words:

"for Gerald with my love. B."

Along with that was the picture that had disappeared, the one with Miranda and Gerald and Simone. I bundled it all back into the bag and tucked it high on a shelf where no one would look.

I went up to Tartakauer's and woke him up.

"You call the police?"

He ran his fingers through his hair and looked down as if he bore a cloak of shame he could never shake off.

"Phosphorus would not convert to Mercury … No."

"Then don't. The woman's dead. She killed Miranda and she killed herself."

"What woman?"

"It doesn't matter. It's over. Somebody else killed Miranda. There's nothing to say. Nothing to tell."

He only looked at me.

"Are you sure? You don't know everything, Milo."

"Yeah, I'm sure. I talked to the cops. Just keep the kid out of it. Okay?"

He held his head, his heavy head bent down with thought. He mumbled something, probably German. Finally he nodded.

"You are right, Milo. Okay." he said and waving me away like trash, that this sordid matter had ended this way. Phosphorus not changed into Mercury.

"We'll talk later," I said and took the stair.

Yet on the way down I couldn't help thinking of something I only partially knew. It came to me and for the longest moment I couldn't get it straight. Then it came again: that Bernice was still there in her way and she was Tartakauer's opposite. What had she done with her nine shots? She had shortened a cursed life with no hope and dismissed a longer life full of grief. If I peered through Spollick's effrontery, I thought she had the autonomy of a fated soul.

Now as I stepped onto the main floor and stood hoping no one would walk by, now there was the problem of breakfast. Two relatively happy people were going to have to be told a horrible story sometime that day. Well, it wasn't my duty; it could wait. After a life of flakery, I could flake for a few more hours. Let Gerald remember some anonymous cop's blank face for the rest of his life.

27. Epilogue

I put the money in a fund for Gerald due when he was 18. 47 K. God knows how she got it. He could go to college with that.

August wore us out with its heat, then it descended into September with cooling rains and tropical storms that were meaningful for people in the Carolinas, which seemed like a continent away. Gerald got used to staying at my place. He developed a curious pattern: when he went upstairs, he would ask me to go with him; as if it was a ritual intended to do in the proper way something that could be abused if done alone. He got used to having Holly around and the three of us would drive her car up the river and have lunch at West Point and other places. The gray blocks of stone, the air of dedication in the way the cadets carried themselves, it all seemed to exhilarate Gerald.

One day a social worker came around, but far from questioning our right to parent, we were praised for what we were doing "until the next of kin could be found." I dumbly nodded my assent. I happily said that would be a great day, which cost me nothing since it would never come.

And one day about then, I saw in the papers how Opov had been arrested for drug dealing, along with several others. I started feeling invincible again. They were off on their own crazy orbits, wherever that would lead them. And I was on mine.

We were on ours.

I took my gun apart and threw the pieces off the Staten Island Ferry, along with the valise weighted down with rocks, junk I never wanted to see again.

Then, late in September, a woman rang the bell, and I let her in. She had a strangely open face, with beautiful large eyes that seemed to see each thing in the world for the very first time. It was Simone, Miranda's sister. When she explained how the attorney for Miranda's estate had searched for her, it made a lot of sense that it had taken so long to find her, given that Miranda's address book had been lost. I asked to see identification and she showed me her driver's license from Idaho: Simone Murphy.

"How many sisters did Miranda have?"

"Why," she said with her open look of innocent surprise. "Just me."

I fished out the picture and showed it to her. Yes, she recognized it. And I recognized her. But the child, the child must be five by now, another person altogether.

"Yes," I said. "At least."

So who was Lyla?

Well, I never found out.

But then in a way that made it clearer: of course they could never catch her, because she had an unknown, or poorly known, relationship with Miranda. She just believed from some deep reservoir of love and hate that Vincent shouldn't get off the way he was going to. And she believed it enough to act. Lyla the surgeon. She was the stand-in for Spollick in a way: she could do what he couldn't do; she alone could take vengeance. She just got the wrong person.

This woman, Simone, so sensitive you thought of a quaking leaf when you saw her, could never take revenge on anybody. She was grateful and deeply pensive on finding Miranda's things, and she shipped them off to Idaho the next day. But I kept Gerald's toys and paintings. I stored them away for another day, when he would be stronger and really want them, or be ready to throw them away himself.

Holly took an immediate liking to Simone, even convinced her to stay another week—and they went on long walks in Prospect Park together. In the end, Simone didn't say goodbye to us so much as she slipped into the mist of another existence somewhere else. Holly wanted to keep in touch, and maybe we would visit one day.

So you couldn't play with time, I decided. You couldn't undo it and redo it as so many people, including me, secretly in our hearts believed. And so when did real life begin? Well, it was obvious; it began when you stopped trying to change the past.

And then one bright morning in October, I called in sick. Gerald was sitting at the table, eating his cereal. We were going up the Taconic for a mid-week drive, and I was walking around the apartment singing something from an old ballad I knew, shaving myself at the same time, when Holly, stroking Gerald's ear, piped up:

"We aren't going to listen to Mr. Fuzzy-Face, with his songs of old dead drunks."

I sang on: "Martin said to his man, Fie, man, fie ..."

"Some wake up giddy, some are born giddy."

"I'm done. All right?"

"Don't know why I'd marry you, given your shady past."

"Crazy enough for you on a stormy night," I said, washing off the razor in the kitchen sink.

"I always wanted a man to be crazy about me."

"Then we inebriated them with tales of our Bowery bar revels. The torpor was shattering."

"Who was it said anything about adoption anyway, I'd like to know."

"She said, wishing a roguish submarine would ransom her from a quiet life."

"Tell me, is there someone else?"

"Yes, but they all look like you."

"I'm dead of envy. Is my makeup right?" she asked.

"I'm afraid to lie to any of them. They all talk."

"Who wants ham and eggs? 'Cause I'm not fixing either one."

We had gotten back to non-sequiturs.